Pears & Bakeries

DYLAN DRAKES

BEARS & BAKERIES

DYLAN DRAKES

BARD IMPRINT (Lighter Romances)

<u>SWEET & STOCKY</u>

Cubs & Campfires

Bears & Bakeries

ROGUE IMPRINT (Darker Romances)

<u>MYTH SHIFTERS</u>

Our Satyr Prince

One Night War

MONK IMPRINT (Poetry)

Stupid Boy Syndrome

Hello, precious pixie! Thank you for reading my latest story, *Bears & Bakeries*. I hope you love this cute and cozy tale about chonky boys frosting each other's cakes!

This section provides guidance on some of the content you can expect, to help you make informed decisions on whether this story is right for you. If you don't want to know this information, turn the page—this section isn't required reading!

This list is not exhaustive. If you have any specific concerns, please reach out via my website (www.dylandrakes.com), and I'll do my best to advise whether that content is present.

Addiction, Abandonment & Trauma

While *Bears & Bakeries* is primarily a sweet and cozy story, it deals with heavier themes than my previous book, *Cubs & Campfires*.

The main characters in this book have experienced significant pain in their lives, including addiction (sex, drug, and alcohol), abandonment and neglect by a parent, financial insecurity, and trauma that manifests in stress, anxiety, and visceral flashbacks.

These traumas are important elements of each character's growth journey and are explored in some detail.

Reckoning with Sexual Addiction

One of the characters in this book has a long history of avoiding sexual activity due to past addictions. This story details their journey of rediscovering their sexual self and finding a healthy balance between impulse and action.

This includes feelings of shame and internal conflict, as well as fears of "relapsing" into past behaviors.

Explicit Sex & Language

This story is intended for an adult audience and features detailed descriptions of sexual activity. It also contains frequent use of curse words.

Consensual Sexual Degradation

The romantic pair in this story enjoy some sexual degradation, such as referring to their partners as *sluts* or *nasty* during sexual activity. This is done consensually.

BDSM

The characters in this story engage in BDSM activity, which is viewed as a loving and healthy part of their relationship. This is done consensually and with the use of safe words / gestures.

To those who hurt.
And to those who comfort them.

ONE

Taking Stock

October 2013

Locky Sorenson was trying to avoid getting a boner.

It wasn't sexy. Like, *at all*.

It might've been, if this were the set of some trashy porn film—standing in a steamy locker room with the 49ers defensive line, all soft lighting and barrels of baby oil and one of those awful soundtracks going *boom-chicka-wow-wow* in time with the thrusts.

If that was how pornos even looked these days?

Locky didn't know.

He hadn't seen one in almost a decade.

But this wasn't a porn set. Or his bedroom. Or one of the very limited spots where getting a boner might be acceptable. This was the break room of SunSpark Industries, the San Francisco tech darling where Locky had been an accounting middle-manager for the last seven years. And he wasn't surrounded by a bunch of sweaty football players, but sixty of his colleagues—none of whom wanted to see Locky pitching a tent in the middle of their cupcakes.

None, that was, except the man currently talking to him.

Locky hadn't met Marty before, a beardy little pocket otter who'd just started in sales. And Locky *really* wished he could stop meeting him now. Because Marty was flirting with him. Like, *obscenely.* Not even attempting to hide his intentions out of fear that Locky might be straight or taken or prone to bursting into red-faced panic whenever cute guys hit on him.

"So, you're the famous Locky Sorenson?" said Marty, looking like he might whisper the word *daddy* at any moment.

Locky tried to ignore the prickles across his skin, but the man was standing too close and smelling of spicy cologne, like sweat and musk and fingernails running down his spine.

"I don't know about *famous,*" said Locky. At least, he was pretty sure he'd said it. He might have just bleated out some random throat noises, like a chubby little Chewbacca. "It's just a few cupcakes."

"*Hardly.* I'd barely got to my desk before people were asking about my welcome lunch. I thought they were just keen to meet me, but apparently they couldn't wait to get their lips around your delicious cakes." Marty gave him a long look up and down. "And I can see why. They're even better than the hype."

Locky gulped. He didn't usually go for younger, shorter guys. But there was something about Marty that made Locky want to pick him up and slam him against the wall. Which was a thought he *really* didn't need to be having right now. "It's . . . It's nothing," he stammered. "I do it for all the new starters."

"And for birthdays and anniversaries and farewells, I hear? You even got the flavor right. How did you know red velvet was my favorite?"

Locky cleared his throat, cursing the fact that he'd chosen today to actually wear a tie. He could feel his Adam's apple bobbing against the knot. "You know Evelyn? In HR? The one who onboarded you?"

"Ah, of course. That *fun facts* sheet she got me to fill out? I thought that was a weird touch for a Fortune 500 company." Marty took a big lick of the icing, holding it on his tongue for far too long before finally swallowing. "If you're free this weekend, maybe I could show you what else I like?"

Locky's lap was hot enough to burn pancakes when he was interrupted by the most blessed sound in the world.

"Damn, Boss Man, you totally nailed these—"

Locky snatched the woman's arm, dragging her away so fast she left a spray of crumbs in her wake. "Adriana! I totally forgot about the . . . thing . . . with the . . . Vanderbilt account . . ."

His voice trailed off as they reached a safe distance. Locky peered through the gap by her elbow, practically hearing his own cheeks sizzling. If she hadn't come along when she did, Locky might have left a wet stain on his suit pants.

What the fuck is wrong with me? Random boners are for thirteen-year-old schoolboys, not thirty-five-year-old accountants!

Adriana—a Puerto Rican skyscraper with sleek black hair and a pants suit to match—raised a sly eyebrow. "You're looking a little hot? Did I interrupt something?"

"Quiet you. Or I'll actually create a Vanderbilt account and make you work it over the weekend."

"*Pffft*, what else is new?"

Locky understood the sass. His team of fifteen had only just finished a super-secret project for the Chief Financial Officer. A whole month it had taken them—late nights and weekends too. He didn't know why they needed an urgent update on the company's accounts, and management wasn't jumping to explain.

"Lachlan, what are you doing?" said a young man by his shoulder. Jared, the second of his junior managers, was dressed like always—an extra from the film *Wall Street*. One who couldn't grasp that business styles had changed since 1987. And that wearing suspenders and aviator reading glasses made him look a smidge serial-killer-y.

Not that Locky could talk. He rode his bike to work most days and always forgot at least one piece of business wear. If it wasn't for the spare stack of shirts that Evelyn shoved into his desk drawer at regular intervals, Locky would spend half his days pretending that his chest hair was a really thick sweater.

Locky sighed. "Buddy, it's been over a year. Are you ever going to call me *Locky*?"

He consciously didn't add, *also, my name isn't even Lachlan.* Because being stuck in this office for fifty hours a week was bad enough without Jared calling him *Havelock.*

"Yes, Lachlan. Sorry, Lachlan," said Jared, not meeting his gaze. "Are you aware it's three minutes over our allowed break? According to subsection 33.6 of the Employee Handbook—"

"*Dude*, chill!" grunted Adriana. "The company owes us one."

Locky perked up. "You're right, dammit! Everyone's been working so hard, why don't I take us to that new make-your-own-pizza place? It's only a few blocks away."

Suddenly, Locky's fears about cute guys flirting with him were swept away on the thought of a counter full of ingredients he could experiment with. A place where he could create his own masterpieces like blue cheese and pear, walnut and prosciutto, arugula and apple!

"Oh, I don't think we could do that," said Jared, rubbing his hands.

"Yeah," said Adriana. "I'll snatch a few minutes on the break, but I'm not heading out for a whole afternoon on company time."

"What's with this work ethic?" Locky huffed. "Who chooses boring spreadsheets over free pizza?"

"People who don't have full blown ADHD?" said Adriana.

"For the last time, I don't have—"

"Oh, did you finally get a diagnosis? said Jared. "That's amazing. Welcome to the neurodivergent family, Lachlan!"

"God, this has really backfired."

"Yup. Sorry, Boss Man. But some of us actually like our boring—"

Adriana's silence was sudden and made even more alarming by the way it rippled through the break room. Soon, every face was glued to the headline on the business channel.

Delphine General in shock buy-out of SunSpark Industries.

Locky's eyes bulged.

Delphine General was the biggest player in the American green innovation industry—four times bigger than SunSpark.

And they didn't buy their competitors to help them grow.

They bought their competitors to *gut* them.

"Oh," said Locky, as the silence turned to panic. "So *that's* why we did the weekend work."

"*Blergh!*" said Locky, tossing his access pass across the food court table.

His housemate, Kai Kimura, stared at it through a mouthful of burger, one of the three on his tray. "The world's most unflattering photo? Thanks, you shouldn't have."

"Keep it. It doesn't even work anymore. I'd just gotten my bike out of the basement when I remembered those socks Evelyn got me. By the time I'd turned around, they'd already locked me out."

Kai sucked the barbecue sauce from his fingers. "Seriously, did you whisk your hair that morning instead of brushing it?"

"Not all of us can look like beefy underwear models in our pass photos!"

"Speaking of," said Kai, reaching for his designer belt, patent black and perfectly complimenting his ass-hugging suit pants. "Want to see my latest?"

Locky ignored the question. He'd spent the last twenty-four hours fielding questions he didn't have answers for. Trying to project stability when he didn't know what was coming.

That had been the worst part, even more than his own sudden unemployment—the fact he couldn't protect his staff, the people who looked up to him.

He'd call everyone over the next few days. Make sure they were adjusting. Offering assistance with their job hunts. Calling in favors and trying to smooth their transitions.

Adriana would be fine, once she'd stopped kicking holes in the wall. And Delphine might even want to keep Evelyn—as soon as they'd made her fire everyone else. But Jared? Poor fucking Jared. The kid was a brilliant accountant, but he was awful at job interviews, having even worse panic attacks than Locky.

Kai was unmoved by Locky's dark mood, inching his pass closer until it booped Locky's nose.

He groaned.

Because *of course* Kai looked flawless.

Kai's mother was of mixed Japanese, Filipino, and Native Hawaiian heritage. Even now, in her fifties, she was so beautiful that she could've starred in tourism ads. Alongside a six-foot-six mountain of Midwestern muscle for a father, no wonder they'd produced a son of heft and height, with skin the color of swaying coconut palms, hair so black it almost glowed blue, and a bone structure that belonged on a catwalk —his high cheeks and square jaw visible even through his thick beard.

Under his perfectly tailored suit, Kai was tattooed and furry and huge. Strong as hell, but with just enough padding to be more muscle bear than gym hunk.

Locky batted the pass away. "What's the gig *this time*? Another startup?"

"Nope, Apex Leisure. They've got resorts all through the Americas. I might even get a stint in Puerto Vallarta and miss the fucking winter."

"You're never letting that grudge go, are you?"

"Seriously! A man from North Dakota and a woman from Hawaii fall in love, and where do they settle down? At the woman's tropical dive resort? Or in a freezing wasteland with more oil rigs than people? I'll give you one guess!"

Locky rolled his eyes. He'd heard this rant so many times he could recite it by heart. "Will you bother learning your coworkers' names this time?"

"Don't get snippy at me for following the money, babes. You could've done the same thing instead of making excuses."

"What excuses?"

"Oh, Kai, I don't want to be an independent consultant like you. I don't want to change job every three months and never know where my next check is coming from. I'd rather work for one company for seven years. Because it's stable and boring and I'm a total fucking pussy." Kai took a big bite from his second burger, speaking through a mouthful of meat. "How many times have I told you: treat jobs in this town like men. Get in, milk 'em dry, then hop the hell off."

"And throw them away when you're done?"

He'd reluctantly concede Kai's point about his career—deep down, Locky knew he'd stayed too long at SunSpark, all in pursuit of some job security that clearly never existed.

But he wasn't going to take *relationship* advice from him. Kai was a pump-and-dump kind of gay. His longest relationship had been three days, and that was only because he'd received a shelter in place alert during a one-night stand.

"Rude," said Kai. "I give repeat performances to some guys."

"When?"

"I mean, I must have? Statistically? Even if only by accident? And stop changing the subject. We're talking about your hideous job, not my delightful sluttiness."

Locky grabbed a napkin, scraping sauce from Kai's beard. "I happened to like my job."

"No, you fucking didn't."

"No, I fucking didn't. But it paid well, and I liked my team. It was rewarding to foster their talents."

"Gross, you sound like a corporate infomercial. Speaking

of, I saw the final stock price. You've been taking your annual bonus in stock, right? Like I told you to?"

"Yes, Dad. Every year."

"*Nice.* So that's a sixtyish grand payout when the sale goes through?"

Locky slumped onto his forearms. "My twelve pieces of silver."

"Oh, please. I saw the takeover terms. Full benefits and a three-month exit bonus for every employee? In a booming job market? Your precious staff will be fine. So chill out and enjoy your windfall." There was an uncomfortably long pause as Locky avoided eye contact. "Havelock Sorenson, you are going to *spend* some of this money, aren't you?"

"Well . . ."

"It's sixty grand! The mother lode! You could buy a boat or a sexy car or go traveling around the world."

"Sure. But wouldn't it be more sensible to put it into—"

"If you say *ten-year bonds* I will flip this fucking table!"

"I'm pretty sure it's bolted to the floor."

"For God's sake, Locky, this is your one chance to get out of accounting. To explore other options. Like your bakery idea. You could finally make that a reality?"

"Jesus, not *this* again. If I wanted to waste the money, I'd just get the boat."

"It wouldn't be a waste! I've told you; it's a brilliant idea."

"Then why hasn't someone done it already?"

"Because most business ideas are only obvious in retrospect. It still takes one person to do it for the first—"

Locky shoved the remaining burger into Kai's mouth. "Eat up, dear. We can't have you wasting away. And are you coming tonight?"

"I sure hope so!" said Kai, chewing.

"To the *meeting*, moron. It's open night. A lot of new people will be there."

"Dude, you were fired half an hour ago. The meeting can survive without you for one fucking night."

"No," said Locky. "I'm their leader. They *need* me."

And after today, Locky might need them even more.

The apartment was dark when Locky got home—blackout curtains to avoid sun damage on Kai's expensive furniture.

The ginger tail of Kai's tabby cat, Apricot, swished against Locky's hateful suit pants. That might be the only good thing about today—he wouldn't have to wear them for a while.

The downside? All the terrifying shit that came with job hunting. Updating resumes and getting references and prepping for interviews. Months of instability and uncertainty and sleepless nights and money stress and—

Locky caught his rising pulse and breathed deep on the dark air. Therapy had been way too costly to do long term, but at least it had given him some killer breathing exercises.

He flicked on the lights, warm and industrial, with those curly filaments you saw in trendy cafés. Apricot sagged like hot mozzarella as Locky placed him on the marble counter, cream and gold and flecked with black. Exactly the kind of tidy glamour you'd expect from Kai.

Locky tapped his crumbling laptop until his favorite online radio station was playing—*Just Jazz*, a mix of ragtime and swing and big band music.

As brassy notes filled the kitchen, Locky looked at the

corner of the media player. It said *live* in glowing green, with 60,000 listeners online.

That made Locky breathe a little easier.

Because that meant he wasn't alone.

Locky hummed the familiar music—"Summer Song" by David Brubeck, even though it was closer to winter than summer. He wrapped a butterscotch-colored baker's apron around his stocky frame, looped over bulky shoulders and tied above his big bubble butt. Kai had recently washed it for him, and the canvas smelled of starch and Calabrian lemon. The smell of promise and possibility.

Kai often joked that it was strangely hot seeing Locky dressed like this—aproned up and with a collared business shirt underneath, rolled over his furry forearms and unbuttoned past his clavicle, letting thick tresses of sandy blond poke out by his well-bearded chin.

An alluring combination of house-proud poppa bear and thick-chested Scandinavian woodworker.

Breathing a contented sigh, Locky laid out his most precious possessions—a complete set of bakeware that he'd bought from a thrift shop after leaving Seattle. It was a sleek mix of vintage steel and ceramic, coated the color of fresh buttermilk.

Even just looking at the pans, set up neatly in their vintage display caddy, calmed him. On those nights when his heart beat too fast and sleep wouldn't come, he'd stay up baking until dawn, creating new and exciting treats. Letting the ingredients tell him what they wanted to be.

As bags were unclipped and jars unscrewed, Locky was kissed by the sweet smell of vanilla and the rich, earthy aroma of baker's yeast. Glass bowls were blessed with snow-soft powdered sugar and the gentle swish of flour through a silver sieve.

As Locky settled into the familiar routine, the tension in his shoulders was replaced with a little bop. The songs flowed like melted butter. The room grew warm with the radiant heat of the oven.

And, just for a moment, the world seemed a little more manageable.

Locky arranged the chairs around the church basement. There was space for twenty in the inner circle, with another thirty against the walls. Usually that would be overkill, but tonight was a Tuesday—open night.

The night when anyone could observe.

Locky had found that a crazy concept at first, having strangers stare at the regulars like they were actors in a really depressing play. But his mind had changed when he'd seen just how many people would watch for weeks or months from the sidelines, only to finally pluck up the courage and join them in the middle.

Locky filled the drip coffee with heaped scoops of a rich, dark grind—far more expensive than the collection bowl covered. He'd never bought coffee this fancy for himself, sticking to whatever charcoal floor sweepings were on sale that week. But when it came to others, he'd much rather welcome people with the best than quibble over a few bucks.

It was the same with the three dozen donuts, pink iced and rainbow sprinkled. He could have just bought a few boxes on the way over, but it was so much *warmer* to cook them from scratch. To make people feel comfortable and welcomed and supported.

Because Lord knows, they needed it.

With everything in order, Locky opened the doors. Familiar faces greeted him. Some he hadn't seen for a week. Some he'd seen only yesterday. And some he'd never seen before—startled eyes and scared glances.

Locky took extra care with them, speaking gently and smiling softly.

Kai came in just before seven, still wearing his suit. He'd never been like Locky—he didn't come every night, and definitely not to the same group. He preferred to go to different meetings around town, mixing it up based on wherever his latest job was. But, asshole though he sometimes was, he'd still come here tonight. Because he knew that Locky would appreciate it. Because he knew that Locky might be struggling.

Kai peered around the room. "Is the witch here?"

"Evelyn's still at SunSpark. I think she'll be working some late nights for a while."

"You *think*? I don't like those odds. I'll sit by the door, so I can make a getaway."

Locky snorted and dragged Kai to the seat beside his. Soon, Locky was the only one left standing, positioned so he could see everyone in the room and anyone else who might enter.

There came a familiar pause as every eye turned to him. Some relaxed. Some nervous. Some ashamed and desperate and hopeful that this time—*this fucking time*—it might be different.

And a brilliant calm swelled in Locky's chest. The knowledge that he was their rock. That he was their certainty.

Because even if he couldn't protect his staff, he could at least protect *these* people.

"My name is Locky Sorenson," he said, his voice as warm as fall leaves. "And I'm an alcoholic."

"Another incredible meeting," said Kai, with revolting sincerity. "I don't know how you do it."

"Ewww," said Locky, in the middle of stacking chairs. The rest of the regulars had already left for the diner, and Locky would join them once he'd tidied up. "Who the fuck is this, and what have you done with Kai?"

"Yeah, that was never going to work, was it?"

"No, weirdo. What do you want?"

"I was thinking about what you said over lunch."

"Come on, man! It's been a hell of a day."

"And there'll be more like it if you get another shitty office job. Just give your bakery idea a chance."

Locky was too drained to have this conversation again— one that came up every few months, whenever Kai tried to make Locky *live his dreams*. "For the last time, the bakery was a throwaway idea. I haven't thought about it for years."

"But you *could* think about it. That's the point. I know you've got baggage about money. And given the shit you went through, I get it—"

"It's not that!" snapped Locky, before forcing himself calm. Kai was only trying to help, after all. And Kai, of all people, knew the pain of *that* particular issue. "Sorry it's . . . Okay, maybe it is that. But it's not *just* that. Even if I wanted to test the idea, which I really don't, I haven't got the first clue how to open a small business. Social media? Marketing? Shop fitting? Making a catchy menu? I don't know how to do any of that. I bake random cakes and I can do accounts. *That's it.*"

"Hello? Kai Kimura here? World-renowned project manager and best friend, at your service?"

"You work for the same Fortune 500 companies as me! You don't know shit about small business permits and niggling state regulations that could send you bankrupt."

"I thought you might say that," said Kai, whipping out his phone and revealing the slick website of a Mr. Benedict Owens, Small Business Adviser.

Locky froze. Because the webpage was having an immediate and counterproductive impact on his dick.

Kai had mentioned Benedict over the years—his old college roommate—but Locky had never actually met the guy.

Which was definitely a good thing.

Because Benedict was *stunning*.

Locky wasn't usually attracted to Kai's business friends, with their expensive suits and stony faces. But there was something about Benedict that fizzed deep into Locky's balls. Thick eyebrows were set above an even thicker beard, complimenting long lashes and round cheeks. It was a roundness that implied a thick-set body that Locky *really* didn't need to be thinking about right now.

Locky coughed. "He looks . . . nice?"

"Yeah, he is. I haven't seen him in a few years, but he's a small business wizard. Helps them get off the ground and navigate the bureaucratic shit." Just as Locky started to protest, Kai added, "Listen, jackass, just meet with him. He's not some sleazy operator. He'll give you an honest assessment of your business idea. If he thinks it's crap, then I'll drop it for good, and you can hunt for another awful accounting job."

Locky gargled in frustration. "And if he's suffered a head knock and actually likes the idea?"

"Then you've got to entertain it."

"Kai . . ."

"Don't *Kai* me. I'm not asking you to open the actual store. Just work with him to make a business plan. Get yourself in a position where you *could* open it down the line. Deal?"

Locky groaned. "*Fine*. Anything to shut you up."

TWO

All Stitched Up

B enedict Owens was trying to avoid a panic attack.

Well, not a *panic attack*. He didn't get those. Because he had nothing to panic about. He lived in a lovely neighborhood and drove an expensive car and was blessed with excellent health. Not including his current chest tightness with crippling inability to breathe, of course.

But that was nothing to worry about.

Because that reaction was expected.

He always felt like this on opening day.

Benedict leaned against the inside of his front door, careful not to crumple his custom suit. He clicked through the music on his phone, finding his most-played track. A rainstorm in a forest, calm and continuous. Like he was alone in a cabin, far from here and far from now.

Benedict set his alarm for ten minutes—ten, tiny minutes of escape. And that was all he allowed himself before grabbing his keys.

Because he was already late.

And he needed to be there for his clients.

The sparkling sky seemed to mock Benedict as he walked toward the shop, currently hidden on the other side of a street corner. The blue above was bright and peaceful, like there was nothing in the world to worry about.

But that was clearly inaccurate—because he had *hundreds* of reasons to worry. Because what if he'd missed something over the last few months? What if he'd suggested the wrong location or butchered the social media strategy? What if he'd screwed up the marketing or been too pushy with a decor idea? What if all the money and all the plans had come to nothing, and he was left staring at an empty store and crestfallen faces?

And it would all be his fault. Because his clients had trusted him as their business adviser.

And he'd fucked everything up.

Benedict stilled himself at the corner, cool in the sharp lines of shade. He waited for his pulse to calm, caught between two worlds. Because this was the final point of ignorance. Once he rounded the bend, he'd be confronted by the reality of his efforts—success or failure.

He thought for a moment about turning back, but forced that idea aside. Because he'd promised Chloe and Castor that he'd be there. And he needed to follow through this time.

For his clients.

For *himself.*

With a ragged breath, Benedict turned the corner.

And he almost leaped in relief.

Stitch Me Up was packed, so full that he had to ease his way through an all-ages throng to reach the store window.

Through the glass, children inspected vibrant balls of soft yarn in peach and chartreuse and ultramarine. A group of college-aged girls in beanies and oversized sweater dresses thumbed bolts of fashionable plaids and distressed denims. An immaculately besuited gay couple gestured to a wall of crochet hooks.

And there, scurrying through the store, was one-half of Benedict's clients—Chloe, all slender tattooed arms and paint-stained overalls. Her partner, Castor, was clacking lacquered black nails against the cash register. Even by their usual standard, Castor's beard looked incredible today, like a Viking had tied their saffron braids with pastel trinkets.

They were the same trinkets that were wrapped in little packages on the counter, which half the customers seemed to be buying.

Impulse purchases, thought Benedict, thrilled that his idea had made their final cut. And in the corner was the sign-up sheet for the sewing classes. That had been another of Benedict's ideas, to help this place feel more like a community hub than a store. It was good marketing, and aligned perfectly with Chloe and Castor's personal—

A tall truck rumbled past the crowd. It was just for a moment, but long enough that the window in front of Benedict clouded, becoming less a pane of glass than a shadowy mirror.

Suddenly, Benedict was staring at his own reflection—a tall, broad man in a navy suit and starched white shirt, pulled together with a deep purple tie and matching paisley pocket square.

The mirror showed a stiffly professional demeanor. The demeanor of someone who had it all. Who *knew* it all.

Which was exactly how he *didn't* feel right now. Because

in that terrible second of shade, the store had looked suddenly empty—ransacked and boarded-up and failed.

The tightness returned to his chest as Benedict pushed his way through the crowd. The same crowd that proved he was being stupid, that there was nothing to worry about. Because the store hadn't failed. There were hundreds of people here. He'd done everything right, everything he could!

But that logic didn't matter. Not to the clench in his lungs and the sheen of cold sweat across his forehead. Not in the awful pressure against his chest, like he was trapped under a pounding waterfall, crushed and drowning and freezing at the same time.

When Benedict finally reached the soft leather of his car, he cranked the heat to full, trying to thaw the ice in his veins.

His fingers were numb when he reached for his phone. He'd thought it would be different this time. That after ten fucking years, he was finally done with this shit!

But nothing had changed.

Nothing would *ever* change.

With his jaw clenched, Benedict blocked Chloe and Castor's numbers.

"I'm sorry," he whispered, tears running down his cheeks. "I'm so fucking sorry."

As he pressed hard against the head rest, Benedict tried to convince himself that it was better this way. That it was kinder.

Besides, it wasn't like he'd need their numbers.

Because Benedict would never see them again.

Benedict's home office desk was covered in neat piles of paper.

He slid the business plan for Stitch Me Up into a clean folder, flicking through the pages of yarn options and logo designs. All the things that Chloe and Castor had thought impossible. All the things that Benedict had helped make real.

With slow solemnity, Benedict closed the folder. Because this was how he wanted to remember them. Bright and clean and orderly. A universe of possibility where nothing had gone wrong yet.

He found a free spot on his floating bookshelf. A hundred other folios were held between tidy bookends, the colors marching in a neat rainbow gradient. He plucked one of them at random and could almost smell the craft beer from the page, grassy and herbal.

It was for Hops and Honey, the brewery he'd helped Dan the football coach create. The man had seemed so rough at first, and Benedict had expected him to make some snide comment at having a black, bisexual business adviser. But he'd actually turned out to be the most doting, marshmallowy father of three little girls.

Like so many people, Dan had thought that his business idea was impossible. That he was too old. That it was too late.

And Benedict had shown him different.

Benedict had let him *dream*.

During his business degree at Berkley, when the rest of his class would conduct mock negotiations over some billion-dollar acquisition, Benedict would shy away from the more ruthless tactics, never understanding why so many students seemed to relish their combativeness, like they were Roman gladiators in front of a baying crowd.

One time, a professor had pulled him aside and told Benedict that he lacked the *killer instinct*. She'd said it mournfully, but Benedict had never been happier. Because he didn't want a killer instinct.

He wanted a *kinder* instinct.

That was why he'd never worked for the big consulting firms. Why he was earning a tenth of his contemporaries. Because *this* was where his sparkle lay. Not in beating someone down, but in giving them a hand up.

Benedict ran a thumb over the page in the folder. There were three photos of three little cuties, their faces turned into different beer labels.

Bridgette, bright and floral.

Esme, cloudy and mellow.

Charlie, red and nutty.

It had been a stretch goal of Dan's—a series of beers named after each daughter. They hadn't been ready when the brewery opened, and Benedict didn't know if Dan had ever made it happen.

Benedict hadn't gone back to see.

Benedict *never* went back to see his former clients.

Not anymore.

"Hellooo? Bro Bot?"

Benedict screamed as the unexpected voice ripped him from a nostalgic haze. He jammed the folio into the shelf like a teenager caught with a dirty magazine, causing one of the bookends—a black cat in a business suit—to slam on its side.

There was nothing inherently startling about his twin sister and housemate, Beatrice Owens, who looked like she needed a foot rub rather than a scream to the face.

"And hello to you too," she said, booping his nose.

Her once-bold morning makeup was softened from the workday. A yellow estate jacket was unbuttoned around her full figure. Long dreadlocks were relaxed across her shoulders, rather than in the loc bun she usually wore at the office. And, like always, her elbow cradled a handbag that was worth more than Benedict's laptop.

"Tris!" he barked, once he'd caught his breath. "What have I told you about sneaking up on me?"

"That I should do it more often?"

Just as Benedict was about to retort, the folios started toppling from the shelf, tumbling to the floor like a row of cliff divers in an old newsreel. Page after page flapped open, revealing little stories about tea shops and interior decorators and after-school education centers.

Once the carnage had stopped, Tris toed a stray folio with a bronze Louboutin. "Have you thought about having a normal bookcase? You know, with edges? Edges are big these days."

"Are you going to mock me, or help clean up?"

"First one, please!" she said, collapsing into his office chair. "How was the day? Good opening?"

"Yeah," he said, with only a slight groan from bending down. "They had a line all the way to Connor Street by the time I left."

"Wow, they got that many people in just five minutes?"

"I stayed longer than five minutes!"

"Ten?" she said, kicking off her shoes. When he didn't respond she added, "Yeah, let's call it ten."

"They were busy! I didn't want to distract them."

"I'm sure they would have loved your *distraction*."

"Tris! They're happily married."

"I thought that made it hotter for you?"

"God, I should never have told you about Vegas."

"Vegas? I was talking about Sacramento. What happened in Vegas?"

"Nothing you need to know about. And fine—if I'd met Chloe and Castor out in the wild, I probably would have gone there. But do you really think I'd be stupid enough to bang a client?"

Tris rubbed her foot. "Speaking of, I caught up with Crina—"

"For the record, I never banged Crina."

"Ewww, no! She's like a hundred years old! I meant speaking of other clients!"

"Oh, that makes more sense."

"Did you hear that she's shutting down her dance studio?"

Benedict's blood froze. His eyes darted to a pink folder halfway down in the scattered pile.

Oh, fuck.

Oh, fuck.

Oh, fuck.

Not Crina. Jesus, anyone but Crina. She was one of the most vivacious people that Benedict had ever met—a former Ballerina from Romania who'd decided at sixty-seven to quit her evening job as a cleaner and return to her first passion.

Depth charges exploded in Benedict's guts. Then the questions followed, cold and shameful.

How did I screw up her business plan? What terrible advice did I give her? How has her dance studio gone broke after only eight months?

Tris rushed to the floor and helped gather the folios. "Shit! Sorry, end-of-day brain. She's not going bankrupt or anything. She's moving to a bigger studio. Her wait list is so long that she's hiring a second instructor."

"Oh," said Benedict, breathing a deep sigh.

Tris picked up a folio from the pile.

Benedict's eyes snapped to it.

It was different from the others.

White.

Unmarked.

Barely touched.

And not because it was new.

It was one of the oldest in his collection.

Tris held her grip as Benedict tried to yank it from her. "And you'd know Crina was successful if you actually visited her once in a while. She asked after you. Said she hadn't heard from you since the opening."

Benedict tugged the folder away, sliding it into the least-visible part of the shelf. "These stores aren't *my* businesses, Tris. I can't hold their hands forever. I'll do everything I can during the planning phase, but once they open, they have to trust their own instincts. Me going back and visiting them? Giving them advice for years and years afterward? That wouldn't help anyone. *Trust me.*"

It was later that evening when Benedict wandered back into his office. Or maybe it was early. It all depended on your perspective.

The rug was soft under his feet. From down the hall came the chainsaw growl of Tris's snoring, although she'd deny it with vicious pillow attacks if he ever brought it up.

Normally he'd chuckle at that, at how insistent Tris was that she never did anything bro-ish like snoring or farting or burping, even when everyone knew that she did.

But he wasn't chuckling now.

Because his mind was elsewhere.

The shelf of folders glared at him, the colors muted in the dark. Slowly, he reached for the white folder from earlier. The one that Tris had grabbed so hurriedly.

It opened to pages covered in curious shapes, all swoops and lines and blocks of color. Paintings that looked like a dream.

A dream that could have made a fortune.

A dream that could have changed the world.

A dream that ended in *bankruptcy*.

With a life ruined.

With a client destroyed.

And it was all because of Benedict's incompetence.

His neglect.

His stupidity!

Benedict eased the folder back on the shelf, the guilt as strong as it was ten years ago. His unread emails provided some solace—some escape. He found a suitable business inquiry from a Mr. Locky Sorenson, sent a few hours earlier.

That made Benedict feel better.

Because wallowing wouldn't help anyone.

All he could do was move on.

And not make the same mistakes again.

THREE

Stiff Patter

Locky paced around his bedroom, weaving between piles of discarded clothes. Those piles only got bigger as he yanked out jackets and jeans, staring at himself in the dirty mirror before tossing them aside.

Why had he let Kai bully him into this meeting? He only had eleven weeks left of his exit bonus, and he had no idea when his stock option would come through. Yes, the takeover was agreed, but it would take months before the paperwork was settled.

Until then, Locky was on a countdown. Every day he wasted was another day he wasn't searching for a real job—something to replace the stability that had been ripped from him.

And what if he couldn't find anything? He'd only got the job at SunSpark because he'd met Evelyn at a group meeting, someone who'd taken pity on a wide-eyed college graduate who was new in town. And Locky had only been promoted because he had the rare trait among accountants of being able to talk with other humans.

But there'd be no kind strangers to help him out this time. He was on his own.

And the clock was ticking.

"Kai?" he barked, wrestling the buttons on a polo shirt. "Does this look weird?"

His voice was raised, half so Kai could hear him from down the hall and half from the terror he was trying to ignore.

Locky wasn't in denial about his charming collection of *mental disorders*—as his one-time psych had called them. But that didn't mean he should fall to pieces over this stupid meeting. Because it didn't mean anything. This Benedict guy would hear half a sentence of Locky's pitch and declare it dead on the spot.

After all, *a late-night bakery*? What kind of idea was that? It was something a kid might scribble on a fast-food napkin.

Kai's voice echoed down the hall. "It looks great, babe. Proud of you."

"You can't even see it!"

Kai poked his head in. He was wearing a loose navy hoody, the UC Berkley logo emblazoned with gold. A heavy gym bag hung against his sweatpants. "Oh, you're wearing *that*? Not the black bow tie from the murder mystery party we hosted last year."

"Wait, should I . . .?"

"That was a joke, moron!"

Locky grumbled as he followed Kai to the kitchen. "Why did you make me take this meeting?"

"Will you relax? You're the potential client. It's his job to impress you. Not the other way round."

"Yeah, but—"

"But nothing. Either he thinks the idea's crap and you go back to your miserable office life. Or he thinks the idea's great, and you explore it for a few months." Kai gave him a kissy face as he reached for the door. "Play your cards right and you might even get a screw out of this. Seriously, how long has it been?"

Before he could answer, there was a knock at the door. Locky's immediate instinct was to dive behind the kitchen counter. But there wasn't enough time. Because Kai was already there, dutifully grabbing the handle.

The door swung open, revealing Benedict Owens.

And Locky had to bite back a gasp.

The man was even more stunning in person, tall and stocky and almost intimidatingly stylish. He wore a three-piece suit that highlighted every inch of his masculinity—and there were a lot of inches to highlight.

His hair was set in a twist out style with faded sides. A powerful brow gave way to full cheeks and a well-shaped beard. His earlobes were stretched to the size of pennies, with white-gold tunnels that glowed against his deep, chestnut skin.

Locky had always loved piercings on a man, and there was something about this combination in particular—the sharp suit and rebellious metal—that gave Locky some very unhelpful thoughts.

Locky tried to stop his gaze at chest level, but his eyes moved beyond his control. His mouth almost dropped when he saw the man's suit pants. His thighs were so beefy, his ass so impossibly thick, that Locky immediately imagined the visitor flat on his back, with Locky holding one tree-trunk leg in each arm.

Shit! No! Bad thoughts!

Locky whimpered in awful realization, but it was too late to stop his bodily instinct. He slapped hands in front of his lap, hoping like hell he didn't look too obvious.

Fortunately, the two other men were distracted.

"What's up, Benny Boy?" said Kai.

"Kai? Oh my God! What are you doing here?"

Locky realized that he'd spent so long composing that initial email to Benedict, he'd forgotten to mention that Kai had referred him. This would be Benedict's first time making the connection.

"Wow, thanks a lot," said Kai in departure, but not before noticing Locky's clasped hands. Kai smirked, waiting until he was just behind Benedict's back before making a series of unhelpful grabby motions and exaggerated licks toward Benedict's ass.

Then there was silence.

And Locky was left alone, trying to hide an infuriatingly sustained erection while staring at the single most beautiful man he'd ever seen in real life.

There were times when Benedict's policy of not getting too close to his clients was easy. But this was not going to be one of them.

The first problem was that Mr. Sorenson was a friend of a fucking friend. Benedict wouldn't have responded to the email if he'd known that. Because that meant trouble. There were too many connections and expectations of familiarity. Plus, the client might show up at some event down the line and want ongoing advice, which would only distract Benedict from his current client.

The second problem was that Mr. Sorenson was hot as hell.

Benedict had never had much of a type when it came to naked friends. Tris had once described him as a pansexual mega slut, which wasn't far off. He was hot for cocks. He was hot for pussy. He was hot for curves and twinks and muscles. He was hot for asses and tits and lips and beards and clits and great screaming squirts and arching jets of cum and just *all of it*.

And for some reason he'd never been able to explain, there was nothing that turned him on more than social awkwardness. People who said the wrong thing or were really fucking adorkable always drove Benedict wild.

Given the choice, he'd always take the nerd in the Green Lantern shirt, breathlessly rambling about their favorite story arc, over the smoldering bad boy in the leather jacket.

And it was this impulse that Benedict really had to push down right now. Because in this moment, with Mr. Sorenson holding his hands over his crotch like some Victorian-era maid, Benedict wished he could give the poor guy a hug. He looked so nervous and so awkward and so fucking cuddly, with the V around his shirt collar revealing a tuft of golden fur so thick that Benedict could've used it as a pillow.

Not that he would, of course. He wouldn't do *any* of that. Because sometimes clients got nervous. Sometimes they freaked out. But it wasn't his job to comfort them. And it definitely wasn't his job to *hug* them.

All he had to do today was get in, do the consult as quickly as possible, and hopefully not wind up with a friend of Kai's as his client. Maybe he'd luck out and the idea would be terrible.

"Mr. Sorenson," said Benedict, mustering his most professional voice. "Benedict Owens. It's a pleasure to meet you."

The hand that took his was burning hot. Mr. Sorenson's other hand remained glued to his front. "Yes. You too. Hello."

Benedict waited for a long beat before saying, "Should I come inside?"

"Yes! Sorry. Would you like some water? You look hot." The man's face flushed even redder. "Hot as in temperature! Not saying you aren't hot in the other way. You are, obviously . . . I mean . . . Oh, *fuck*."

"Water would be great," said Benedict, having to suppress the unhelpful sparkles that radiated from the man's nuclear awkwardness.

Mr. Sorenson scurried into the kitchen as Benedict took in the surrounds. He'd never visited Kai's apartment—they'd gone their separate ways after college, only seeing each other incidentally at conferences.

Neat wasn't a strong enough word to describe the decor. It was almost regimented in its tidiness. The kind of place where even the label-maker had a label.

And that was classic Kai. He certainly couldn't imagine Mr. Sorenson, with his un-ironed polo shirt and frayed jeans, being responsible for it.

"What can I help you with?" said Benedict, sinking into a cognac-colored couch. He usually let the client choose where to sit, but if he didn't make the first move they might conduct the whole meeting standing, like soldiers on parade. "You mentioned an idea you wanted to discuss?"

"I did, didn't I?" he said, rushing back with brimming glasses. "And please, call me Locky. I'd say Mr. Sorenson was my father, but good luck finding him!"

Benedict laughed dutifully at the joke, trying to ignore how adorable Locky's awkwardness was. Benedict wasn't thrilled about using first names—not in the beginning anyway

—but the last thing he needed was to make the man more nervous. "And what would this idea be . . . uh, Locky?"

Still standing, Locky gulped his water like a thirsty camel. His forehead was sweat-beaded. "It's dumb. I know it's dumb. But Kai's forcing me to explore it."

Benedict pulled out his tablet from a leather messenger bag. "Let's not be hasty with those kinds of judgments. Why don't you sit down and tell me all about it?"

Locky sat stiffly. There was a long pause before he finally spoke, fast but soft. "It's a bakery. But one that only opens at night."

Benedict paused the stylus.

He'd heard all kinds of business ideas over the last ten years, but it had been a long time since he'd heard something truly original. His mind drifted into a million curious thoughts. A bakery that only opened at night? What would that even look like? Who would the customer be? How would you market it?

It was a tantalizing thought, full of unexpected possibility.

"Interesting," he muttered, tapping the stylus against his chin.

Locky shot up from the couch "I knew it! You're right. It's crazy and dumb and it would never work. I'm so sorry for wasting your time."

"*Whoa*. Don't beat yourself up like that. That wasn't a bad *interesting*. I was just surprised."

"Surprised because it's a stupid idea! Because it would never work! Because it's the dumbest idea in the history of . . . *history*!"

Benedict froze, fighting two instincts.

The first was the obvious one, the one that rested deep in his bones. The one that said *for God's sake, give the poor guy a hug!* That was the instinct carried by an eight-year-old boy who burst into tears whenever the news showed a video of a natural disaster. The kid who always asked his parents for spare change to put into every hat on the street. The instinct that didn't care whether it was appropriate or socially acceptable or part of a wise business strategy—if you saw someone crying or freaked out or struggling, you gave them a fucking hug.

But the second instinct was newer, and all the stronger for it. It was the learned instinct of life. The instinct carried by a thirty-six-year-old man who knew the taste of reality, and the consequences of swallowing it. The instinct that said you couldn't go around hugging clients. Because you had to keep that part of yourself separate. *Safe.*

For your protection.

And for theirs.

Locky was almost vibrating now. His breaths were short and stunted. Words were coming out in half-formed syllables.

It was a reaction that Benedict knew well. A reaction he'd seen in his own mirror—glassy-eyed and vacant and wishing it would all just fucking *stop.*

And that . . . that was too much for him. Against his better judgment—against everything he knew he shouldn't do— Benedict dropped the tablet and came to Locky's side, running a firm grip along each arm.

Locky shook under Benedict's touch, like a frightened puppy in a storm. "It's okay. Everything's okay."

Throwing caution to the chaos, Benedict wrapped his arms over Locky's shoulders, drawing him into his chest.

Locky didn't return the hug, although he pressed ever so slightly into the warmth, causing the soft curls of Locky's blond hair to run through Benedict's beard. He smelled of green apple and woody spice.

But that moment didn't last long. Because Locky let out a strangled squeak and pivoted suddenly from his hips, like a lounge chair halfway through unfolding. Now, Locky's forehead and feet were touching Benedict, but his midsection was as far away as it could possibly be.

Benedict let go of Locky on instinct, but the man chose that moment to return the hug, stopping Benedict from stepping back.

Benedict blinked in confusion. "Are . . . you okay?"

"Yes!" said Locky, far too quickly. "Everything's fine. Nothing's the matter."

Benedict looked around, wondering if Kai had set this whole thing up as an elaborate prank—some joke about the perils of working with small businesses? Something the rest of his old classmates could laugh at during their next reunion.

It was while looking around that Benedict finally saw the cause of the problem.

And it was a *very* big problem.

"*Whoa!*" said Benedict, snapping his gaze up from Locky's crotch.

"Oh, God. Oh, God," muttered Locky. "This isn't happening."

"I'm pretty sure it is," said Benedict, biting his lip to stop himself laughing. He couldn't see Locky's face, but the embarrassment was radiating off the man's head. "Should I . . . take it as a compliment?"

"This isn't funny!"

"You're hugging a stranger while trying to hide the biggest erection I've ever seen. It's *a little* funny."

"I'm sorry. I'm sorry. I'm so fucking sorry."

As much as Benedict wanted to joke about offering Locky a hand—and as much as this moment would be taking top spot in Benedict's awkwardness spank bank—he felt genuinely sorry for the guy. "Did you want me to get you a pillow? Or leave the room? Or . . . something?"

Locky whimpered. "Why don't we just go our separate ways, and I can write today off as the biggest disaster of my fucking life?"

That offer hung in the silence that followed.

Because here was Benedict's out. The one he'd wanted. Offered on a silver platter.

Benedict knew that he should take it. Friend of Kai's or not, Locky was a walking disaster. And that was the opposite of what Benedict needed. He needed sensible, self-directed clients who took advice, opened their stores in an orderly fashion, and moved the hell on with their own lives.

And yet, something stopped him. Something he'd once believed a whole lifetime ago: *that those with the biggest problems deserved the biggest help.*

Even Benedict was surprised when he said. "If I left now, I'd never hear this bakery idea of yours."

Locky glanced up, still holding the hug. Eyes as blue as the summer sky were set against cheeks so red he looked like he was wearing blush. It was such a bleak look, so small and so helpless, that Benedict almost broke in two. Because all he wanted to do was tell this poor guy that this wasn't a big deal and that he didn't need to look so devastated.

"You can't be serious?" Locky squeaked.

Benedict shrugged, the movement lifting Locky momentarily to his tiptoes. "I've had worse. One guy got so worked up talking about custom picture frames that I had to call an ambulance."

Locky at last shifted to a more regular posture, their bodies separating. Benedict resisted the urge to look down and see if there was any remaining evidence of the problem.

"Was he okay?" asked Locky.

"He was. But it proves that you shouldn't feel bad. Some people get a business idea and rush it straight into production. For others, even talking about it can make their bodies do weird things. I'm guessing it took a lot of courage to tell me about that idea? To even contact me in the first place?"

"I . . . I suppose so."

"Then let's focus on that. Forget about everything else and celebrate that as a step forward."

Locky looked him over, searching and curious.

After a long time, he finally nodded.

"So, baking, huh?" said Benedict, as though the last five minutes had never happened.

"Yeah, it's how I wind down from . . . well, I supposed you've seen from what."

Benedict gestured toward the kitchen. "I think a wind down's probably in order?"

"You mean *bake*? Right now?"

"If you don't mind? I find it useful to see the source of someone's inspiration."

There came another searching look.

And, eventually, another nod.

Locky shuffled into the kitchen, turning on the spot a few times. "Where should I start?"

"Wherever you'd like? Just pretend I'm not here."

"I guess I'd usually put some music on? I don't like cooking in silence. It reminds me of . . . well, I just don't like it."

"Fine by me," said Benedict, taking a seat at the counter.

An orange cat pawed into view, rubbing its cheeks against Benedict's well-polished boots. "And who do we have here?"

Locky looked up from the most battered laptop Benedict had ever seen—held together with frayed silver tape. "Oh, that's Apricot. Kai's cat. I can put him away if you like?"

"Is he usually out here when you bake?"

"*Always*. Usually hoping to get some cream. He normally sits on the stool next to you."

Benedict pulled the neighboring stool back and Apricot leaped up, eyeing him with a cocked head.

At first, Benedict considered not engaging—getting close to a client's pet could lead to accidentally getting too close to them as well. But he settled on this entire day being so screwed up that it hardly mattered.

He scratched under Apricot's chin, eliciting a deep and contented purr.

Locky returned to the sound of brassy jazz—the last genre Benedict would have expected. "What should I bake?"

"Whatever you'd like. You're the expert."

"I just usually bake for other people, is all," said Locky, pulling on a sturdy-looking apron. His expression was light and carried an adorable shyness, which somehow emphasized the way the apron wrapped around his frame, like a big caramel hug. "So it's really whatever *you'd* like."

Benedict thought about this for a moment. "It's hard to go wrong with chocolate chip cookies?"

Locky's face shifted in the most beautiful way, like clouds parting after a storm. "Oh, I make *great* chocolate chip cookies. Do you want them straight up or with a curveball?"

"Let's have the curveball. That's usually a good thing in business."

Locky spun around, scanning the kitchen before grabbing a plump orange from a neat fruit bowl.

"A chocolate chip cookie with orange juice?" asked Benedict.

"*Zest*," cautioned Locky, waggling the fruit in his direction. "You don't want excess liquid in a cookie batter."

Benedict chuckled as Locky rushed around the kitchen, grabbing bowls and pans and whole armful of ingredients. "My apologies, chef. Tell me more. I bet you know all the secret techniques?"

Locky took the bait, just like Benedict had hoped, launching into a passionate demonstration of egg temperature and sifting strategies and the ratios between white and brown sugar.

And, suddenly, the man was transformed. Gone were the nerves, and in their place was a keen-eyed nerd who'd been waiting hours for someone to ask about their special subject.

Benedict tried not to grin at his own tactics. He'd been through situations like this in the past. Well, not exactly like *this*—he'd never found himself in an accidental boner hug before. Some clients would barely let you through the door before they'd monologued their entire business idea. And then there were people like Locky, who needed a little time before they opened up.

He waited until Locky was spooning flour into a gleaming stand mixer before trying his luck. "So, a nighttime bakery? What inspired that?"

"It was an idea I had with Kai. I run a nightly meeting, and we were talking about how there's nowhere good to go afterward. Well, nowhere that isn't full of bad choices and temptation and . . ."

Locky gave Benedict a curious expression. Not *scared* exactly. But cautious maybe? Uncertain?

And then it hit him.

He hadn't seen much of Kai in recent years, but there was one trait from their college days he'd always found admirable. "Sorry, I should have clicked. So you're like Kai? You're . . ."

"*Sober?*" said Locky, with a surprisingly warm laugh. "You can say the word. It's not offensive. The first step is admitting you've got a problem. And I am *well* past the first step. I'm the meeting leader, I'll have you know!" Locky flicked the mixer on, the hum low beneath the gentle flow of jazz. "It was an idea I had after one of our meetings. They finish at eight, and some of us like to head out afterward. We usually go to this diner nearby, which is fine, I guess. It's just kind of soulless. Day-old drip coffee and cheesecake that's been sitting there for weeks. The kind of place you visit because nowhere else is open."

"You couldn't go to a restaurant?" said Benedict, before quickly adding, "I'm not trying to shoot you down. Just focusing on market gaps. If that's okay?"

Locky nodded. "Restaurants get weird if you don't order a full meal. Besides, you'd never wander around and talk to new people at a restaurant, like you would at a bar."

Locky filed that away—the desire to have a bakery with the characteristics of a bar. Not just a place to eat but a place to socialize.

It was fascinating, but too big to delve into now.

"A coffee shop then?"

"Good luck finding one. The whole *coffee shop that's open until midnight* is a figment of 90's sitcoms. They don't exist anymore. Even the ones that stay open until nine have the same issues as the diner: coffee that's been steaming all day, with tired staff mopping under your feet to clear you out."

"Yes, I can see the problem," said Benedict. "So what about your store? What kind of things would you serve?"

Locky's easy expression stiffened. "I . . . I don't know. I hadn't really thought about the menu."

"Oh, well, that's fine too. It's what I'm here for. To help you explore all of that."

Locky sighed. "Yeah, but what's the point? None of this will ever happen."

"Why not? It's a very innovative idea."

"I've been around enough marketing types to know that *innovative* is another way of saying *risky*."

"*Ahhh*. Let me guess. You're thinking about five-year leases and ten-thousand-dollar fit-outs and being stuck with mountains of debt?"

"Isn't that what a small business is? A massive money sink?"

Benedict collected his tablet from the couch. "What if you could test out your idea without any of that risk? Not just the plan, but actually opening a store?"

Locky scowled. "How?"

Benedict knew that he should pull back from the casualness of this conversation. That it was getting too familiar. And yet, he didn't. "Trade secrets, Mr. Sorenson. Trade secrets."

Locky drummed his fingers on the counter, clearly as confused as he was intrigued. "So . . . I wouldn't need to sign any leases?"

"Nothing long term, no."

"Or make any risky decisions?"

"Nope."

"Or—"

"Locky," Benedict chuckled. "I can take you all the way to the final decision, with everything ready to go. With a location lined up and a menu in place and a social media strategy primed. With a beautifully formatted business plan in place. And you won't have to commit to a single thing before that moment. Or follow through if you don't want to. We can explore all the different options without you spending a cent beyond my services—which, I might add, are very reasonably priced. There's no risk here. Only reward."

Locky rubbed his hands. "And . . . you really think it's a good idea? You're not just saying that?"

Benedict bit back a frown. "I would never, *ever* give a client false hope, Locky. If this idea didn't have potential, I'd tell you. I promise."

"So . . . God, how would this even work?"

"Well, I usually recommend location hunting first. Why don't I line up some options that won't break the bank?" Benedict glanced over at the stand mixer. "Also, I'm no expert, but shouldn't that have stopped a while ago?"

"Oh, fuck!" said Locky, diving for the machine. A beige scoop of batter fell from his finger, almost bouncing off the rim of the mixing bowl. "Well, that's ruined. Unless you want your cookies as tough as an old boot."

"Let's bake them anyway. No point wasting it."

Locky looked horrified. "I couldn't do that. They're *your* cookies. They should be perfect."

Benedict looked the man over. "Perfect is a good goal, Locky. But sometimes things are better when they're a little messed up."

FOUR

Different Strokes

Locky kicked an empty cola can down the pavement.

It had been three days since his meeting with Benedict and the shame still burned hot. Just thinking about it made him want to curl up and hide. Because here was this kind, handsome man, expecting a serious client, and what had Locky given him? An emotionally unstable sex freak who couldn't control his nerves or his nads.

Locky still hadn't called him back with a final answer.

He wasn't sure Benedict would even pick up.

He knew he had to make the call. He'd promised Kai as much. And he had tried, picking up his phone a dozen times and thinking about it. About apologizing for what happened. About shoving this shame aside and imagining what it would be like to say *yes*.

To be taken on as a client?

To be a baker? A business owner?

To let this crazy idea *breathe*?

Last night, Locky had punched in Benedict's number, his thumb hovering over the call button. But before he could press it, his whole body had started to shake, his mind flooding with thoughts of shuttered windows and bankruptcy notices and men in rusty removal vans.

Not that *Benedict* was intimidating, even if his fees were suspiciously low. But maybe that was part of the ploy? Something to suck him in? Some trick that would drown him in debt and throw him back on the streets and—

Locky snapped to reality at the sound of a slamming door. They were standing in front of an immaculate Edwardian townhouse, all rich navy siding and glinting bay windows.

Evelyn Abruzzo stared at the bronze door knocker. Other people might have muttered something under their breath, but Evelyn was more of a *scream down the street* kind of gal.

"And the same to you, *puttana*!" she bellowed, with a kick of cherry-red Doc Martins against the wood. She dragged Locky away with a whip of sundress and a flounce of silver curls. "Honestly, the people these days. Where are their manners?"

It was impossible for Locky to keep up. Evelyn was only nipple-height, but she scurried ahead like a terrier tugging on the leash.

"What exactly is a *marbled murrelet*?" said Locky, glancing at her clipboard. It was hard to keep track of Evelyn's causes. She helped out with homeless organizations and AIDs research and a million different environmental charities.

She'd spent twenty years working HR in the logging sector before finally seeing the light and joining the solar industry in the nineties. That's probably why she took on new causes like she was making up for past sins.

"It's a bird, *Picciriddu*. Scruffy little bastard, like it couldn't decide what color it should be and just rolled around in the most boring ones. But that doesn't mean it deserves to go extinct." As always, her voice was fast and sharp. "And stop changing the subject. This business offer, how can you be second guessing it? You bake beautifully. The best I've had. *Mamma, perdonami.*"

Locky blushed, half from the praise and half from the mini sprint they were doing between houses. It had been a mistake to mention his meeting with Benedict, but Evelyn had a knack for extracting information. And while Locky appreciated her concern, he wanted to see how *she* was holding up—finally being fired from SunSpark after helping offboard everyone else.

"It was nothing," he said. "Just a dumb meeting. Besides, the money—"

"Which your stock option will cover."

"Yes, but—"

"And you don't have to sign anything?"

"True, but—"

"Then it's settled," said Evelyn, rapping at the next door and launching into a breathless speech. "Honestly," she said to Locky, once a startled man's signature was extracted onto her petition, "you make too much fuss. It would do this city good to have somewhere like your bakery. In America, the night is only for the young, with everyone meeting when they're too *sbronzo* to stand. But what kind of connection is that? Back in Sicily, the night was for everyone, and you won attention through your wit and your charm."

"I know, Evie. But I can't spend all that money on myself. Think of the good I could do with it. The difference I could make."

"You already do so much for others. How many celebrations have you hosted? How many meetings have you chaired? You can't feel guilty for chasing your own happiness.

The world doesn't get better by good people destroying themselves, but by everyone else doing a little more."

Locky tried to argue but Evelyn slowed their walk. She looked at him lovingly until Locky finally sighed.

Evelyn didn't need to say anything. She was his closest friend in the city—although he'd never admit that to Kai. She knew where Locky had come from. What he'd been through. All his quirks and fears.

And while Locky did genuinely hate the idea of spending thousands of dollars on himself when others had nothing, it wasn't the whole concern.

He looked away, feeling shame at the admission, even though she already knew the stories. "What if it all goes wrong? What if I lose everything and end up in debt and . . . I just can't go back to that, Evie. I *won't!*"

When Locky finally looked back, Evelyn's eyes were soft. "And this young man making the business plan? What could go wrong with that?"

"Nothing, I suppose. But if I follow through and actually open the store . . ."

She took his hand with bony fingers, small but strong. Her skin was cool—welcome against his rising heartbeat. "You know our mantra better than anyone, *Picciriddu.*"

Locky nodded, breathing out the stress. His pulse slowed at the affirmation: one that had helped him through the darkest time in his life. "One day at a time?"

She squeezed his hand. "One day at a time, little goat."

Benedict stared at the dark ceiling of his bedroom.

What the fuck was that?

It was three days since his meeting with Locky, and that one question had bashed around his head ever since.

What ... the ... fuck ... was ... that?

Benedict had gone into that first meeting with Locky just like he usually did. With strict rules and tight control. With a promise that he'd keep things professional and not become too friendly. That he'd get the hell out of there when the job was done.

He wasn't supposed to be patting cats and hugging clients and staring at their fucking dicks! That went against every rule he'd established. Every protection to keep his clients safe.

But Benedict had thrown all those protections away. It was stupid and reckless, and he didn't know what had come over him.

Benedict checked his phone for the hundredth time before tossing it back on the pillow beside him. He'd been hoping to see a message from a certain someone. But it was blank.

The disappointment hit him sharp and strange, just as it had for the last few days. It was a disappointment he couldn't explain. Because he'd done hundreds of initial consultations over the years, and lots of them didn't pan out. Maybe the business idea was trash. Or maybe Benedict wasn't the right fit for the client. Either way, Benedict had always shrugged it off.

He'd been fortunate to never struggle for potential clients, with five offers for every available slot. And it wasn't like he needed the money. He certainly didn't *dwell* on those rejections. Just like he didn't compulsively check his phone to see whether they'd messaged.

But rather than dusting himself off and getting a different client, Benedict was just waiting around like an idiot. Because there was something about Locky that had stuck with him.

Maybe it was the contrast of the man—so big in size but so small in ambition? One minute terrified to the point of having a breakdown, the next utterly at ease in the presence of a glass bowl and some cookie sheets.

Which was to say nothing of his *other* problem.

Benedict pressed his eyelids shut, consumed with the madness of the memory. It wasn't every day you met someone who could get that aroused from a hug. And while they were in an emotional state, too. Benedict couldn't imagine his own dick leaping to attention in the middle of a panic attack.

Not that he had panic attacks, of course.

He tried to shove those thoughts aside. Because Locky was still a potential client, for God's sake, and he didn't need to be thinking about clients that way!

But no matter how hard he tried to focus on the laptop on his belly—full of neat spreadsheets and design software—he kept coming back to that image over Locky's shoulder.

Benedict had never received complaints about his own proportions, apart from those who needed him to ease a little more slowly into the occasion. But that brief glimpse of Locky was a different story. The man was *huge*, like he'd stuffed a lead pipe down his jeans. Benedict had actually seen the outline of Locky's cock jutting through his pants pocket, like a really thick meerkat peeking out for a better view.

It was such a contrast with the rest of the man. Because you wouldn't think someone so lacking in confidence would be packing a tool like that? If you were *that* hung, surely you strutted into every room like you owned it?

And yet, Locky had been so *awkward* about it.

At how big it was.

At how hard it was.

Benedict realized that his own cock was growing against

his gray sweats, a spot of darker charcoal swelling by his hip bone.

Seriously? Now?

The outline pulsed against the cotton, bouncing up in sustained throbs, causing the fabric to cling to his cut head and show off his prominent veins.

Benedict decided that he'd just ignore it. Sure, Locky was awkward and cute and sweet and nervous and hung like a fucking ox, but that was all the more reason *not* to think of him that way. Because that kind of mindset was dangerous. That kind of mindset led to mistakes—mistakes he couldn't take back.

Locky was a client, plain and simple. And he didn't think about clients that way.

Except . . . was he *really* a client?

It had been three days since their meeting. Three days since Benedict had given him the best pitch he could. And Locky hadn't called him back. Not to ask follow-up questions or seek clarification or to ask for more time.

Nothing.

Moonlight filtered through Benedict's window as he mulled the decision.

Eventually, with a conspiratorial smile, Benedict ran fingers along his t-shirt covered chest—slow as he could manage, biting his lip and letting out a little sigh as the sparks gathered in his balls. He felt hot and urgent and lazy in the same stuttering breath.

This was fine, he convinced himself. Because Locky was probably never going to call him back.

So what's the harm?

Benedict stripped out of his clothes, calm and unhurried. Not because he needed to mask the noise, but because he wanted the slow pulse of this moment to surround him. To send his head back against the pillow. To allow him to float away on the sparkling sensations.

Benedict licked each thumb in turn, tongue tip warm against his fingerprints, and rubbed lightly against his nipples, hard and prominent, hot from the skin but cold from the silver bar that pierced each.

His belly arched toward the ceiling at that teasing touch, and it took every ounce of restraint not to press down harder, to feel the arc of energy that always gave him goosebumps.

"Ohhh, *fuck* . . ." he whispered, running his thumb tips in slow circles against the sensation. Each flick against metal caused his cock to throb up, uncaged by fabric now. There was a warm drip by his deep belly button with each solid pulse, the energy arching from his nipples to his cock to his swelling balls —so fucking full and so fucking sensitive.

The slick precum turned the circle of his Prince Albert piercing without needing to be touched. The steel slid rapturously inside his slippery cock head with each thump of blood.

Still, Benedict resisted the pull, rubbing his toes languidly against the Egyptian cotton sheets. Steadying himself. Letting the material embrace his big thighs and well-built calves.

When that became too much, he raised his knees and spread them wide—revealing himself to the otherwise empty room.

And yet, the room became much less empty when he closed his eyes, allowing himself to slip into world of dreams and fantasy.

Where anything was possible.

Where *anyone* was possible.

Benedict whimpered as strong fingers pushed against his thighs, shoving his knees against his chest.

The dream-like shimmer of Locky kneeled on the bed like a fucking god. His pelt of sandy blond was thick across his impressive stock, almost connecting to his beard across those beefy pecs. Light pink nipples poked through the thatch, hard and pointed and begging to be licked. His belly was hefty and hairy, leading down to golden tufts of pubic hair, unkempt and rugged.

And his cock.

Oh, *fuck*, his cock.

His shaft was creamy white, revealing a cockhead the size and color of a juicy plum. Its straight length was hard as hell, pulsing at everything Locky was seeing—like there was no man in the whole world more attractive than Benedict.

But even better than his body or his dick was Locky's smile. Awkward, yes, but wide now. Warm. Absent the stress or the nerves of their first meeting. Instead, blue eyes beamed down at Benedict, glowing above a grin, toothy and dimpled and ever so slightly shy.

And in that singular look, Benedict knew that it had been his touch, his *words* that had tamed those terrors. Because there was no pain anymore. No hurt.

Only contentment.

Only joy.

And this, right here, was Benedict's reward.

Locky kissed down Benedict's calves—fantasy yes, but suddenly feeling so very real. Soft lips were replaced by a hot tongue. Benedict shuddered at the heat and the hunger as Locky moved from his hips alone.

A slick pressure kissed Benedict's hole, calling deep into his soul.

And now, delay was impossible.

Never breaking eye contact, Locky ground his body forward, sliding his big head in—thick and overwhelming and so fucking perfect.

Benedict groaned from his core. There was no teasing here. No gentle half-thrusts to get him used to the sensation. Instead Locky slid all of himself inside Benedict—all the way to the balls in one thumping blow.

Benedict grunted hard at the overwhelming fullness, emphasized by how Locky pulled himself halfway out, stopping when his huge, bulbous glans were throbbing right against Benedict's prostate.

Benedict tried to squirm at the sheer heat of that act, at the hardness of the direct stimulation, pressing so roughly inside him. But Locky held his legs in place, making him feel every twitch, sending a bolt of gooey pleasure into his nuts as Locky bulged against his most sensitive spot.

Benedict lost track of how long they stayed like that, willing the fantasy to life. Hours maybe. Days. Grinding slow and hard against his soul. Teasing him. Making him beg for more—for harder, for deeper. Making him say the words of command.

Fuck my brains out, Locky!

And in the fantasy, Locky obeyed.

He moved in quicker strokes, grinding back and forth against Benedict's swollen spot, dragging his slicked piss-slit against the place that made Benedict moan the loudest.

Those moans turned to gasps at the depth and the pace of the thrusts. Now it felt like someone was smacking against Benedict's detonation switch, the spark fizzing along his fuse —wrapped tight around his balls and buzzing up his shaft.

Benedict burbled as Locky angled himself even harder.

The directness of the sensation was making Benedict shake, unable to hold back the bursts of precum, splattering to his nipples each time Locky bottomed out with his thick cock.

Benedict grabbed the man's forearm as he was fucked harder, stocky muscle and dense blond fur. With each thrust Benedict dug nails into hot skin—urging him on, letting Locky know just how fucking good it felt.

Locky took the hint, quickening his pace. Fucking him harder and deeper and taking control of Benedict's body.

In one movement, Locky rose from his knees, standing up without withdrawing his cock. Soon, Benedict was folded in on himself, his whole weight balanced on his broad shoulders, with his knees digging into the pillow by his own ears.

His precum dripped heavily from his straining cockhead, just half an inch from his panting mouth. The clear slick ran along the silver of his piercing, gathering into bigger drops, before finally drooling in long, sticky strands over his outstretched tongue. Those drips soon turned to clear squirts across his lips as Locky hit his prostate so aggressively that Benedict's knees were shaking uncontrollably, like his whole body was imploding.

Benedict wanted to grab his cock. He *needed* to grab it. But he didn't want this feeling to end. This mix of heaven and hell. The joyous and the overwhelming.

"Open your fucking mouth," Locky growled, somehow finding even more pace. "I want to see you swallow your load."

Benedict did as he was told, grasping his cock desperately, his fist already slicked. He stroked his seven inches, so thick he couldn't close his hand around the girth.

That only spurred Locky on. "You want a mouthful of your own cum, you nasty little slut?"

"Yes!" Benedict screamed, barely able to keep his eyes open. Everything was a blur of sparkling silver.

Locky growled at his eagerness. Monstering his ass. Fucking him harder. More direct. More quickly.

"Say it again, you filthy fucker!" Locky snarled. "Tell me how much you want it!"

"I want . . . I want . . ." Benedict whimpered, his voice distant.

"Fucking say it!"

"I want . . ." But Benedict couldn't inhale now. Couldn't remember a time when he could. "Oh . . . Locky. Just there. Just there! Oh fuck. Oh, fuck! *Oh, fuck, fuck, fuck!*"

The first jet of cum slapped Benedict across the face so hard that it sent splatters over his chest and thighs. His body seized at the force—dynamite and napalm.

Barely conscious, Benedict opened his mouth wider as the hot salt sprayed across his tongue, each jet drowning him and sending him cross-eyed. He tried to roar out in ecstasy, but his mouth was overflowing, the jets coating his face and eyebrows and hair. He tried to breathe, but all he could do was gargle his impressive mouthful of cum, spluttering desperately for air through blasts wouldn't fucking stop.

The smash against his prostate continued. Through the orgasm. Around the orgasm. Inside the orgasm. Shaking him and shattering him over and over again. It ground him down, slapping him around until all he felt was the slow, pulsing inferno of bliss.

And then—with warm waves washing across his sweaty skin—Benedict opened his eyes.

Well, he opened *one* eye. The other was glued closed.

Benedict found himself folded up like a pretzel, with his favorite prostate massager buzzing violently in his ass.

He had no memory of getting it out. Not that it mattered. It had clearly done its job.

Benedict swallowed deeply on his huge mouthful of cum, savoring the heady taste, before uncoiling himself in a sweaty heap, neck sore and limbs heavy against the comforter.

His breathing slowed as he melted into the bed. And as he drifted through the afterglow, Benedict could almost sense a bearded chin resting on his chest. Almost feel the sensation of thick blond hair running through his beard—the scent of green apples and spicy wood.

That momentary comfort was interrupted by a flash from his phone, just outside the splash zone.

Benedict stared at the screen.

Locky—the real one—had finally got back to him.

And it was a *yes*.

Suddenly, all that warmth was replaced by something cold.

Regret.

Shame.

Knowledge that he'd fucked up—despite everything he knew. Despite everything he'd tried to change.

Benedict gritted his teeth.

This evening? This moment? It was an error of judgment. A stupid fantasy that he'd allowed himself to indulge in.

But he had to put it out of his mind.

Locky turned beneath his sheets. The air was cool, but his skin was burning hot.

He tried to ignore it—the pulse and the sizzle and the

wicked little voice telling him that no one would know if he reached down and tended to the fire.

Locky was good at brushing away these temptations. At saying no when his body said yes. But it was harder when he was stressed. When he yearned for the simplicity of past comforts—sex and drink and pills—as familiar as they were destructive.

The voice in his head was sweet as wild honey. Saying how easy it would be to break his vows. How easy it would be to shatter everything he'd fought for.

But Locky was stronger than that—ten years stronger.

And he didn't succumb.

Eventually Locky found sleep, restless and vivid and terrifying. A demon haunted him through plains of pure regret, brown eyes and brown skin. Lips like pillows and legs strong enough to lift the world.

Then came words—sweetest words.

Begging him.

Praising him.

Drawing out the shameful sensation of his own lust.

The nightmare rolled through Locky, heat and hatred, desire and devastation. And as much as Locky fought against it, as much as he called on his restraint, it was no use.

His resolve drained away.

His conviction turned to ash.

And in this terrible nightmare, this ceaseless moment, Locky allowed the lust to overtake him.

And he gave in to the demon.

He tried to stop it. Screamed to stop it! But the scene bloomed like a bloody rose in front of him—like he was watching himself from a distance.

Fucking the demon.

Devouring the demon.

Being devoured in return.

Until there was nothing left.

Locky awoke with a jolt, heart racing and forehead slicked with sweat. He knew it was just a bad dream. That he hadn't really given in!

But right now, it didn't matter.

Because he'd felt every stab of failure.

Every twist of regret.

In the darkness, Locky buried his face into his hands.

And he cried.

FIVE

Locating the Problem

Locky blinked. Not because it was bright—it rained overnight, and the early morning was thick with fog, drifting in cold and muggy.

The blink was because this first location was *awful*.

The warehouse was painted the world's dirtiest yellow, with concrete rendering so lumpy it might have been applied with a frosting knife. The windows were high and small, matted with grease so he couldn't even see inside. Pipes snaked around the front, weather-worn and dripping green moss over a faded sign reading *Big Pete's Paints*.

"I know what you're thinking," said Benedict, adjusting his purple silk tie. "But trust me, this place has charm."

Benedict's sister snorted. "This place doesn't *have* charm. It *needs* a charm to vanquish the monsters."

"Tris! Stop making me look bad in front of my new client."

"Apologies," she said without emotion, flicking through her folio. "For your enjoyment, valued human, feast your eyes on this well-equipped commercial building in charming Bret Harte."

"Isn't that a pro wrestler?" said Locky, recalling scratchy images from nineties television.

Tris didn't look up. "Such humor you have. Almost as abundant as the amenities of the surrounding area—such as broken streetlights, cracked pavements, and best of all, rabies."

"Tris!"

"What? This place is crap! I'm only showing it because you wanted the cheapest place on my books."

Locky bit his cheek. This whole situation was pointless. Adriana and Jared from his old work were coming around tonight to talk interview tactics—with both of them already back on the job market. Meanwhile, he was out here wasting what little time he had left.

Plus, things between Benedict and him were . . . strange. The relaxed, supportive guy who'd watched him bake cookies had vanished, replaced by the tight-laced businessman who'd first walked through his door.

Locky pulled his hoodie closer. The quicker they got through this, the better. "Can someone *please* explain why we're in an industrial estate?"

Benedict placed a hand over his sister's mouth before she could speak. "Gladly. Consider this location an imperfect—"

"He means hideous," said Tris, muffled.

"*Thank you.* Consider this a *hideous* example of a bigger concept. If you want to maximize value, then old industrial zones are perfect. You get lots of real estate for a fraction of the cost. The parking is phenomenal. And the atmosphere can be truly unique."

Locky looked around. "I think the atmosphere might be unique here for a reason."

Just as Benedict was about to respond, Kai's silver Audi pulled into the driveway, the headlights diffuse in the fog. He stepped out, Armani loafers dangerously close to a shattered beer bottle.

Evelyn stumbled from the passenger side, gasping. "Air! Sweet air!"

"Shut it, old woman! It wasn't that hot!"

"*Picciriddu*, help. He was trying to roast me alive!"

"If you want roasting, I'll show you roasting," grumbled Kai, struggling to button his trench coat through mitten-covered fingers. "Fuck! Satan, just take me now! At least Hell has a fire going!"

"Bah. You know nothing of the cold. Back in Sicily—"

"If you mention Sicily one more time!" snapped Kai, breathing hard onto his hands. "And I know Sicily is one of the hottest places in Europe, by the way!"

Evelyn ambled over, dragging Locky's face down for a wet kiss on each cheek. "You see how he treats a feeble old woman?"

"Feeble? I've seen you punt a mugger in the balls!"

Locky sighed. It had been a mistake to put Kai and Evelyn in the same car. He'd originally thought to stuff everyone into Tris's car, but he'd realized too late that it was an eco-friendly micro hatchback with a *Let's Get Realty* logo on the door. Tris, Benedict, and himself were already swelling into each other's space. And it wasn't like Locky could drag everyone around on his bike.

He could feel a headache coming on—alongside the desire for warm jazz and the smell of vanilla. "Where did you both go?"

"Don't blame me," said Kai. "For some reason, the satnav thinks this whole street has been condemned."

Tris coughed. "Funny you should say that . . ."

Benedict and Tris were a few paces ahead of the group, walking to the next warehouse.

"Seriously? A condemned street?" Benedict hissed, flicking through the property folio.

"It's not *condemned*, condemned. The appeals have been stuck in Town Hall for years. It's still leasable, just on a month-to-month basis."

"You could have warned me! Look at this listing: *A charming slice of post-modern chic, for those wanting an industrial edge to their brand?*"

"Good, isn't it?" said Tris over to the click of dagger-sharp stilettos. "That's why they pay me the big bucks."

"Who's *they*? You own the company."

"Me, then. This is why I pay *me* the big bucks."

Benedict groaned. "What a way to screw up a morning."

"Bro Bot, what did you tell me? Make it cheap, cheap, cheap. Well, I lined up a dirt-cheap property with a very convenient rent structure. No lock-ins and no risk. Isn't that what your precious client wanted?"

"You don't understand. He's already nervous about this process. I just want to make it easy for him."

"Or make it hard for him? Like, really, *really* hard?"

"Jesus, Tris. *No*, I obviously don't want—"

Benedict looked up and was confronted with a startling flashback on the road ahead.

The truck.

The cracked street crossing.

That particular shade of navy on the warehouse.

Zoe's Planet of Plants!

Without input from his brain, Benedict spun on his heels, his voice a tiny squeak. "I think the next street over would be faster!"

Locky was too busy keeping Kai and Evelyn from fighting to notice the sharp shift, but Tris chuckled under her breath. "What's the matter? You don't you want to see Zoe?"

"Oh, shut up," he said, whacking her arm with the folio. "Or I'll tell Mom and Dad that you're asexual."

"They know, remember? I told them last Easter? That dinner you thought would be full of shouty fireworks? They literally just shrugged and said, *that's nice dear*?"

"Oh, damn. It was so uneventful I forgot. Fine, shut up or I'll tell Mom that you bought her Cartier watch at a half-price sale."

"You wouldn't dare!"

Locky dodged a blow-up skeleton. The rubber was half deflated, making its sinister grin look more glum than menacing. "Pretty sure someone's already renting this place?"

"Correction," said Benedict, standing beside an obnoxiously large *80% Off* sign. "Someone *was* renting this place. But it's a week after Halloween, and they're clearing out, ready for the next tenant."

"And that tenant could be *yooou*," said Tris, flatly. She grabbed one of the movers, dressed in dirty overalls. "This crap better be out by dusk. If I see one fucking cobweb, I *will* charge you for another day."

"Ah," said Evie, from by the front door, holding a plastic pumpkin bucket. "This would be perfect for *dolcetto o scherzetto.*"

Kai groaned, his large frame squashed between two cauldrons. "Why do you do that? It's *trick or treat.* You know it's trick or treat. You've lived in this country for almost forty years!"

Locky did his best to ignore them. Five warehouses they'd been to, each one filthy and cold and tainted by their constant bickering. The headache that had started at Big Pete's Paints was now a deep throb in the back of his skull. One that wasn't helped by all the questions that Benedict and Tris kept asking.

Do you love this place?

Is it big enough?

Is this the kind of street you'd like?

What decor ideas do you have?

What do you want?

What do you want?

What do you fucking want?

Locky stifled the urge to sob. It felt like pop quiz he hadn't prepped for. Because he'd never sat down and figured out costs —he did enough of that at work. Just like he'd never thought about footfall, and parking density, and profit margins, and whether he was *clustered with the right kind of stores.*

Because he hadn't thought about the bakery at all.

It was just a dumb idea.

A half-formed thought.

And it was becoming really clear, really fast, that this wasn't enough—no matter what Benedict said. Because everyone kept expecting him to walk into these places and *get inspired.* To say things like, *yes, marvelous, we'll hang the chandelier over there and deck the counter in rich mahogany.*

And Locky wasn't getting any of that. The only thing he was getting was an increasingly panicked sense of emptiness.

"Another *day*?" Locky asked, once Tris had unhanded the mover. Despite the hot prickles up his neck, he was trying to play along with everyone's effort. "You rent this place out by the day?"

"Of course," said Benedict, his shoulders stiff. "If warehouses aren't your vibe, then *pop-ups* might be the answer. They're perfect for testing an idea out. You build buzz, get lines around the block, and then clear out before the interest dips. All upside, no risk."

Benedict stared at Locky, expectantly. His eyes were hard but sparkling, as if saying: *Isn't this perfect?*

And it was. Of course it was. It was everything Benedict had promised him. No risk. No lock-ins.

And yet, the thought of leasing somewhere like *this* made Locky's stomach churn. Because each dragged-away decoration revealed what this place really was—a white, soulless box, stripped clean and made ready for its next tenant.

That image gave Locky a sense of dread, at just how easy it was to unpack a dream. Merchandise that was once hand-picked and fawned over, being tossed into a grubby truck and hauled away.

Locky didn't know what he wanted the bakery to be, but it wasn't *this*—some disposable novelty, swept aside and forgotten like a one-night stand. It was just . . . *wrong*. And worst of all, he didn't know how to make it better. Because he didn't know what to ask for, or what he could afford, or what his dreams even fucking were. Because those dreams were supposed to be *vivid*, and all his brain was serving was slack-jawed drools.

Benedict's glow dimmed. "Damn. Another miss?"

Locky swallowed. "No, it's brilliant. You've done a great job. Why . . . why don't you show me around?"

Benedict's heart sank as he dragged Locky around the city, doing everything he could to find a good match.

But nothing seemed to work.

Locky kept saying he was fine when he clearly wasn't—looking detached and defeated all through the afternoon.

And as they walked side-by-side, with Locky's shoulders slumped and his gaze trailing along the footpath, Benedict kept having the strange urge to hug him again. To tell him that it was normal to feel overwhelmed. That they'd look back on this moment in a few weeks and laugh.

But Benedict fought back those instincts.

Because he needed to keep himself in check.

Locky's kitchen was a blessed relief after the day he'd just had. And it was made even better by the company.

"What was wrong with that answer?" whined Jared from across the counter, looking like he'd stepped out of an MTV audience from the late 80s.

Adriana stirred a big pot of *asopao de pollo*, a Puerto Rican chicken stew with peppers and olives and swelling grains of rice, filling Locky's kitchen with the heady aroma of herbs and salt. "For the last time, dummy, you have to talk about what *you* did. Stop talking about me and Boss Man and the rest of the team. It's all about you, you, you."

"But . . . it wasn't just me. The whole team worked on that project."

Locky laughed as he buttered some copper ramekins for his dark chocolate and chili lava cakes. "I know, buddy. But that's not how job interviews work. They want to know what *your* skills are. That you didn't rely on other people."

Jared stared at his meticulously prepared notes. "But I *did* rely on other people!"

Adriana took a sip on her red win. "*¡Ay bendito!* This is going to be a long night."

An outsider might have considered that rude—drinking alcohol in front of a sober person—and it was definitely something Locky had wrangled with over the years. But the truth was, situations like this were complex and deeply individual. It depended on so many things, like what stage of recovery someone was at, and what their triggers were, and their personal preferences.

Some sober people avoided temptation entirely and asked others to do the same. Which was totally fine.

Others would feel awful if Aunty Pat couldn't whip up her famous eggnog for the rest of the family at Christmas, or if their cousin tried to make their whole wedding dry just to accommodate them. And that was also fine.

Because everyone was different, and that was the point.

Kai had been sober since he was fifteen and had no issues with people drinking in front of him. If anything, he thought those long, boozy lunches made for better negotiations, sipping on seltzer while his rivals slurred their way into bad deals and unintended revelations.

Whereas Evelyn was the opposite, avoiding any scenario where alcohol might be present.

Locky usually found himself somewhere in the middle. Every year he treated Evelyn to a nice dinner out rather than attending the work Christmas party, with that level of debauchery being too much even for him. But having a friend enjoy a few glasses of wine on a relaxed evening—particularly when Adriana asked every time if it was okay—was something he'd grown comfortable with.

And that was the right word to describe the evening.

Comfortable.

The candlelight was as warm and sparkling as the conversation. Jazz swooned around them, adding a husky magic to the air. Jokes came as easily as the food, hot and spicy then sweet and tempting, spoonful after delicious spoonful, until all three of them were contented puddles on the couch, laughing off recent events and reminiscing on shared memories.

And in that moment, a certainty washed over Locky—that *this* was what he loved about baking. The comfortable and the inviting. The ability to make people feel special and loved and welcome.

And there was no cold warehouse or white-walled pop-up that could give him that feeling.

So why even try?

"And what have you been up to, Boss Man?" said Adriana, slipping him an elbow to the ribs.

He hadn't told either of them about his business exploration. And right now . . . well, there wasn't any point, was there?

Locky smiled back at her, suddenly more certain than he'd been in weeks. "Just a dumb side quest. But it's over now."

Pier 7 was one of those San Francisco gems that always made Benedict feel conflicted. During the day it was overrun with people. But right now, just before dawn, it was beautiful and peaceful and almost meditative—with the neatly spaced lamps washing across weathered wood and wrought iron. In the distance, the lights of the Bay Bridge twinkled over an expanse of calm water, the sky blushing from inky blue to dark peach.

Because, on the one hand, Benedict wanted to tell everyone about this place. About how perfect it was to just sit and think, feeling that curious mix of connected and disconnected.

And yet, the more people that knew about it, the more it would lose the calm that made it so special in the first place.

Not that he was experiencing much calm right now. Not with the email he'd woken up to.

The one he hadn't responded to.

The one he couldn't stop staring at.

Benedict,

Thank you for taking the time to discuss options with me. Sorry again that I've been such a mess.

I've decided against doing a business plan. I really hope you don't think it's about you. You've been way more patient than I deserve.

It's just not the right time, and it probably never will be.

~ Locky

Benedict read it over and over, uncertain why it was

hitting so hard. Because clients came and went. Some lasted a few days, some stayed for a few weeks, and some never called back at all.

And that was fine.

In some ways, it was better.

But Benedict didn't feel *fine* about this, tapping his phone whenever the light faded, making the words stand to attention against the dark.

He kept doing that for another half hour, until the bench creaked beside him—the arrival of the only person Benedict could think to call.

"What kind of hour do you call this?" said Kai, stretching out and catching his gym shoes on the rails. "And this better not be about a loan. If you're stupid enough to work with small businesses, that's your own fault."

Benedict relaxed at the arrival of his old friend—their interactions still familiar despite their time apart. "Oh please, *new money*. My trust fund could crush your salary any day of the week."

Kai's shoulders bounced in little laughs. They sat in silence for a while, the stars fading against golden clouds. "Locky bailed on you, huh?"

"He told you?"

"Nah. But you don't live with someone for seven years without picking up on things. And he seemed way too happy when I got home last night."

Benedict stared at the lapping water.

Eventually he handed the phone to Kai, who gave a low sigh. "Yup, he's an idiot alright."

"So that's it? It's over?"

"If it was me? Sure. But brooding on a pier suggests you've got other ideas?"

"I just . . . I don't understand why he's so reluctant to follow his passion? He's obviously trapped in a career he hates, just so he can make money he doesn't want to spend? Seriously, what's *that* about? And I've seen him bake—he's clearly creative and loves doing it. But that creativity doesn't extend to imagining what his bakery might look like?"

Kai tapped his sneaker against the railing, sending a dull pulse through the beams. "He's a complex guy, Benny. I had to nag him for years just to talk to someone like you. It sucks that he wants to bail, but he's a big boy and it's his call."

Benedict stared at his old friend. "What aren't you telling me?"

"Lots of stuff? It's not my place to spill someone else's trauma."

The word hit Benedict like a punch. *Trauma?* What the hell had Locky gone through to make him like this?

Even though the silence grew around them, there was nothing quiet in Benedict's head now. Because one line from the email kept looping over and over.

It's just not the right time, and it probably never will be.

That line scratched beneath Benedict's skin. Because it didn't feel like a delay. It felt like an execution. Like this was a crossroad that would affect the rest of Locky's life. Like if he didn't take the chance now, he might never do it.

And even though it went against every defense mechanism Benedict had built—even though he knew it was risky and stupid—he couldn't stand the thought of Locky walking away from his dream forever.

Not like *this.*

Not without asking him to reconsider.

Before Benedict could respond, Kai groaned. "It won't make a shit of difference, but he'll probably be at the Chat Street Diner tonight. He heads there most nights with some of the regulars."

"He won't take the night off? Even after *this*?"

"He never misses it. Honestly, that group would fall apart without him."

Benedict scoffed. "I just figured he'd be hiding under a pillow or something."

Kai stared for a long time across the water. "No, Benny. He got more than enough of that shit as a kid."

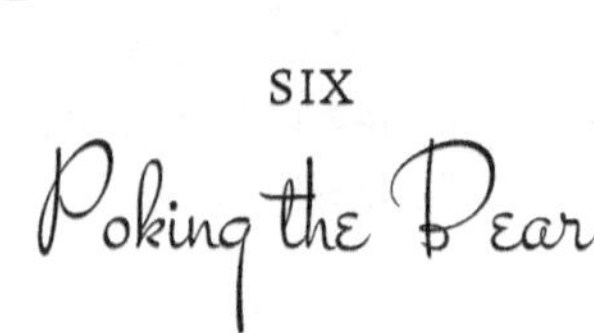

Benedict had never much liked diners, particularly their habit of blaring unflattering fluorescent lights at all hours. It was an especially bad look for this one, with its authentic 1970's decor—all earthy browns and scratched-up vinyl flooring. There was a fine line between nostalgic and decrepit, and this place was drowning in the latter.

"Oh . . . my . . . God!" came a familiar voice. "Benedict Owens? What are you doing here? I am shocked. *Shocked!*"

Kai slapped his cheeks, *Home Alone* style, to add to the effect.

There were a dozen or so people across two booths on the otherwise empty floor. Evelyn was one of the three people Benedict recognized, sitting as far from Kai as possible but still close to the blond man in the middle of the mass.

The man who was giving Benedict a long and weary look.

Locky shunted into Benedict's booth, far enough away that the others wouldn't hear them. He hadn't told everyone about exploring a business plan, just like he hadn't told Kai or Evelyn that he'd abandoned the idea. Although judging by his housemate's terrible acting, Kai had already figured this out.

Benedict at least had the decency to look apologetic. He was wearing one of his fancy suits, but there was something crumpled about it, matching his expression. "Sorry, I didn't mean to interrupt."

"Yes you did," said Locky. "Unless Kai told you I'd be alone?"

"Well, no, but—"

"Then you knew I'd be with people, *my people*, and you gate-crashed anyway."

Benedict opened his mouth but shut it again. He'd probably expected the timid and anxious Locky. Not the Locky who'd step in front of a bus for his people, protecting them from threats and outsiders.

And Benedict was an outsider. Just because Locky had told him about the diner, didn't mean he had any right to show up.

"I guess I deserve that," said Benedict. "For what it's worth, I am genuinely sorry for the intrusion. But I needed to talk to you."

Locky pinched the bridge of his nose. He'd lodged seven job applications today, each one leaving him relieved and certain that he'd made the right choice. The last thing he needed was talking through whatever injured pride this guy was nursing. "What do you want, Benedict? Didn't your parents teach you to take no for an answer?"

"My mother's the head of a child literacy charity, and my

father's an engineering professor with more patents than friends. We're more of a *try, try again* kind of family."

Locky crossed his arms. "Well, go on. Have your second try."

Benedict adjusted his tie. "I . . . I messed up yesterday. I should have asked a lot more questions before I flooded you with locations. Things that could have gotten those creative juices flowing. Like if there's any existing stores you'd like to emulate? Or something from a movie or TV show that you've liked? Or maybe somewhere from your past you've got fond memories of?"

Somewhere from my past . . .

Heat spiked in Locky, sudden and savage. "Oh, *sure*. Let's draw on some treasured childhood memories, shall we? Actually, there was this precious little malt shop my mother and father took me to every single year on my birthday. It was our special treat as a happy family, where I got banana splits and triple-stacked waffles and a unicorn of my very own. It was filled with soda jerks in these *darling* little paper hats and all the waitresses were called Peggy! You've got it, Benedict! I'm going to open up a 1950's malt shop full of greasers and poodle skirts! Why didn't I think of that?"

Locky was snarling by the time he finished.

It would have been better if Benedict had joined him in that anger. If he'd marched out at Locky's rudeness.

Instead, Benedict looked him over with a deep sadness, like Locky was a ripped-up teddy bear that needing stitching back together.

Locky's anger morphed into a creeping guilt. Because Benedict didn't deserve that. He was just trying to help. Just trying to understand.

Locky searched for words to explain his outburst but came

up empty. Because how could he explain a little without explaining all of it? Without going into the long, lonely nights on scratchy sofas and cold floors. Of being awoken by slurred singing and filthy thumps against the wall as his mother paid for their presence. Of moving every few months whenever his latest father figure got sick of them. Of going to school hungry and being too ashamed to take the free meals. Of bourbon-soaked whispers as he pretended to sleep—a thousand broken promises that tomorrow might be different.

That tomorrow she'd stay home.

That tomorrow she'd stay sober.

I swear, Locky Bear. I swear.

Locky bit back those memories, but a tear blinked down his cheek, doing what his body did best, denying him the smallest shred of dignity.

To his surprise, a hand threaded between his own, cool against his burn.

Locky gripped Benedict back on instinct. He didn't want to, because he knew how fucking selfish that was. Because this poor guy didn't need any more of Locky inflicted on him. He didn't need this broken toy scratching at his perfect skin.

But Locky couldn't bear to let go. Because right now, with the memory of all those dark nights, Benedict's hand felt like the only stable thing in the world. And Locky felt like a drowning man against a crashing current, fearing he might never make it back to the surface.

More tears came as Benedict moved beside him, strong and stable in a way that Locky knew he didn't deserve. The glass of Locky's self-preservation creaked under the strain of the moment, telling him to resist, telling him to hold it all back, before finally shattering into a million shameful shards.

Locky burrowed deep into Benedict's frame, too big and

too powerful to be shaken by the flood of his tears. Broad arms wrapped around Locky's shoulders as he wept a tide he couldn't bring himself to stop.

And Locky hated how much he needed that strength right now. How small and how safe it made him feel.

When his tears finally settled, all Locky could bring himself to say was, "I don't have those kinds of memories, Benedict."

The bigger man stroked his back as Locky stared at the damp patch he'd left on Benedict's shirt, tears and snot against designer cotton.

And Locky almost laughed at just how fucking perfect it was. Because that's all Locky would ever be—a dirty stain on beautiful cloth.

When he turned up to face Benedict, he was shocked to see that the man's cheeks were also wet. "Then maybe it's time we made some?" Benedict whispered.

Locky almost tripped into the darkness, still wallowing in his earlier outburst. He didn't know why he'd let Benedict drag him here—wherever *here* was—except that Benedict understood what he was feeling right now.

Locky crooked a finger into a stray beam of moonlight, drifting in through a gap in the newspaper-covered windows. His skin hung silver and alien in the dusty air.

Then, like some great vault being revealed, the L-shaped room roared with a warm and welcoming light. It was a restaurant—at least, Locky assumed it was, given all the tables.

It was about the same size as the Chat Street Diner, but the similarities ended there.

Because this place was like nothing he'd ever seen.

There was a 1920's vibe to everything, although Locky didn't have the words to describe it. Art Deco? Art Nouveau? Either way, black wallpaper was patterned in gold velvet, all fancy flowers and peacock plumes. Clamshell lights were spaced between old record players and vases full of white feathers. Tall bookcases were stuffed with faded, leather-bound classics—surely more for show than to actually read. And every corner was filled with the sharp green fronds of potted palms.

It looked like a much more luxurious version of every Gatsby party Locky had attended in college. Like it should smell of cigars and rich perfume, full of people saying things like *gee willikers*.

"*Pizza My Mind*?" said Locky, reading the bright neon swirl over the counter. His voice echoed among the still.

"Hey, puns sell," said Benedict, pulling a napkin from the dispenser and inspecting the logo.

Locky wandered through the circular tables that dotted the room's length. There were also a dozen intimate booths running along each side, green leather and cream marble. To his surprise, a little stage was tucked at the far end of the L, with a lighting rig bolted to the ceiling and a space cleared for a little dance floor.

The decor left an odd impression on Locky. It was heavy-handed, yes, but also strangely warm. Playful in how absurdly overdecorated it was. So committed to a long-lost aesthetic that it almost coaxed a smile across his cheeks.

"Why are you showing me this, Benedict?" he said, genuinely confused. It wasn't like they'd talked about coming here. The drive over had only been five minutes, and Locky had spent most of that time kicking himself for how much of an asshole he'd been. For how he'd let himself collapse in front of this man *yet again*.

"Think of this as the wildcard option. I know it doesn't scream *bakery*. But you said you liked the vibe you got from bars—the liveliness and the socializing—you just didn't want the alcohol? Well, I can see that happening here. Plus, there's something about this place that fits with your baking? Jazz and aprons and interesting recipes?"

Locky didn't react to that premise—*that the store fit him*. Because he wasn't considering this place. He'd already made up his mind, already applied for the jobs, and that was final.

It didn't matter that there was something strangely appealing and unexpected and, yes, completely absurd about this place. A bakery that looked like a prohibition speakeasy mixed with a Depression-era hotel lobby? With gilded furnishings and a dance floor? No one would expect that. No one would *want* that.

And neither did he—no matter the unfamiliar fizz that was forming on the edge of his thoughts.

But . . . still. He'd already put Benedict through enough these last few days. The least he could do was humor him.

Locky walked behind the counter and peered into the kitchen. Compared to the main area, it was almost intimidatingly undecorated—professional white and steel, with big commercial mixers and enormous ovens. "This can't be another pop-up?"

"Nope, this is a normal business with a normal lease. But the pizza shop is on hiatus. The owners had to go back to Texas to take care of some family stuff. But they've got this lease they can't get out of—paying rent even though they're not bringing in money. They're looking for someone to sublet the last chunk of time while they figure out what to do."

"How long is *a chunk*?"

"About four months. Until the end of February. And they've put some pretty specific conditions down. That's why I didn't think of this place originally. Plus . . ."

Benedict gestured to a long run of silver tubs beneath the counter. It was a cocktail bar—currently empty.

Locky wasn't bothered by that.

After all, it wasn't like he *had to* stock it.

He leaned against the counter, eyeing the antique cash register. It had buttons that probably went *ping* when the drawer sprung open. "And what are these *conditions*?"

"The owners are fine with replacing the neon sign with your own. And with changing the napkins and lamp shades and things like that. But nothing more permanent. They're hoping to come back and reopen the pizza shop at the end of the lease."

Locky drummed his fingers on the counter. Pleasingly, it was at the perfect height for him. "So someone could rent this place for a few months and then just walk away? With no obligation?"

"Exactly. And the owners might never come back, meaning the temporary tenant could start a new lease of their own. If they wanted to. No obligation, though."

"Interesting," said Locky, giving the space a closer inspection. It was in surprisingly good condition for a shuttered store. Apart from one wonky light up back, everything seemed to be working.

A curious sensation came over Locky as he dwelled on the long room. Even though it was quiet, there was something almost alive in the decor. Like he could hear the soul of the place—jazz drifting over laughter, deep and rich. People dancing to swing and big band music. The gentle clink of crockery and the scents of cinnamon and nutmeg and dark, toffee caramels.

And among it all was the chatter of the customers, talking about how amazing it was to find somewhere like this. Because finally they'd found somewhere welcoming. Finally they'd found somewhere they could feel safe.

The unexpected click of a phone camera made Locky turn back.

"Sorry," said Benedict, coming around the counter and showing him the photo. "You just looked really fitting behind the counter. See?"

Locky almost gasped as broad fingers brushed against his back, the tip of one coming dangerously close to sliding under the waistband of his underwear.

Suddenly, Locky was aware of every inch of the man beside him. Of the soft chest against Locky's shoulder. Of the strong chin by his forehead. Of the wide hip merging against his own belly.

Locky realized that Benedict wasn't trying some sleazy move. He seemed totally unaware of the effect he was having, talking excitedly about social media strategies. And yet, the texture of the moment had changed for Locky. A few seconds earlier, he'd been relaxed. Now it felt like a gale roaring against a brushfire, stoking a dangerous and unwelcome flame.

Benedict smelled of cologne—sweet and pink and far more playful than Locky would have expected. He'd been too distracted to notice it the last time he'd burrowed into Benedict's chest. Or the last *times*, Locky supposed, cursing how often he'd found himself in that pathetic position.

The scent didn't project itself like some did, resting close to Benedict's skin. That only made it more alluring, making Locky want to press his nose deeper into the man, taking in all of that sweet aroma. Just like it made Locky want to slide his own hand against Benedict's lower back. To run the tip of his pinky along that point between shirt and belt. To burrow his fingers beneath both, finding bare flesh, hot and tactile.

Locky tried to avoid the imagery, but it came anyway, fiery and glowing. Images of Benedict's shirt being ripped from his broad frame. Of Locky running his tongue along Benedict's belly. Of taking Benedict's enormous ass in both hands, gliding a thumb from the dimples above each cheek to the firm globes below—squeezing that flesh, warm and animal, with his tongue already extended.

Ready to taste the man.

Ready to *prepare* him.

Locky bit his cheek as the crackles collected in his groin. Because it wasn't like Benedict was trying to cause this reaction. It was just Locky's fucked-up mind, unable to control these thoughts and these feelings and these—*Jesus, stay the fuck down!*

No sooner had Locky registered how hard his cock was getting—stretching out his jeans in a slow, snaking growth— than he also realized just how bad a direction it was growing in. Because it was heading right toward Benedict's hip, like a shark sneaking up on its prey.

Locky tried to pull away, to free himself of the slow-motion car crash.

But it was too late.

Locky felt a hard press against his cockhead, throbbing right against Benedict's hip bone.

Benedict stopped talking mid-sentence, raising a confused eyebrow.

And then he looked down.

Benedict tapped on the walk-in fridge. "Are you okay in there?"

"Go away!" came a muffled voice from inside. "Let me die in peace."

"Yeah, that's what I'm worried about. The fridge isn't running, and you've been sitting in a well-sealed room for the last fifteen minutes. When the police come, the first thing they'll ask is *why didn't you open the door?*"

"Would anyone care if I ran out of air?"

"Okay, that's enough of that," said Benedict. "Ready or not, here I come."

He was met with a warm, antiseptic stillness. The fridge hadn't been turned on in months, but it was well cleaned, with nothing left inside but empty wire racks and one defeated man, slumped in the corner.

Benedict sat beside him.

"I'm really fucking sorry," said Locky, hiding his face.

Benedict gave a sad smile, even though Locky couldn't see it. "You've said that about eighty times now."

"And I'll say it eighty more! I'm really, *really* fucking sorry."

"You don't need to do that, Locky," said Benedict, reaching out a comforting hand but pausing before it made contact, hovering awkwardly in midair for a brief, shameful moment, before finally completing the journey.

Locky's shirt was damp.

The skin around his neck was burning.

Locky looked up from the burrow between his knees, like Benedict had just pressed his hand into poison ivy. "Aren't you worried I'll go feral again?"

"I wouldn't call getting a boner *going feral*."

"It is when it happens just from hugging. Or putting a hand on my back. What the fuck is wrong with me? Why can't I just . . ." Locky pinched his lips, the skin around his mouth going white against the blush. "Never mind. I'm just . . . I'm not like you, okay? I'm not perfect and put together and professional. I'm fucked up, and I'm damaged, and you're welcome to just leave. You've already dealt with enough of my shit."

A truck could have driven between Locky's words and his body language. Because his words screamed for Benedict to leave—and Benedict knew that he could. That Locky wouldn't blame him for driving away and losing his number and never seeing him again.

But Locky's body said the opposite, curling in on itself like an injured animal. Desperate to be held.

Benedict knew that leaving was the logical option. He'd been so disciplined with himself for so many years. Kept his distance and blocked countless clients, no matter how loudly his instincts had pleaded with him to stop.

And yet, right now, Benedict couldn't bring himself to do that. Because if he did, he'd always wonder what story was trapped behind those blue eyes.

And Locky wanted to talk about it—Benedict could see that. The words were like prisoners behind his tongue, bitten back and swallowed out of fear. The fear of spilling your guts onto a sea of blank stares, were no one understood your pain. Of not knowing how to explain the weird little walls you'd built around yourself over time, all to make it through the next day. The next hour.

How everything inside you wanted to scream and stay silent at the same time. Because speaking would get it all out, but it would also make everything too fucking *real*.

That complexity was something Benedict knew all too well.

Even in he'd never talked about it.

Not even to Tris.

Not even . . . to *himself*.

Because he'd never let himself dwell on all the shit he'd done. On all the ways he'd fucked up.

And here was Locky, thinking that Benedict was *perfect*?

It was heartbreaking.

When Benedict spoke, it was like he was watching himself from a disbelieving distance. Because these words couldn't be coming from *him*. After all these years of denial and deflection, he couldn't be sharing something so intimate, so painful.

Not now?

Not here?

Not with this man of all people—a virtual stranger?

Benedict swallowed hard, his mouth dry. "Do you remember when we were looking at warehouses? And I made us turn around quickly and switch streets."

Locky looked up. "Vaguely? I just thought we'd taken a wrong turn?"

"No," said Benedict, his blood running cold. His tongue felt like a rusted fishhook, trying to catch the words before they left his mouth. "We were about to cross in front of a former client's store. And I freaked out."

And there it was. Spoken aloud for the first time.

Benedict expected some kind of condescending pity from Locky, and was shocked to feel fingers against his own, warm against the cold fridge floor. When Benedict turned back, he wasn't met with the same man—shamed and shy. He was met with the man in the kitchen. The man with blue eyes that projected a certainty he probably never reserved for himself.

"Was it a bad experience with that client?" Locky asked, his voice steady.

"No! She was lovely. I just . . ." For a split second, Benedict thought about lying. About making himself seem *slightly* less pathetic. But the words had momentum now. Rushing out in a way he couldn't stop. An avalanche of admission—all his fuck ups, all his failings. "I don't visit my former clients. I block their numbers and pretend they don't exist when we're done. Because I can't stand the thought of seeing them go bankrupt. Of knowing that I fucked things up for them."

Benedict looked away, shamed by his admission, by his weakness and his stupidity. Because he knew what Locky would be thinking.

Is that it?

Because of course it wasn't enough to cause the pain that it did! Thousands of businesses folded every damn day. It was the reality of the world. It wasn't something that should cause him to fall to pieces like this. Only *real* trauma should do that. *Real* pain. All those people who'd suffered far worse and didn't bat an eyelash.

And here was he, letting himself be so weak and so fucking selfish! Letting himself abandon all those clients without explanation.

Their faces washed around Benedict, like a dam wall seizing under the strain of a flood. How many had tried to contact him? How many thought it was their fault—that they'd done something wrong or offended him?

But Locky didn't scoff. Whether out of mercy or just plain pity, he actually delved deeper. "I'd like to know more? If you're okay talking about it?"

Locky's voice was unexpectedly reassuring.

Like Benedict's pain wasn't ridiculous.

Like it was *justified*.

"I . . . I screwed up really badly in my first few years," Benedict continued. "I got too close to my first set of clients and kept giving advice long past their stores' opening. Helping them select new stock and expand locations and deal with unexpected issues. And it all just built up over time, one became five became thirty. There were too many people and too many stores and too many things to remember. I was giving each new client less and less time, just trying to keep up with all these former clients. And by the time Malcolm came along . . ."

The words seized in Benedict's throat—just like he'd kept the man's memory locked away in its plain white folder on his shelf.

But as much as he didn't want to relive this memory, Locky's warm grip spurred him on.

And so, through tears and awkward pauses, Benedict told Locky about Malcolm Robinson, his thirty-first client overall.

The one that he'd fucked over.

The one that he'd sent *bankrupt*.

Malcolm was an eccentric modern artist of the *my five-year-old could paint this so why is it worth fifty thousand dollars* school of painting. And unlike Locky, Malcolm had known exactly what he'd wanted—an expansive, impressive art space, with mazelike corridors and kooky installations and dramatic light shows. Benedict had helped as much as possible, but Malcolm's mind moved at a million miles a minute, and Benedict was caught up giving advice to all his previous clients. And somewhere in that fray, Benedict had missed some crucial details—like Malcolm wanting to sign a five-year lease in luxurious Union Square, completely unaffordable and based on impossible profit assumptions.

But Malcolm rushed ahead. And by the time Benedict realized, it was too late. The ink was dry on the lease, and the bankruptcy notice soon followed.

Benedict suddenly remembered how badly all of this would play into Locky's own fears. He scraped the tears from his cheeks, cursing himself for breaking down like this in front of a client. "You don't need to worry. I only ever take on one client at a time now. Giving them all my focus. I won't miss things like that again. I promise."

"That's not what I was worried about," said Locky, squeezing his hand tighter. "I was worried about you."

And in that strange moment, sitting in an empty fridge with a man he'd only known for a few days, Benedict believed him. Because there wasn't a space in those eyes for selfishness.

"So," said Benedict with a bitter laugh, gesturing broadly to Locky's lower half and desperate to change the subject. "I'm assuming you got a few less *sex is perfectly natural* talks and a few more *God is always watching* lectures?"

To Benedict's surprise, Locky shared the laugh. "No, that's . . . well there was a bit of that. A lot of it, actually. But that's not the issue. My mother was too much of a hypocrite for that stuff to stick."

"So . . . why all the boners?"

Locky exhaled slowly. "That stuff. *Sex*. It was always part of my drinking. Going out and partying and taking someone home? If I was having sex, then I was drunk. And if I was drinking, then I was looking to fuck. I don't even remember most of the sex I've had. I'm . . . I'm not sure I can remember any of it, actually."

A familiar expression of shame washed over Locky, and Benedict squeezed his hand firmly, encouraging him, just as Locky had done.

"And when I finally made the decision a decade ago to stop drinking, I stopped doing all that other stuff too. I was so fucking afraid that it might be a kind of doorway. That one thing could lead to the other, you know? So I just stopped. I forced it back. I used bargaining and shame, and every single thing I could think of. Until I just didn't do those kinds of things with other people. Or even with myself."

Benedict let those words sink in—that this handsome, beefy, virile man hadn't had sex or jerked off in almost a decade. "Wow," he whispered, unable to think of anything else to say.

"Yeah, *wow*," snorted Locky, looking Benedict over like a newly discovered land. He laughed again, small and sad. "We're a pretty messed-up pair, huh?"

"Maybe," said Benedict, running his thumb across Locky's palm. "But like I said—sometimes things are better when they're a little messed up."

Locky led them back through the restaurant in the glow of an odd kinship, two relative strangers who'd just shared something more intimate, more secret, than they'd ever told another person.

"I do like this place, you know," he said as Benedict reached for the lights. "It's such a random choice. But that makes me like it even more."

"So I should pencil it in as a maybe?"

"I . . . I wasn't lying when I said it's not the right time for me. I've already applied for a bunch of jobs. Things have moved on."

"And how long until the offers come in?"

"A few weeks, I guess? They want to have things in place by Thanksgiving. But I don't want to waste your time when I'm never following through. That wouldn't be fair."

"Even if you never open the store, Locky, I'd still like to help you to dream about it. Because maybe, one day, the time will be right."

Locky considered that, surveying this strange, special space with new eyes. And in that moment, he did wonder, for the very first time, what it might be like if all of this was his.

Even if only as a dream.

"Okay, *fine*," he said. "It's not like I'm doing anything else for the next few weeks."

SEVEN

Sweet & Sticky

The wind rustled Locky's hair, cool and pleasant below the late fall sky. Hazelnut-colored roofs peeked through amber leaves. Down the steep street was a picturesque view of Alcatraz, like a private resort in the twinkling bay. Which, in its own way, it kind of had been.

Locky hadn't ridden a cable car in years, although right now, alongside the sunshine and the high ring of the bell, he couldn't remember why. Maybe it was because he usually cycled everywhere, hitting the sloping streets with a clench of well-worked booty and that amazing feeling of struggle.

Benedict relaxed beside him on the outside seat of the carriage, with nothing between them and the rushing street below. Locky had never seen him without a suit before, although he still looked impossibly crisp—wearing jeans that gripped his tree-trunk thighs and a white t-shirt so simple it probably cost a fortune. He'd paired it with a Berkley letterman jacket, royal blue and sunburst yellow, alongside white Wayfarer sunglasses that matched his unmarked sneakers.

It shouldn't have looked as good as it did. There were too many pieces of 80s teen movies and 90s Jerry Seinfeld. But the way he was just sitting there, with a casual ankle across one knee and an arm draped over the wooden seat slats, he looked like every boy that Locky had been too afraid to talk to in high school.

Like he didn't have a single problem in the world.

But Locky knew that he did. Because Benedict had shared that with him—something nerve-racking and personal and so deep that the man had buried it down to his core, until he'd picked the strangest moment and the strangest partner to reveal it to.

Benedict was terrified of his clients going bankrupt, and he went to extreme lengths to avoid knowing what happened to them after they'd opened their stores.

Locky had thought about that these last few days—how lonely Benedict must have been. Playing the professional part in front of each new client. Hoping that this time, *this time*, it might turn out different. Only to have the car crash happen again and again.

Locky was lucky. At least he had a support network for some of his issues. But Benedict? He'd been alone through all of this—fear and panic and confusion.

Locky had also considered the irony of that. A few days ago, Locky had been trying to get away from Benedict. And now, their roles were reversed. Because that's what Benedict would do to him, wasn't it? If Locky actually followed through and opened his store, he'd become just like all the clients before him?

They hadn't talked about it explicitly, but the truth still hung between them. Even if Benedict wanted to help Locky, in just a few short weeks he might cut him off, blocking his number and tossing him aside.

And for reasons that Locky couldn't quite explain, that thought made him strangely sad.

Benedict raised a good-natured eyebrow—one that perfectly hid the storm behind the smile. "What are you looking at, stare bear?"

"Oh, nothing. Just wondering what your secret plan for the day is. Beyond *menu development*?"

"I could tell you, Mr. Sorenson," said Benedict, peering over his sunglasses like a judgmental librarian. "But that would ruin the surprise."

Locky stifled a smile. *Mr. Sorenson?* Benedict hadn't called him that since they'd first met—when Locky had specifically asked him not to. Usually, he hated *Mr. Sorenson* as much as he hated *Havelock*, with either making him sound like an old Scandinavian fisherman.

And yet, right now, with the gentle breeze and the soft sun, it didn't sound so bad. Not with the sly little grin that Benedict was giving him.

Locky dropped his drugstore sunglasses so low they almost slid off his nose. "Maybe I don't like surprises, Mr. Owens?"

"Oh, you'll *definitely* like this one."

Red paper lanterns draped over bustling streets. Footpaths pressed tight below the awnings of gift shops and jewelers, with towering vertical signs nestled between fire escapes and ornate metal balconies.

Locky spun through morning shoppers as he took it all in, relishing the hustle and the noise. He couldn't remember the last time he'd come to Chinatown—the last time he'd even had the chance. Not with his eight o'clock starts and weekends filled with even more work.

Sometimes he felt like he'd lived his entire life in the office, one day rolling into the next, month into month, year into year. But walking through the press of people here, at ten in the morning on a random Thursday, it felt surreal and almost wondrous. The earthy aroma of ginseng and medicinal teas rose up to meet him. Bright pops of color glowed from painted murals on red brick walls. The upturned corners of tiled roofs glinted with golden dragons.

Locky was so distracted by the magic of it all that he almost didn't notice when Benedict took them on a sudden detour, leaving the lantern-filled street for a single block, only to rejoin it a few minutes later.

There was a brief silence as Benedict shot him a glance— his shoulders pinched, jaw tight, as if wondering whether Locky would say something.

Locky considered that for a moment, whether he *should* say something. Yes, he understood what Benedict was going through—there was clearly a former client that Benedict hadn't wanted to walk past. And yes, Locky wanted to be there to talk when the moment was right.

But he also knew that sometimes you didn't want to talk. Sometimes you just wanted to push through and let it pass without discussion. Because dwelling on it only made it more real.

Locky had already shown Benedict that they could talk about these things. But right now, with that look on Benedict's face, Locky wanted to show him the opposite.

That they *didn't* have to talk about it.

Instead of raising the detour, Locky pointing to a window filled with bronze burnished ducks, succulent and glinting. And there was something in seeing Benedict relax, in seeing the realization that he didn't need to explain himself, that warmed Locky even more than the morning light.

"This is a test, isn't it?" said Locky, standing in the shade of a decorative streetlamp. "Something to do with menu development?"

"*What?!* Why would you say that?" said Benedict. His smile was both infuriating and adorable, making his cheeks go all chubby.

Locky had never been a fan of puzzles. But maybe he needed to learn? Because setting up a business *was* like a puzzle. With dozens of pieces that had to fit just right to make a full picture.

Locky took in the shops on the three street corners.

The first was an ancient-looking building selling fortune cookies, with a distant view of old ladies behind clanking machines. He'd heard about this place—that fortune cookies were invented right here in San Francisco, even if LA had *views* on that.

On the second corner was a compact bakery, barely big enough to fit five people but packed high with incredible treats. Buns were filled with lotus and pineapple, with red bean mooncakes and jeweled sesame balls. Locky's mouth watered at the sight, and he wasn't surprised to see a line stretching down the street. But what did surprise him was the way most customers seemed to be getting the same thing—egg tarts, with flaky pastry and golden yellow tops.

On the third corner was a tiny soup restaurant, dishing out steaming bowls of noodles and dumplings. As Locky peered closer, he noticed there wasn't a permanent menu, just a well-used blackboard on the counter, listing a few options for the day.

Locky snorted as Benedict's puzzle pieces came into view—the three options for his business plan.

He could open a store selling just one kind of thing, perfected over the years. Or a store that had a wide range of options, with a signature dish or two that people flocked for. Or maybe he could open a store of pure experimentation, making up the menu every single day.

Locky cleared his throat, fumbling for a sentence he couldn't quite start, not without sounding like a stereotype of himself.

Benedict saved him. "In case you're wondering—not saying you were—but the financially safest option would be the first one. It would involve fewer ingredients, a more consistent workflow, and much easier branding. Plus, you can still mix things up a little, like having a store that only sells cupcakes. They might all be the same thing, but you can still experiment with flavors."

Locky gave a grateful exhale at not needing to ask the questions about money and security. Of having Benedict already know what his biggest fears would be. It was a strange kind of familiarity, as comforting as it was confronting.

And now it was Locky's turn to sneak glances toward Benedict. Wondering if the man would judge him for taking the safe option. For not being bolder and taking bigger risks.

It was only a *plan*, after all. Locky could do what he liked, propose what he liked. Because it was never going to actually happen.

But Benedict didn't call him out. Instead, he patted Locky on the shoulder as the crossing blinked green. "Hungry?"

Locky stared at him for a moment before nodding. The strong hand stayed there until they were safely on the other side of the street. Like he wasn't worried that Locky's body might go feral on him again.

And as they stepped into the cool shade of the fortune cookie store, smelling of baked sugar and rich vanilla, Locky cursed himself for not wearing sunscreen.

Because he could feel the heat glowing against his cheeks.

It was a day later and Benedict was flicking through the draft business plan, clean white paper resting against the black leather of the steering wheel.

The folio glowed in the overcast morning. The plan was barely started, just page after page of pro forma boxes, most without a single scribble. But they would soon be filled. He'd seen to that. Because he'd managed to convince Locky to trust him. That the dream was worth developing, even if he didn't intend to follow through.

Benedict ran a well-manicured thumbnail over the empty sheets, thinking back to their moment in the fridge. He still couldn't believe that he'd admitted all those things. Things he'd never told another soul.

Of course, Tris knew half the story. He'd never told her explicitly, but she knew enough of his former clients to piece it together.

But he'd told Locky all of it. Said the actual words out loud. After ten years and hundreds of clients and doing everything he could to keep those fears hidden, he'd really just admitted it all. And to Locky Sorenson, no less—someone who was just as messed up as him.

It was strange to realize that those confessions were out there now. Strange, but also kind of nice, even if Benedict didn't know where this situation left him. Because he couldn't avoid getting too close to Locky, like he would with a normal client—they were way past that. But he also didn't know where their boundaries now lay.

Should he try to maintain some level of distance? Did he even need to? After all, Locky wasn't like a regular client—he'd made it clear he wasn't going to open his store. That meant there was no danger of his idea failing.

So . . . what was the risk in getting closer?

As Benedict stepped out of his car—golden leaves collecting on the polished roof—he did think, just for a moment, that it might be nice to not run away this time. To talk a little more about these feelings that he'd buried for so long. To let Locky unpack his own issues.

To just . . . be messed up together?

Benedict's eyes bulged as he stared at Locky's living room.

Over practically every surface were bits of notepaper torn into rough squares. There had to be hundreds of them, scattered over the coffee table and stuck to the curves of the couches and even covering the glass of the television. On every single one was the name of some dessert category, alongside a handful of messy notes like "keeps well" and "comforting" and "visually appealing."

And standing in the middle of them all was Locky.

There was an irony to his appearance, because even though he was dressed like he'd just rolled out of bed, his face looked like he hadn't slept in days. He was wearing a tight-fitting white t-shirt, chest hair cascading from the collar, alongside a pair of gray sweats that left *nothing* to the imagination.

Benedict did a double take at that, looking away before sneaking peeks at his thick-all-over client. Not that Locky noticed Benedict's attention. Or that he'd let himself in through the unlocked door. Locky was too busy spinning on the spot and muttering to himself.

That spinning didn't help. Because as much as Benedict tried not to stare, the sweats were gripping Locky's butt even more than his dick, showing off ass cheeks that were big and bouncy and stuffed into the light cotton like two bulging bike helmets.

It wasn't like Benedict hadn't noticed Locky's ass before— it was pretty hard to miss. But right now, it was like those cheeks had a gravitational pull on Benedict's eyeballs, making him imagine how firm and furry they would be under his touch, with nothing but that thin layer of fabric hiding them from view.

Kai appeared from the hall, fully suited apart from his tie, which was threaded in loose strands around his unbuttoned collar. He approached Benedict for what appeared to be a greeting hug but turned into a throttle. "I should have left you on that damn pier," Kai hissed, shaking Benedict back and forth by his lapels. "He's been like this all night. You broke the wall on his imagination and now my sofa is covered with his dream splatters!"

"That sounds kinda hot?"

"Shut up! If you don't fix him, I'll get one of those cages you take dogs to the vet in!"

"You don't own one already?"

"Mask, yes. Tail butt plug, also yes. Cage, not yet. But, so help me God, if I come back tonight and it still looks like this, I'll go full pup master on his ass!"

Benedict didn't have time to respond before Kai slammed the door, the noise finally catching Locky's attention.

"Oh, thank God you're here," he said, dragging Benedict into the cyclone of paper. "It's all gotten a bit out of hand. But I did what you asked."

Benedict stumbled into a section of paper marked *European Spiced Cookies*, inadvertently kicking the *speculaas* onto the *pepparkakor*. "I didn't have *this* in mind when I said *come up with a few menu options*."

"Well, if I'm going to specialize in just one kind of treat, I've got to make an informed choice."

"Has . . . anyone ever talked to you about ADHD hyperfocus?" Benedict said, delicate as he could. "You know, where someone goes from a scattered mess to strangely organized over one specific thing?"

Locky waved a dismissive hand. "You wanted options, I've delivered options!"

Benedict was going to say, *I didn't tell you to catalog the entire history of sugar meeting flour*, but was met by an expression from Locky that was dangerously close to pride. And that, Benedict had to admit, was a big improvement over confusion and shame.

"Well, excellent," said Benedict, trying to find a place to sit before giving up. The only available stool was occupied by Apricot, who eyed him with a mocking stretch. "I guess we should start whittling these down?" Benedict picked up the nearest piece of paper. "For example, I'm pretty sure you shouldn't specialize in *Asian Cakes and Pastries— ESPECIALLY EGG TARTS*, all capital letters."

Locky snatched the paper. "That was your fault for taking me to Chinatown. I've been thinking about the tarts for days."

"It was yesterday, Locky. And you ate seven of them."

As Benedict hung his suit jacket over the nearest lamp, he couldn't help notice how Locky's gaze darted away when Benedict turned back around—almost like Locky had been taking his own survey of Benedict's curvy ass.

Locky froze for a moment, before he half-walked, half-sprinted out of the living room, not stopping until he was safety behind the kitchen counter. "Coffee?" he squeaked, his voice as high as the red-velvet blush that was spreading through his hairline.

Benedict stared at the counter full of ingredients. There were containers of flours and sugars and identical-looking white powders. Beside them was a tower of jars, full of viscous liquids that Benedict had never heard of before, like treacle and golden syrup. He didn't know what they were. And right now, after six hours of whittling, he didn't want to ask. Not when they were finally making progress.

"Right," he said, sipping his sixth cup of coffee. "Down to the final duel?"

"Cupcakes versus pies," said Locky with a sage nod.

"Honestly, I never saw this coming. I thought cheesecakes would've made the top two."

Benedict squinted at the big pieces of paper taped to the living room wall, listing pros and cons in Locky's haphazard handwriting. "If you'll recall, Mr. Sorenson, you decided there were too many other stores specializing in cheesecakes, that they universally relied on dairy, and even though they keep quite well, you derisively called them *a bit too brunchy*?"

It hadn't been an intentional decision to call Locky *Mr. Sorenson* when they were bantering, it had just popped out a few times and Locky hadn't corrected him. Plus, there was something strangely relaxed about the title. Relaxed and, if Benedict was honest, ever so slightly bratty.

"Not *derisively*!" said Locky. "There's just something more ten a.m. brunch about cheesecake than ten p.m. swing dancing."

Benedict bit back a laugh. Because Kai was right—the dream wall had broken. A few days ago, *Pizza My Mind* was just someone else's store. But now, Locky was already imagining what the evenings might look like in *his* store. Imagining that little stage playing swing music at ten p.m.

And the best part was, Locky probably didn't even realize the daydreams were forming. And Benedict certainly wasn't going to draw attention to it.

Instead, he clapped his hands together. "Well, cupcakes or pies? I guess you'll have to do a bake off?"

"Correction," said Locky, reaching behind a tall cupboard door. "*We* will have to do a bake off."

Locky returned holding a second apron, matching his own. He waved the neck loop invitingly and Benedict marveled, not for the first time, at just how different the man seemed when he was on this side of the bench. Because it wasn't like Locky was pretending to be a different person here. It was more like he finally became himself. And there was something incredibly hot in seeing the playful, obsessively nerdy side of Locky. The man who'd write down a hundred different baked goods or get so focused on something that he'd wander around obliviously in bulgy sweats.

Benedict cocked an eyebrow. "Baking isn't exactly my strong suit."

"Come on. It will be fun. You can be my sous-chef."

"Who's Sue? Never met her before?"

"It means second in command, Mr. Owens. If you're interested in working under me?"

"Sure! That sounds hot," said Benedict instinctively, before realizing what he'd just said.

And who he'd just said it to.

It would have been so much better if Locky had laughed. Or if Benedict had laughed. Or if either of them had carried on without drawing attention to the moment. Because that would have meant it was just some casual rib, some throwaway joke between acquaintances.

Instead, both of them mumbled synchronized apologies, which only emphasized how much it *wasn't* a joke.

It wasn't news to Benedict that he found Locky hot. The man was handsome and awkward, and Benedict had already given plenty of nocturnal attention to the thought of the big bear fucking his brains out. Just like he knew the feeling was mutual. He'd seen Locky's physical reactions to his touch enough times. And he'd literally caught Locky checking him out this morning.

But they'd never shared a mutual recognition of this fact before. And now, it was just like their conversation in the fridge—something had been revealed that neither of them could take back.

Not that Benedict would ever follow through on it! Locky had his abstinence, and for damn good reasons. It was all tied up in his sobriety, and Benedict would never do anything to challenge that. Just like Benedict had his own reasons for keeping his distance. He'd already gotten closer to Locky than any client before him. But that didn't mean he'd toss every preservation instinct aside and try to *fuck* this guy.

Benedict gathered himself. "Sorry, I didn't mean . . . *So, baking, huh?*"

"Yes, *baking*, yes!" said Locky, his fair complexion unable to conceal the heavy blush. He cleared his throat and made an odd little movement toward the counter, pressing his body flat against the marble. "Do you have any experience?"

"Tons. I'm an expert," said Benedict, knowing that he shouldn't make the joke, but still wanting to see just how far he could make that blush spread. "Oh, sorry. You mean with *baking*? Not really. You'll probably have to guide me pretty closely."

To Benedict's delight, the blush spread all the way down Locky's neck. "Well . . . I . . . I promise I'll be gentle with you."

And it took all of Benedict's willpower not to say *I'd really rather you weren't.*

Benedict sifted the flour, making a snow-dusted halo around the glass bowl. He was awful at this, but Locky didn't say anything, looking over with these little glances that made

Benedict want to lean him against the cupboard and kiss his cute nose.

"You never actually told me how you got into baking?" said Benedict, the moment filled with soft jazz and the gentle purr of Apricot from the edge of the counter.

"I mean, it's not exactly a fairy-tale story. None of that *Gran and I used to make cookies in her cozy kitchen* crap."

Benedict remembered what Locky had said in the diner—about not having those kinds of memories from his childhood. He thought about dropping the subject, but curiosity got the better of him. "I'd still like to hear it, if that's okay?"

Locky appeared to consider this, spooning powdered sugar into a stand mixer. "If I didn't cook as a kid, I wouldn't have eaten."

Benedict stopped mid-sift, the words ringing hot in his ears. "Jesus, Locky . . ."

"Right? My mom was all about the clubs, always on the hunt for the hottest spot and the hottest guy. I was the unhappy accident from one of those hookups, although she never narrowed it down beyond a dozen candidates. Just like she never let my arrival slow down her lifestyle. There was always another night, another club, another man." Locky paused before finishing in a low voice. "Another fucking bottle."

Benedict reached for Locky's hand across the counter, and the man took it gratefully.

"At night, I used to turn the cooking channels on in the background, just so I could pretend I wasn't alone. Or I'd play the jazz station on an old portable radio, imagining I was hosting these fancy dinner parties."

Locky rubbed his face against a thick bicep, seeming annoyed that something this awful might cause the emotion to well up. "And you know how the story goes. Boy grows up, and what does he do? Chases the same clubs and the same men, just like his mama taught him. Drugs, drink and dick. Crying in the gutter with his whiskey-soaked *woe is me*-s." Another tear ran through Locky's beard, this time joined by a bitter laugh. "Such a fucking stereotype, right?"

Benedict squeezed hard on Locky's hand. "How did you get out of it?"

Locky gathered his breath. "I was supposed to catch up with a friend from high school. One of the few I still had. We hadn't seen each other in ages and she put on this big feast for me. And I just never showed up, never even remembered that we'd made the fucking plans. Instead, I was drunk or high or in the middle of some fuck pile. And I know people might scoff—*oh, it's just one missed dinner*. But it fucking broke me. Because when I saw her again, she told what her night had been like—sitting alone in her apartment, waiting for someone that would never come. I just thought: like mother like fucking son, huh? I've finally become just as reckless and selfish and unreliable as *her*."

An unexpected calm washed over Locky, a darkness he must have long ago reckoned with. "And something just snapped in me, you know? I knew I didn't want to be like that. That I was *better* than that. So I found my first group meeting. I saved up and went to college, for the most boring, stable thing I could find. I cut out everything from that former life, everything that might tempt me back. And I just tried to be better. To get that nine-to-five and be as normal as possible."

Benedict exhaled slowly. Suddenly, Locky's contradictions made sense. The fear of sex? The fear of spending money? Why someone as creative as Locky would trap himself away in a profession he didn't love.

Because, despite everything he'd gone through, despite everything he'd endured, Locky just wanted to be a better person.

"I think you've come a really long way, Locky," said Benedict. "And I think you should be really fucking proud of that."

Locky resisted the urge to intervene, despite how unevenly Benedict was trimming the pastry. Because there was something charming in seeing him like this, with his shirt sleeves rolled up and his tie discarded.

Benedict stared at his handiwork. "I . . . completely butchered that, didn't I?"

"No! Well, yes. A little."

"A little?"

"Okay, a lot. But pies are meant to look rustic."

"Should I add that to the list of pros on the pie list?" said Benedict, gesturing a pastry-crusted hand to the wall. "That you can screw them up and they still look good?"

"Maybe wash your hands first? If you get butter on Kai's Rubelli wallpaper he'll kill both of us."

Benedict snorted. "He finally got his Rubelli, huh? Just like he always wanted."

"I keep forgetting you roomed with him in college. What was little twink Kai like?"

"The same but skinnier? If he wasn't talking about boys, he was talking about brands. He was so obsessed with shaking off his rural upbringing. He always said that when he made it big, he'd only work for Fortune 500s, and only drive a German car, and he'd live in the right neighborhood and wear the right suits and yada, yada, yada." Benedict looked around the apartment. "I guess he made it happen."

"I don't think *you* can talk much about suits, Mr. Owens."

"Touché. Although you can blame my parents for that. And Tris. She's always argued that small businesses owners should act like big time CEOs. That it makes your clients feel like they're getting the diamond club experience, even if they're only paying for bronze. At least I managed to avoid the Fortune 500s?"

"You weren't tempted to be like Kai? Take a trip down millionaire's row as a high-powered consultant?"

"I'm lucky that I can offer my services for a reasonable price. Money isn't exactly an issue in the Owens family."

Locky thought about that. "Not that I'm asking for a handout, but why charge at all, if you don't need the money?"

"I tried! The first few months after I graduated, I thought I'd offer my services for free. Handing them out to whoever needed them most. But it didn't work. Clients always felt bad about the situation, like they were exploiting me, or they'd rush through everything so fast I couldn't do a proper job. I didn't hit my stride until I started charging."

"So you'd do this work for free? If you could?"

"Yeah, I would. I remember helping some family friends when I was still a freshman. It was just some basic business advice to streamline their boutique, but it doubled their sales in just a few months. And that stuck with me. You aren't just making tiny tweaks on a spreadsheet with small businesses, you're literally changing someone's life."

"So that closeness wasn't something you always avoided?" said Locky, before quickly backtracking. "Sorry, I didn't mean . . . You don't have to talk about it if you don't want to."

"No, it's fine. God, you've shared so much about yourself, I'm probably due. I actually loved that about the job. Getting to know these funny, weird, passionate people with clever ideas but no clue how to make them real."

Benedict laughed as he launched into the greatest hits of his former clients, captivating Locky with the hijinks. There were unbelievably niche business permits and last-second deals to secure rugs from Belgium, and a live dog-grooming display that went horribly wrong after a prized poodle got a tummy bug.

And with each story, the glow around Benedict seemed to brighten. The way his face lit up as he remembered these people.

And then, the glow faded.

Locky wrapped Benedict in a hug as the tears came, sudden and sharp. Just like Benedict had done for him. Just like Benedict deserved.

"Sorry," sniffled Benedict. "It's so fucking stupid. It was just one client, one fucking bankruptcy. I know I've done a lot of good, that I've helped a lot of people. So why can't I just get over it? It's not like I went through any *real* trauma. This is nothing compared to what you experienced."

Locky rubbed Benedict's back, his jaw set by something he encountered far too often in his nightly meetings. "Please don't do that to yourself, Benedict," he said softly.

"What do you mean?"

"Don't minimize your suffering like that. Don't tell

yourself that your pain is invalid because it isn't big enough, or that other people have been through more. Because down that path lies shame instead of healing. Life affects everyone differently. Some people get bitten by a dog and shrug it off. Others spend every day of their life terrified that it will happen again. There's no rhyme for these things. It isn't about how weak or strong you are. And it isn't for other people to decide whether or not your trauma is real. It *is* real, because you've lived it."

Benedict didn't respond to that. But Locky could have sworn his breathing became a little easier.

"So how does your panic manifest? Like, is this a problem? Being here with me? It's okay if it is. I won't be offended."

Benedict gave him a tragic smile. "You're not going to open your store, right?"

"Not even a little bit."

"Then I think we'll be fine. It's low risk, you know?"

Locky nodded, the relief building in his chest— confirmation that Benedict didn't plan to cut him off once they were done making his business plan. It was a relief Locky didn't know he'd been craving.

"And with your regular clients?"

"It's hard to explain. Not getting close is more of a logical defense than a visceral one. Just to make it easier at the end? The actual nerves don't start until closer to opening day. Then the thoughts creep in—all the second guessing. What if I've forgotten something or given bad advice? What if someone's trusted me and I've put them in a position to fail? And by the time their store actually opens . . ."

Benedict's lip quivered and Locky could see the guilt wash across his face. All the people that he'd abandoned. All the people that he'd pushed away. The connections that had been severed before their time. The friends that had been forgotten before they'd been made.

This time, Benedict held the emotion back, blinking it gone. "Thank you for putting up with this," he whispered. "You've got enough going on without taking on my shit."

"Funny," said Locky. "I was about to say the same thing to you."

Locky could have bottled the smell of his kitchen—spicy cinnamon and sweet vanilla, deep chocolate and the fragrant tang of green apples. It was just on dusk now, and the room seemed to glow like a crackling fireplace.

Benedict leaned over the counter and took a deep breath. On the left were red velvet cupcakes, their ruddy crumb topped by an obscene amount of pearl-white frosting, double the height of the cake. On the right was a Dutch apple pie, the crisp golden crust giving way to a Christmas-warm crumble, the caramelized spots swirling with a dark, sweet resonance.

Locky sat on the living room floor with his laptop, finding some fitting background music to enhance the tasting experience—just as Benedict had suggested. He selected "Fly Me to the Moon," by Frank Sinatra and Count Basie, filling the room with a rich and mellow ambience.

They were both in socks now, with Locky tapping his foot against the thick rug. And rather than summoning Locky back, Benedict brought the desserts over to him, sitting with his legs folded into the space between them, their feet close but not quite touching.

Now, the only thing left to do was make the final decision.

Locky took the spoon first, digging the glinting metal into crisp pastry. Apple pieces flowed from the crust, the sauce sweet and sticky.

And as Locky held the spoon up to the light, a thought overtook him, making his hand pause and his heart beat faster.

Because this feeling—this strange and curious feeling—was new to him.

No, not new.

Forgotten.

And Locky's defenses told him to keep it that way. That he was being stupid. That he shouldn't indulge this sudden desire. That it was too risky and too much could go wrong.

And his defenses were right to think that. Of course they were. They'd kept him safe for so damn long.

But in this moment, in this place . . . Locky didn't want to be *safe* anymore.

Locky turned the spoon around and brought it slowly to Benedict's lips. "I owe you the first bite," he whispered, his fingers shaking. "After those awful cookies I gave you last time."

Benedict looked at his hand curiously, and Locky feared that he'd misread everything. That all the comments and touches throughout the day had been nothing more than two broken people finding platonic comfort in each other.

Locky made to pull his hand back, feeling foolish. But Benedict stopped him, resting fingers against Locky's elbow. Those same fingers slid slowly up Locky's forearm, the touch ticklish, before finding their grip against Locky's wrist—thumb curled against his palm, fingers holding the back of his hand steady.

"Nothing you make could ever be awful, Mr. Sorenson," said Benedict, his big brown eyes fixed on Locky as he brought his mouth to the metal, holding out his tongue ever so slightly, pink and soft against the silver. And Locky could have sworn, just for a moment, that Benedict pressed his tongue tip along the smooth curve of the spoon before wrapping his lips around the shaft.

The look on Benedict's face was one that Locky would savor for as long as he lived. Because he looked like he was basking in warm sun on a spring day. Like he'd never known a moment of pain.

Benedict licked his lips and swallowed slowly, seeming to savor the taste. Locky's stomach was filled with butterflies—imagining that he was that spoon. Imagining that he was feeling that pink and delicate tongue sliding across his skin.

Benedict's fingertips brushed across Locky's knuckles as he took the spoon for himself, carving out another divot of apple pie. He offered it to Locky, sweet and steaming.

Fingers still shaking, Locky returned the gripping gesture, running fingers up Benedict's forearm before coming to rest against his hand. Locky was barely able to handle how much his chest was pounding or how wide Benedict was smiling.

The spoon came softly across his own tongue, held out slightly, just like Benedict had done.

The warm sweetness swelled through Locky's mouth, rich and heady. And in that moment, Locky didn't know if it was the song or the spice or their long day together, but nothing had ever tasted quite so wonderful.

Locky was surrounded by a strange sensation, like moonlight drifting through smoke. The sound of laughter, sweet as cinnamon. The rise and fall of notes as people danced the stars to sleep. And through it all that taste of butter and vanilla. Like a promise that everything would be okay.

And then, for the first time ever, with a clarity that almost made him gasp, Locky could *see* his bakery.

When he finally opened his eyes, Benedict was grinning. "Pies?" he asked.

Locky let the taste linger, before finally nodding. "Pies," he repeated. The music tempted Locky's focus as he turned to the laptop, the words forming as the smoke faded from view. "You . . . said puns sell, right?"

Benedict's grin grew wider. "I did. Do you have a good one?"

"Maybe? What do you think about the name . . . *Pie Me to the Moon?*"

He'd expected Benedict to laugh. But instead, Benedict's expression set Locky's skin aflame. Because Benedict looked at him like was fine art in a gallery, precious and curious and wonderful. "You, Mr. Sorenson, are far too fucking adorable."

Locky shuddered under the praise, under the heat of how it was said. Because it wasn't made as some playful comment. It was said with fire—in a voice that practically pinned him to the rug and laid warm kisses along his neck.

Benedict seemed to realize this as well. "Sorry, that was . . . I'm not trying to break your rules or anything."

Locky's stomach sank, struggling to find the right thing to say. Because of course Benedict would respond that way. After everything Locky had said about his decade without sex, it would be cruel for him to do anything else.

Worse still, Locky didn't know where to go from here. Because what was he even asking? What was he even offering?

Was he just playing around with a desire—just entertaining the thought? Or was he actually proposing something real—something *physical*?

Locky didn't know. Not for certain.

The only thing he knew was that he didn't want this moment to end. Or for Benedict to stop touching him.

And if he didn't say something now, the moment might pass.

When Locky finally spoke, chest pounding and skin prickling, it felt like ten years of fear and torment were dancing across his tongue. "I . . . I think a decade might be long enough? You know?"

Before Benedict could respond there was a burst of hallway light as Kai opened the front door. He looked down at them with a raised eyebrow, and it took Locky and Benedict a surprised beat before they ungripped each other's hands, like teenagers caught under the bleachers.

Kai gave them a shit-eating grin. "As much as I'd love to mock whatever *this* is, you know your meeting starts in fifteen minutes?"

Locky scrambled for his phone, knocking over the uneaten cupcakes. "Oh, fuck! Oh, fuck! Oh, fuck!"

Kai waved a hand. "Breathe, Babycakes. Daddy will drive you."

Locky ran toward his bedroom to change, before remembering the conversation he'd just been having. He turned around sharply, only to run into Benedict's chest.

He looked up at Benedict, cold reality slapping Locky across the face. Because why the fuck had he said all that stuff? He'd only just found Benedict, broken and vulnerable and finally having someone to talk to, and Locky had taken it *there*? It was so fucking selfish of him. Benedict needed someone to help him, to understand him, not someone who'd use his vulnerability for their own twisted desires!

"I'm so sorry," said Locky. "That was stupid of me. Just forget I said anything, okay?"

But rather than being relieved that he could now ignore Locky's offer, Benedict leaned in by his ear, so close that Locky could almost taste the cinnamon on his breath. "And what if I don't want to forget about it?" said Benedict, his voice flickering with fire. "What if I really liked where that conversation was going, Mr. Sorenson?"

EIGHT

Gimmie Moiré

Locky and Adriana were trying to calm Jared, whose twitchy footsteps were echoing through the cavernous lobby, all sharp lines and blaring white lights. Office buildings in San Francisco generally went one of two ways—friendly, open-aired lofts, or sterile steel hangers—and the entrance to Dellacor Industrial was definitely the latter.

It was a decor that made Jared's polka-dot tie and double-breasted suit stand out even more. The look wasn't helped by the crumpled paper bag he was huffing on, something Locky had only seen in movies.

"Buddy," said Locky, as Jared paced circles around the gray leather lounges. "We've talked about this. You've got great skills and great references. And the fact they want to interview you shows they're interested."

"Yeah," said Adriana, trying to keep pace with Jared's frenetic speed. "And we went through interview questions like a *million times* yesterday. They worked for my interview with White Stone, and they'll work for you too!"

Jared pulled his face from the paper. "They *won't* work for me! What if they ask something we haven't prepared for? What if they hate me and think I'm weird and I screw everything up!"

"Jared," said Locky, stepping delicately into his path. "Did you like working at SunSpark?"

Jared looked up from the floor and nodded, the bag crinkling as it inflated.

"And what did you like about it?"

Adriana plucked the bag away and basketball shot it into a nearby trash can, leaving Jared with nothing but a guilty look. "I just . . . I liked putting things in order. The green energy industry is growing so fast, and there were always new deals and new clients and new contracts. I liked finding order among the chaos."

Locky reached over and straightened Jared's tie. "Well, Dellacor is big into 3D printing. A leader in an exciting new industry. Lots of new deals and new clients and new contracts. So tell them exactly what you just said, and I promise they'll love it."

Before Jared could respond, a woman appeared by the elevators, calling his name.

Locky patted Jared's chest companionably, feeling the pounding heartbeat beneath. "You got this, buddy. I know you do."

When Jared was gone, Locky and Adriana slumped onto the lounges—careful to avoid a Tupperware cake carrier. They shared an exhausted look, having spent the better part of two days helping Jared prepare, including several interventions to stop him canceling the interview altogether.

Not that Locky had minded the distraction.

It had given him an excuse to not see Benedict.

Not that Benedict had done anything wrong! Even if

Locky did get skin-prickles and butterflies thinking about their long day of baking. Of running fingers up each other's forearms. Of the final words Benedict left him with:

What if I really liked where that conversation was going, Mr. Sorenson?

Locky gulped at that memory—at the way Benedict had said it. Because, yes, Locky had started all this. He'd changed everything between them with his *suggestion*.

But now, Locky didn't have the first clue what to do. Benedict was interested in *where that conversation was going*—helping Locky break his sexual drought. But how would it happen? And when? And how was Locky supposed to behave now?

He had a social media session booked with Benedict in a few days' time, and he was already nervous about how their dynamic would shift. Like . . . should Locky waltz in wearing nothing but a jockstrap and just go for it? Or should he wait until Benedict made the first move? Or was he supposed to just act normal and go with the flow?

Locky's ten years of abstinence had never felt so obvious. Because he didn't have the first clue how to flirt anymore. It used to be so easy! Walk into a club, find someone with a vaguely appealing face, and just go for it. But now Locky knew that he'd be overanalyzing every look and touch and tone of voice.

It wasn't like he *wanted* to rush things along. This was new and sweaty and scary. But this current situation, where the sex might happen at any moment, was putting him on edge.

"What's the cake for, Boss Man," said Adriana, lazily tapping the plastic container with an acrylic nail.

"You remember Grace in marketing? It's her thirtieth

wedding anniversary. What? Don't give me that look. She was there when I started, and she was always lovely to me."

"Are you going to cycle cakes around town forever?"

"Not *forever*. Just until everyone is settled into new jobs."

Adriana clicked her tongue, her expression somewhere between disbelief and admiration. "You really are something, you know that?"

Locky looked away awkwardly. "It's nothing. Everyone would do the same thing."

"No," said Adriana, giving him a gentle flick on the forearm. "They really wouldn't."

There was no phrase in the English language worse than *act natural*. Particularly when Locky had completely forgotten how his hands worked.

Seriously, where did he normally put them? Jamming them by his side made him look like he was hiding in a broom closet. Crossing them in front of his apron made him look like a toddler apologizing for breaking Granny's best vase. And shoving them on his hips made him look like he was about to launch into a rendition of *I'm a little teapot*.

"Wow, so natural!" said Benedict, looking up from his chunky digital camera, the one he'd been wielding for the last half hour around the Pizza My Mind kitchen.

"I told you I'd be terrible!"

"No, come on, you look great! The pinstriped business shirt and rustic apron is a very sexy vibe."

Locky tried to stomp down the blush before it started. It felt like he'd spent their last few meetings as a KitchenAid.

If anything, Locky's twitchiness was worse than he'd anticipated—a twitchiness that Benedict didn't seem to share. Because why would he? Benedict had already told him the situation. Locky wasn't going to open his store, so he was low risk. That meant Benedict wasn't going to get nervous about this arrangement. He could be as relaxed and flirty as he liked.

Which might have been why Benedict seemed particularly playful today. Like everything carried a little more meaning.

It would have been frustrating—well, it was frustrating—but it would have been even more frustrating if that playfulness wasn't so damn effective. Because after ten years, the last thing Locky wanted was some slick nightclub bad boy, strutting around with an impersonal chat-up line and treating him like a piece of meat. He wanted someone who understood his situation. Someone who could make space for things to go wrong or be awkward or for Locky to freak the fuck out.

"Do we have to do social media?" Locky groaned, after far too many shutter clicks. "Couldn't we finish the menu development? Choosing pies for the permanent menu actually sounded fun."

Benedict scooted around, grabbing different angles. "And we will, Mr. Sorenson. But the social media package takes time to finish. So it's better to start now."

Locky huffed, not even trying to pose anymore. Because what was the point of social media?

He hadn't stayed with his therapist long enough to pinpoint exactly what his *mental disorders* were. General anxiety disorder? Sure, he got nervous about certain things, but not persistently enough to tick that box. A phobia of spending money—or *chrometophobia* as Dr. Jenkins had said with his smug little smirk? On himself, absolutely. It wasn't an accident that he rode a third-hand pile of rust everywhere, or that he paid cut-price rent to a friend when he could've started his own mortgage years ago. But that didn't explain his lack of concern spending money on other people, like buying good coffee for the nightly meeting or donating to Evelyn's charities or treating his team to a celebratory lunch at the end of a major project.

In fact, the only thing Dr. J had completely ruled out was a social anxiety disorder—assuring Locky that his fear of getting a boner in public was more of a justifiable aversion to getting fired for lewd conduct.

If anything, Locky *liked* being around people. Preferred it, in fact. He even liked crowded spaces, which let him fade into the noise and momentum of an area.

In those first few months after he found his sobriety, he would often just sit in the mall food court with his eyes closed, listening to the sounds of normal life around him, mundane conversations and the clacking of trays and the notices over the speakers—the sounds of people who woke up and went to work and didn't stumble into a stranger's bed at 4 a.m.

But, as social as Locky was, social media had never appealed to him. Because how did sending messages over the internet create friendships? How did posting photos of your breakfast bring people together?

"And this will definitely be private?" Locky asked, over the endless camera clicks.

"Yup, I'll make up a website and create the social media profiles, but I'll set them all offline, ready for you to take over down the line—and yes, I know you don't have any intention of actually doing that." Benedict scrolled through his handiwork on the camera screen. "Right, that's enough stills. Time for some video!"

Locky threw back his head. "Seriously?"

Benedict slid Locky the box of ingredients they'd brought from the apartment. "Come on, grumpy pants. The website will look more professional if there's video of you getting all cute and artisanal."

Locky grumbled as he unpacked, again having to supress the blush at Benedict calling him *cute*. "Couldn't we have done this back home?"

"Trust me, the white-and-silver vibe will make everything pop. Plus, the owners begged Tris to give you a free day in here. They seem pretty desperate to get a tenant in." As if on cue, a beam of sunlight drifted through the window. "Oh, that's perfect! Just pretend I'm not here. Try to—"

"Act natural?"

"*Exactly!*"

"Huh?" said Locky, the half-kneaded dough running thick and sticky through his fingers.

Benedict stared at the camera. "Crap. It looks like we've got moiré."

"What the hell is moiré?"

"It's a camera thing. Fine patterns can sometimes go weird on video. See?"

Locky could indeed see the problem, although it wasn't the first thing he noticed. The framing of the video was surprisingly beautiful, with the white walls and golden sunlight making everything look far more professional and high-end than he'd expected. The only problem was the way the pinstripes of his business shirt were blurring into one hideous splodge. "Oh, God. Is there some button you can press to make it go away?"

"Unfortunately not. Sorry, I should have told you to wear a solid color."

Locky stared at the screen. As much as he hated having his picture taken—and he *really* did—there was something almost magical about the image playing back. The colors seemed even warmer than real life, like honey had been brushed over every surface. The ovens in the background faded off into a beautiful blur. And the way he was centered at the bench, with his apron flour-dusted and his sleeves rolled up . . .

Locky realized that he'd never seen himself bake before. And right now, in this video, with the sunlight and the framing and the way he was kneading the dough, he just looked . . . *right*.

He looked like a real baker.

"So we can't do anything to save it?"

"Sorry, it's just one of those things. But we can set up at your apartment. Change clothes there?"

Locky glanced out the window, at the golden light that wouldn't last long. And then he looked at Benedict, wearing his light gray suit. He wasn't wearing a tie today, which was new for him, but he was wearing a crisp white business shirt, without a single pattern or pinstripe to be seen.

"Could we . . . maybe swap shirts?"

To Locky's surprise, Benedict immediately tugged off his jacket, revealing the swell of his broad chest and shoulders. "Great idea! Quickly, let's try and keep the light."

As Benedict reached for his shirt buttons, Locky tried to speak—to explain that he hadn't meant getting naked it front of each other right here!

But he was too late.

Benedict had already removed his shirt.

And Locky forgot entirely about the video.

Sunlight glowed across Benedict's neck and shoulders, silhouetting a strong and stocky chest with tight black curls of hair roaming over his full belly, as if directing the eye to wander over all his masculine heft. His arms were pure bulk, not toned exactly, but adding beautifully to the width of the man. And yet, despite the allure of Benedict's exposed skin, Locky's gaze was drawn to something else entirely.

Something he hadn't expected.

Something that set his stomach aflutter.

"Your nipples," said Locky, gulping at the two glints of steel among the obsidian. "You . . . you have them pierced?"

Benedict had already undone the top button of his suit pants when he'd freed his shirt, revealing a peek of bright red waistband. But now he paused from his haste, taking in Locky's expression.

And suddenly his demeanor changed. Before he'd been undressing as function, to swap clothes quickly and not lose the light. But suddenly he was grinning.

Suddenly he was *hungry*.

Oh, fuck. Oh, fuck. Oh, fuck, thought Locky, as Benedict stepped closer. *Is it now? Am I ready? Do I even want this?*

His cock answered the physical part of the question for him, rising rapidly beneath the apron, like a loyal soldier called to war.

Locky's skin prickled as Benedict walked toward him. So big and handsome and with such intent in his eyes. Eyes that wanted to touch Locky. To kiss him. To consume him.

Locky's dick throbbed hard at that, confirming that it wanted those things too. And yet, against that urgent arousal were other thoughts. Darker thoughts. Thoughts about what might happen afterward—of the bad habits he might fall back into.

Benedict stopped mid-step, clearly seeing the conflict on Locky's face. But rather than disappointment, he smiled—not with the ravenous glare of moments earlier, but with a gentle, beautiful understanding.

Benedict took a cloth from the counter and wiped Locky's hands free of their remaining flour. Then he leaned down and kissed the back of each hand.

His lips were broad and soft as marshmallows. His touch was as warm as a purring cat. And when he looked back at Locky, his eyes seemed to carry a little of the season with him. "Just because we push boundaries together, doesn't mean you have no voice, Locky. I want you to feel empowered to take risks. But I never want you to feel obligated."

Guilt smashed through Locky, that his conflicted expression had ruined—

Benedict squeezed Locky's hands. "No, no," he said, in a voice like cinnamon sugar. "Never feel guilty about your fears —because that might stop you from speaking. And I want to hear your voice, okay?"

Locky pushed away as much of the guilt as he could, finding some small measure of relief. He'd never had anyone talk to him like this before. To acknowledge his fears so openly. To invite him so intimately into the moment. "Okay," he said through heavy breaths, before adding, "do you . . . know the green, yellow, red system?"

Benedict's knowing expression made Locky's cock pulse beneath his apron. "Well, aren't you full of surprises, Mr. Sorenson."

"It wasn't always my thing!" he stammered, his mind

racing at what it meant for Benedict to be immediately familiar with a system of kink consent. "But if other people were into that kind of stuff . . . I was pretty open to it."

"Well, I *definitely* know the system," Benedict said, stepping closer, like a jigsaw piece sliding into place. "And I am *definitely* into that kind of stuff."

Locky gripped the back of his own neck, hot and already sweating. "Really?"

Benedict almost purred. "Oh yes. And if I remember my training, Mr. Sorenson, green means I'm okay for now. Yellow means that I'll stop what I'm doing, but stay with you in the moment, waiting for you to tell me what you need. You'll use that if you need a second to think, or if you aren't sure, or if things are moving too fast. And red means I'll stop entirely. I'll step back and the play will be over." Before Locky could object, Benedict laid another soft kiss on the back of each hand. "And I promise I won't be angry if you make that call. These words are your tools, Locky. Your powers. And I want you to feel like you can say them without fear. I promise that I'll respect those words, if you can promise that you'll use them?"

Locky drifted on the staggering lightness of Benedict's understanding. "Yes," he whispered. "I promise."

"*Excellent*," Benedict chuckled. "And I know this must be a lot for you. So we don't have to do anything today. Just because I take my shirt off doesn't mean we have to—"

Benedict had made to step away, but Locky shocked himself by slipping a hand behind Benedict's broad back, holding him in place. It hadn't been a conscious choice. It was instinct. Because this man—so kind and so caring—was far too beautiful to let walk away.

Locky's heart pulsed as he glanced from chest to eyes—the

final decision heavy in his heart, knowing that he could just let go, that he could save this for another day.

And yet, right now, so close and so possible, Locky didn't want to wait another moment. Because ten years had already been far too fucking long.

"I don't know how this will go, Benedict," he whispered, stomach twisting as hard as his cock pulsed. "I can't even tell you what I want, or don't want, or what I'm comfortable with. And I don't know if I'll be any fucking good at this. But . . . *green*."

He'd expected Benedict to ask if he was sure. But instead, the bigger man eased himself back into the crook of Locky's thighs, grinning wide and wicked.

And Locky realized why Benedict hadn't second guessed him. Because Locky had said green. And those were his words to wield. His power. His control.

Just like Benedict had told him.

Just like Benedict had *promised* him.

And Locky knew right then, with a certainty he couldn't explain, that Benedict meant what he had said. And that he would respect his words: be they green or yellow or red.

The knot in Locky's stomach relaxed as Benedict hooked fingers under the straps of his apron, running knuckles slowly from Locky's chest to the back of his neck. That touch sent little sparks through the cloth, like metal against a grinder.

How long had it been since someone had touched him like this, so delicate and so full of promise?

Locky let out an involuntary exhale as Benedict slid thumbs up his neck and toward his jaw, easing Locky's face up. Making him look at the man in front of him. Making him *want* the man in front of him.

And sweet Mother Mary, he *did*. In this moment, Locky

had never wanted anything more. He wanted Benedict to teach him. To show him. To remind him of the pleasure he'd denied himself for so long.

"So," said Benedict. "You like my nipples, huh?"

"Yes," whispered Locky, his voice low and hot.

Benedict glanced down to see the impact he was having on Locky's body, very obvious, even through his apron. "You like them *that* much?"

Locky nodded, forcing back the instinct to cover his bulge. That conflict was strong, but the moment won out. Because Benedict wasn't ashamed of seeing Locky's reaction. If anything, he looked fucking thrilled.

Benedict leaned in and Locky's heart flipped like a pancake on a skillet, thinking Benedict was going straight in for the kiss. Instead, Benedict brushed past his lips, hot cheek against hot cheek, beard thick against his own. Benedict's skin radiated warmth, smelling of sweet, pink musk.

Benedict's lips moved in tiny circles on the path to Locky's ear, "Why do my nipples make you so fucking hard, Locky?"

Locky's skin crackled at the closeness, at words so dirty and so raw. "Because you're not supposed to pierce that part of your body."

"Why?" said Benedict, running hands back down the neck loops of Locky's apron, slowly tracing across his shoulders and chest, before stopping at the edge of Locky's pectorals.

Benedict's thumbs rubbed knowingly at that spot, just an inch from each nipple. Locky's shoulders twitched as Benedict eased his thumbs under the apron cloth, closer and closer to the sparkling center of nerves, but not yet touching them.

I'll get there, Benedict's thumbs seemed to say. *But where's the rush? I'm going to take as long as I like with your body, Mr. Sorenson.*

Out loud, Benedict said, "So piercing there is *naughty*, huh?"

Sharp shivers ran through Locky.

Naughty.

The word he hadn't let himself be in a very long time.

Locky brushed his cheek back against Benedict's, wanting more than a passing touch. Wanting to feel that skin press hard against his own. "Yes."

Benedict growled at Locky's enthusiasm, a rumble that made Locky want to give himself over even more. To do whatever the man wanted. "Want to know something even more naughty?"

Locky's whole body shook as his mind raced with possibility. "What?"

"My cock's pierced too."

Locky jolted as a tongue tip traced the edge of his earlobe. And he jolted even harder as Benedict's thumbs completed their journey, finding his hard nipples under the apron.

That touch sent crackles of unfamiliar pleasure through Locky, and he bucked his hips on impulse, feeling the slick of precum glide beneath his foreskin, sliding gently back and forth with each movement against his denim cage.

The sensation against his nipples was so sharp and so unfamiliar that he almost couldn't stand it. Locky was suddenly brutally aware of how long it had been since he'd felt anything like this. Since he'd *allowed* himself to feel anything like this. It was a rage and a rapture that had been imprisoned for far too long.

"Don't . . . don't you feel that all the time, though?" Locky whispered through the bolts of pleasure. "Wouldn't a cock piercing make you want to do this all day long?"

Benedict dragged his cheek back until the two of them

were forehead to forehead. Locky's own vision was filled by Benedict's hungry gaze. And somewhere deep inside Locky yearned for that hunger. The way those eyes were wanting him. The way those eyes were devouring him.

"All fucking day," Benedict growled. "Every time you've ever seen me, I've been primed to fuck you." Benedict pressed their noses together, until their lips were just inches apart. "Just like *now*."

Locky whimpered at the reality of the words. At how horny Benedict looked. "Like . . . now?"

"I'm so fucking hard for you right now," Benedict said, shameless with his arousal, grinning like the demon in his dreams. "Just like you are for me. Right?"

Locky nodded, unable to deny it. Not wanting to deny it. Because he wanted Benedict to know the effect he was having.

"*Good*."

Benedict's fingers moved slow from Locky's nipples, brushing over Locky's belly and pausing to take in his curves. The man's growls intensified as he did so, making Locky feel more desired than he ever had before. What little he could remember of his past experiences had been fast and furious affairs. No one had ever *savored* him before—taken their time on his body, like they never wanted the moment to end.

Benedict ran knuckles down Locky's hips and over the substantial curves of his ass, before finally coming to rest on the edge of Locky's thighs, where the apron was bunching over his bulge.

Benedict's thumbs brushed that fabric threshold, like guards patrolling a city wall. The touch was intimate, promising the next direction of their play. Promising something that Locky hadn't experienced in ten fucking years.

The bigger man looked deep into Locky's eyes as he leaned

in. Their lips almost touched, stopping just before the kiss took place. He was so close now that Locky could taste his breath, sweet as caramel and clove. "Do you want to feel my pierced cock, Locky?"

"Yes," he said, faster than he'd meant to. The voices of dissent were still there in his head, like always. But that stare, so close and so intimate, was louder than they could ever be, anchoring Locky to this moment and this man.

"And I can touch yours?"

"Yes!" Locky said, urgently. And to his shock, there was no doubt in those words. Because he wanted Benedict's hand around his cock. Just like he wanted his own around Benedict's.

"Can I kiss you, Mr. Sorenson?" said Benedict, his hands already sliding under the apron's hem. Each fingertip was spread against Locky's thick thighs, drawing toward his target.

And rather than respond, Locky did what felt right. What he'd been wanting to do for far too fucking long.

He kissed Benedict.

Benedict grunted in surprise, before kissing him back, firm and fiery.

Warmth swelled through Locky, huge and hot and bigger than his body could contain. In one burning instant he felt more complete than he could remember. All this time, all those teasing touches, had been like electricity arching between two distant rods. But now they were entwined in their contact, bolts bright and blue and making the air buzz.

Benedict's tongue came next, hasty against Locky's own, spiking an urgency that Locky didn't know he had. Because, suddenly, it was like there wasn't enough time to do everything he wanted.

Benedict thrust his hand beneath Locky's apron,

wrapping fingers around Locky's bulge. He slid his grip up the already wet denim, gasping at just how far he had to go to get to the tip.

Benedict's touch, even through his jeans, made Locky's foreskin glide against the mess of precum in his underwear. He squirmed hard at the sudden sensation, but didn't break the kiss. Wanting both parts of the man—his mouth and his hand.

Locky returned the gesture, finding Benedict's cock jutting out of his half-open fly, slicked and thick in his own underwear, already hard beyond description. Locky ran his thumb along the underside of Benedict's shaft, reaching his cut cock head through the thin fabric, flared and rigid.

And then, with his own tiny gasp, Locky found the piercing—solid steel and far hotter than he'd thought it would be, even through Benedict's underwear. It was a ring, a little thicker than he'd expected, closed under his thumbprint by something like a ball-bearing. To Locky's surprise, it rotated effortlessly under his touch. The soft cotton and the slick of precum making the ring glide at even the slightest twitch.

The effect was instant.

Benedict broke the kiss, shaking involuntarily and muttering tiny *oh, God*-s under his breath. Locky relished that —the way those tiny movements, *his* tiny movements, could bring this man to heel, making it so Benedict could barely string words together without shaking.

Locky moved the ball slowly around to Benedict's urethra, then slid it back to just below his frenulum, allowing the full circle to move back and forth in its slippery rotation.

Benedict's eyes fluttered with each twist, like he didn't know where he was anymore. Like he was completely overtaken by the sensation.

Locky held Benedict's gaze, marveling at the intensity of

his reaction. At how the precum grew heavily beneath his touch, so wet that it started dripping in thick, clear strings, even through the fabric.

Benedict seemed barely able to keep his eyes open, jolting hard at the sensation. The bigger man reached around Locky's neck and pushed their heads together, already coated with sweat. "You . . . are so fucking good at that, Mr. Sorenson."

The pressure around Locky's midsection eased as Benedict undid the apron. His hands were impatient now, snapping open Locky's fly—his cock so hard that the lightest touch made the buttons pop apart.

Benedict pulled Locky's waistband out and down, causing his cock to bounce out into the free air. The precum was overflowing against his furry belly in clear, salty strings.

But it wasn't free for long, because Benedict immediately gripped around Locky's cockhead, sliding his thumb under the foreskin.

And now it was Locky's turn to jolt.

Benedict's touch was firm—no light flicks or gentle grazes. Instead, he pressed hard against the sensitive triangle of skin on the underside of Locky's glans.

Locky kissed Benedict hard at that, swallowing gasps of pleasure as Locky returned the favor, tugging Benedict's underwear to his knees with an audible slap of dick against belly. Benedict's cock seemed even thicker in Locky's bare hand—so girthy that he couldn't close his fist around it.

That hard flesh pulsed as Locky slid his hand along the shaft in fast strokes, slicked wet and with plenty more precum drooling out with each pump.

Locky knew that he should slow down and let the moment play out. But ten years of frustration where boiling inside him, sizzling at just how fucking hard Benedict's cock was under his attention.

The piercing rotated under his wet palm, each stroke sending it back and forth inside Benedict, making the man whimper and swirl his hot tongue faster around Locky's mouth.

Benedict returned that perfect punishment. He gipped Locky's foreskin and slid it down, exposing his pink glans, prickly and sensitive and desperate for more. No sooner were they out than Benedict glided the foreskin back up, sending a pulse of intense fire down Locky's shaft and deep to his balls. That fierce sensation was so unfamiliar, so forgotten, that Locky vibrated at how overwhelmingly *complete* it felt—sharp and soft and sensitive all at once.

Faster and faster they stroked each other, like they were fighting to make the other lose control first. Their tongues were a singular storm as they both struggled to maintain their composure, gasps and growls and mad mutters into each other's mouths.

Locky stroked Benedict faster with each groan, relishing the power of his girth and the hardness of his head. Locky couldn't get enough of it. He wanted to feel every bulging vein. He wanted to squeeze every inch of smooth and sensitive skin.

That ferocity made Benedict reciprocate, sending the slide of foreskin back and forth in fast flicks.

Soon they were fisting each other's cocks, both of their knuckles soaked with strings of dancing precum.

It was a foolish war for Locky to wage. No matter how horny Benedict was, he didn't have ten years of frustration pent up inside him.

Suddenly Locky felt the pressure build in his balls. It came on fast and ferocious—far quicker than he'd expected—the pleasure morphing from low threat to imminent explosion in a matter of seconds.

"Benedict," he warned, realizing how close he was to the edge. Each word was a struggle against the sensation. "We should . . . we should slow . . ."

But before he finished the sentence, Benedict kissed him back hard, grabbing a handful of Locky's hair as their tongues blurred together.

And to Locky's surprise, Benedict lost the battle.

Benedict grunted hard across Locky's tongue as the first jet of cum splashed between their bodies and across their chins. The sheer force of the shots took Locky by surprise, but he jerked the man's cock even faster, causing bolt after bolt of salty warmth to blast across their cheeks and beards and up onto their lips, the shots somehow growing in volume and force.

Benedict held Locky's head in place as he kissed him with an outstretched tongue, leaving hot air between their lips. Suddenly, one of the cum jets smacked against the underside of their tongues.

That taste of boiling cum—primal and filthy and so long forgotten—sent Locky over the edge.

His first shot slapped hard across Benedict's chest like cannon fire, sending beads of cum splashing everywhere. But that was the only shot Locky felt in full, because everything after that blurred into volcanic fury. Benedict held him close as tectonic explosions rocked Locky's whole body, deep from his pulsing balls and through his rock-hard cock. All Locky could feel was the fury of the pulses, the blissful sensations so hot and sticky that he couldn't stop. Each soul-shaking blast soaked the cavern between them, like someone had flung a bucket across their chests.

Locky tried to speak, to apologize, but Benedict only stroked him harder, kissed him harder. The man was growling at how much Locky was cumming, and that only made him shoot harder, spraying huge blasts that made his whole body feel like he might implode into this moment. Into this man.

Because all this imprisoned bliss needed to be freed from his aching balls. It needed to roar to life. It needed to scream from his body, all the deprivation and neglect banished in a moment of pure ecstasy.

When the sensation at last stilled, Locky opened his eyes, having to blink a few times to refocus against the intense haze.

Benedict looked back at him, panting and drenched with both of their enormous loads.

And Locky wasn't sure he'd ever seen anyone smile so brightly.

Benedict's room was neat and ordered and cold—the opposite of how Locky felt right now.

Because there was nothing *neat* about the sensations across his skin, the remnant stickiness in his beard, even though he knew he'd washed himself clean.

Just like there was nothing *ordered* in his mind, twisting confusion and wrenching disorientation. The way he'd given himself over to the furious heat of his carnal urges. And yet, that terrible shame was battling against great air-punches of pride for having the courage to break his drought.

Just like there was nothing *cold* through Locky's soul right now. Not with Benedict here, holding him tight beneath the sheets.

Locky's frame was folded into the bough of Benedict's body, strong and secure. One arm was wrapped over Locky's heart. The other held him by the belly, fingers running gently through his sandy fur.

And even though Benedict had offered for Locky to stay over—and even though Locky didn't want the embrace to end—he still felt guilty for needing Benedict's touch, protecting him against whatever might happen next.

"It's okay if you want me to leave," whispered Locky, praying that Benedict wouldn't take up the offer.

And instead of kicking him out, Benedict kissed the back of Locky's neck. The hands around his chest squeezed tighter, holding him steady against the confusion and the chaos. "You care so much for other people, Locky," said Benedict, his voice as light as a prayer. "Isn't it time someone took care of *you*?"

NINE

Afternoon Tease

"Is charcoal wool too utilitarian?" said Tris, thumbing an elegant trench coat dress.

"That's a sentence no one's said before," muttered Benedict, tucking his arms tight to his body. He might wear expensive suits, but he'd always hated stores like this, with so many things that could get knocked over by stray elbows.

As big as he was now, it had been even worse as a high school junior, when he'd towered over the rest of the class. He could still hear his parents hissing at him to keep his hands in his pockets whenever they walked into a Nordstrom. They'd probably have a heart attack seeing him in Prada.

"Philistine," Tris said with an exaggerated huff.

"Better a philistine than blindly buying whatever's in season. Seriously, do you even like this shit?"

"God, no! But you remember what Mom said at her last winter gala? After I dared to wear that black-and-gold Christian Siriano number from 2008?"

Benedict did his best impression of their mother, a mid-Atlantic twang that her Oakland upbringing had no hand in creating. "Darling, just because the *gala* is for charity doesn't mean the *dress* needs to be."

Tris scowled. "Damn right. I don't care how much it costs, or how much tailoring it needs, I'll be wearing something *new* this time!"

"You worry too much about her opinions."

"Easy for you to say, Prince Charming. If I wear earrings that aren't perfectly *en vogue*, she'll talk about it for months. Meanwhile, she didn't say one word when you drilled holes into yours."

"I thought you liked my earrings! You said they made me looked devilishly handsome."

"Yes, Bro Bot, they do. But I still wish she'd get a *little* outraged at your proclivities."

"I mean . . . I could tell her about my other piercings?"

"*La la la!* Please no! Hearing that story once was bad enough. Besides, if I wanted the gory details of your junk, I could ask your new client."

Benedict froze. "Wait . . . What? . . . We didn't . . . We haven't . . ."

"Oh, please. Do you have any idea how loud a pair of bears snoring is? I could have heard you two down the block. If you didn't want to get caught, you should have gone to his place for your little sleepover."

Benedict grumbled. "Okay, fine. We hooked up. And we didn't go to his place because he was feeling really vulnerable, and he'd just called in sick to his nightly meeting—which he *never* does—and his housemate might have been home, and . . ." Benedict stopped at Tris's beaming expression, realizing the level of detail in his story showed it hadn't been some impulsive one-night stand. "Oh, shut up. We only did it once."

"Really? *Once?*"

"Yes!" said Benedict, tactfully ignoring the 2 a.m. jerk off they'd also shared, when they'd both woken up hard and already kissing. Locky had been so fucking ferocious that time, emboldened by the cover of sheets and the breaking of his drought. He'd groaned like a wounded animal when Benedict had jerked them both off with a single hand, their shafts sliding together, ensuring they felt the exact same sensation with each stroke.

Benedict also didn't mention the shower they'd taken shortly after, and how soaping each other off had led to slippery hands and swirling tongues, with Benedict jerking another few loads from the shaking, pent-up bear.

It had all been a bad combination. Or maybe a *really* excellent one. Because each time Benedict had made him cum, the guilt washed over Locky. Which only made Benedict want to hold him close and stroke his hair and tell him that everything would be okay. Which, *eventually*, led to Locky's body firming up once more, ready for another round of temptation.

No wonder Locky was a walking boner machine. Benedict had never met someone so damn horny. He couldn't imagine how Locky had survived all these years without tending to those needs.

"Are you seeing him again today?" said Tris, making goo-goo eyes.

"No, he's doing job stuff with his old work friends. But we're doing a taste-testing afternoon tea later in the week to settle his final menu, if you wanted to hang?"

"*Afternoon tea?* Really? Shall we stroll through London and pick posies with the governor?"

"Be nice, it was his idea. He thought *afternoon tea*

sounded better than *let's make three people gorge themselves on pie until they pass out.* Are you in? He asked for you specifically —wanted to thank you for swinging that free day at the pizza shop."

"Pie, praise, and a pretentious setting? How could I say no?" she said, inspecting a slightly more flattering dress in a tan plaid. "Speaking of, is he ever going to rent that place? The owners have been up my ass about it."

"Sorry, but your ass ain't getting no relief. He's applied for a bunch of accounting jobs. No chance he's following through on the store—we're just killing time until the offers come."

Tris placed a mocking boop on Benedict's nose. "I think you've forgotten how good you are at your job, Bro Bot. He says that now, but you might end up convincing him. Even if you don't mean to."

She said it lightly, as if it was some silly sibling joke. But there was nothing funny about her words.

Because Benedict had assumed they really *were* just killing time. That the business plan was something Locky would slip into a drawer and pull out on rainy nights. After all, Locky had been adamant about that—that he had no interest in making this idea a reality.

But . . . was that still true?

Locky was already getting daydreams about the store, wasn't he? Benedict had seen that across his face. Heard it in the little details Locky would mention out of nowhere. How everything was getting a little more *vivid.*

So maybe all these experiments and tests *could* lead Locky to change his mind? To actually open his store?

And what would happen then?

Would Benedict really abandon him? Just like all the other clients?

His gut told him no, of course not. That he'd taken a different step with Locky. That they'd shared something deeper and more special than any of his past clients.

But that was easy to say now, when his hands were still and his heartbeat calm. But it would be different if Locky followed through. As the bills came in. As the decisions became real. As they got closer to opening day and those terrible instincts took over.

The fears would be mounting then, just like they always did—insidious and devoid of logic. All the ways that Benedict must have fucked up. All the mistakes he'd made. How it was just a matter of time until his reckless incompetence ruined another life. And how he had to get away—had to run, run, *run*—before he could see it.

It might be cute kisses and silly jokes now, but it could all go so wrong, so fast.

He knew that.

He'd experienced it more than enough times.

A strange sensation tugged at Benedict. Because half of him was suddenly terrified at the thought of Locky changing his mind. Of what that might mean between them.

But the other half of Benedict swelled with pride—that Locky might be brave enough, might have *grown* enough, to actually live his dream.

And right now, Benedict didn't know which of those two feelings were real. Or which might win out. All he knew was that last night had been fucking incredible. That *Locky* was fucking incredible, and sweet and vulnerable and caring and awkward and amazing.

And Benedict didn't want last night to be a one-time thing.

"Bro Bot?" said Tris, holding up two pairs of earrings.

Benedict blinked himself back into the store. "Oh, the pearls, I guess."

Locky had never felt quite like this before. It was a strange mix of every extreme emotion, scared and overjoyed and guilty and proud.

Because, on the one hand, he'd done it—he'd finally had sex. Something that had scared him and embarrassed him and caused God knew how many awkward situations for ten long years. And even more importantly, nothing bad had happened afterward. He hadn't crawled out of bed in the middle of the night and gone to the club, picking up exactly where he'd left off. There'd been no desire to do any that—much preferring to stay gripped in Benedict's arms. *And* in his slippery fingers.

Which, on the other hand, was exactly the problem. Because they hadn't just had sex once, but four times. Maybe five, depending on how you counted it—going all night and into the morning. And Locky had been unhinged in those moments, giving himself away to that carnal urge.

Yes, they'd only kissed and jerked each other off, but they'd still done it like animals, barely able to keep their hands off each other.

And even if Locky hadn't gone to a nightclub, there was still something in that frenzy that worried him. In the uncontrolled pleasure seeking of it. Because Locky had been to that kind of place before—gluttonous and uncontrolled.

And he knew where it could lead.

Worst of all, Locky had been so overwhelmed by that first time with Benedict that he'd asked Evelyn to lead the meeting for the night. And that had *never* happened. Sure, there were times he'd had the flu, or had to fly back to Seattle to attend some wedding, but he'd never once been here, in town, available, and still canceled.

And that . . . that was confronting. Because what did that make him? Someone who'd just abandon people when they needed him? Someone who'd discard his responsibilities to indulge in his own pleasures?

Someone who was just like *her*?

"Hello, Boss Man?"

The voice cut through his haze, and Locky stared into a dozen upraised glasses of Coke, joined by the wafting gloriousness of freshly cooked pizza—bubbling cheese alongside his own creation of prosciutto and pear and bittersweet chocolate.

"Sorry!" he said, charging his glass with the others— Adriana and Jared and most of their old team, enjoying the meal he'd promised them before their world had flipped around. "I'd like to extend my heartfelt congratulations to Jared Miller for his new role with Dellacor Industrial. And a very special congratulations to Adriana Rivera, for her *promotion* to team leader with White Stone Investments!"

"And," said Adriana, among the whoops and applause, "to our noble leader, who'll no doubt have his own job to celebrate in just a few weeks!"

Locky had to regather himself at that. Because he hadn't expected the attention to turn back to him. Or his own job hunt. Such as it was.

Before anyone noticed his hesitation, Locky's phone buzzed, giving him a distraction.

Not that the message helped.

It was from his bank.

His stock option had just been paid out.

"Don't judge me, I swear it's not that many pie dishes!" said Locky, faintly embarrassed.

All yesterday he'd thought about this moment, when Benedict would help him bake options for the final menu. And all day, Locky had run circles in his head wondering how it might go down—given this was their first meeting since they'd gotten physical.

Would it be warm, with Benedict greeting him like a lover? Telling Locky how much he appreciated their night together?

Or would Benedict be aloof, showing that he could separate professional and personal and not get too clingy?

In the end, Benedict struck the balance with infuriating mastery, greeting Locky with a hug that was neither too familiar nor too distant. In fact, the only thing Benedict seemed bothered by was the teetering pile of pie dishes on the counter, all fifteen in different colors and materials. Some were black Teflon with crimped edges. Others were avocado-colored ceramic with fluted peaks. Others were made of clear Pyrex or dark cast iron.

"That's . . . quite a setup?" said Benedict, with a tone that Locky found strangely hesitant. Strangely unlike the Benedict he'd come to know.

"They weren't expensive or anything. I thrifted most of them. Easier to bake everything at once rather than doing a million batches."

"That's fine," said Benedict, flatly, pouring himself a cup

of coffee without making eye contact. "I didn't say anything bad about it."

"No, but . . . I thought you might worry that buying these dishes meant I wanted to follow through with opening the store."

And I know that would make things weird, he silently added.

The words hung in the air between them, as Benedict paused for a terribly long time. Locky could see from the way his back rose and fell that he was struggling to control his breathing.

And an awful spike of fear ran through Locky. That maybe Benedict regretted their night together. That maybe Locky had been just as bad as he'd feared. That maybe Benedict was worried he'd have to do it again out of obligation!

Locky thumbed the edges of his apron. "Are . . . are you okay?"

As quickly as it had come, the tension left Benedict.

In one sharp movement, the bigger man came to Locky, *rushed* to him, and kissed him deeply, running his free hand up Locky's back and into his hair. He held Locky like he was making an apology with his lips alone. Like he'd thought a thousand thoughts and this was the only way to communicate his answer—to a question Locky didn't know and didn't understand. There was passion there. A passion so deep that Locky wasn't sure he deserved it. But there was pain too—in the way Benedict gripped Locky like he thought he'd lost him. In the tears wet down Benedict's cheeks.

Locky didn't know what was happening, and he didn't care. Because Benedict was here. And that was all that mattered.

When Benedict finally pulled back, he rubbed his nose against Locky's, like he couldn't bear the thought of their skin parting. "Why would it be a bad thing if you opened your store, Mr. Sorenson?" he said, his voice mournful with a pain that seemed so very far beyond this moment. "I wanted to help you dream about your bakery. And I'd never want to crush your dreams."

Benedict had gathered himself by the time they were buttering the pie dishes—all fifteen of them. That newfound collection might have been exactly what Locky said it was, an innocent way of saving time with their big bake today. Or it might be something bigger—a sign that Locky was already investing money in his future bakery.

Benedict didn't know which it was. And maybe Locky didn't either. Not yet.

But it didn't matter. Not anymore.

Because Benedict wasn't going anywhere.

He hadn't been certain when he'd come here—he'd spent too long these last few days pondering those same questions he'd had with Tris at the boutique. What he'd do if Locky showed signs of reconsidering. What he'd do if Locky decided to open his bakery. Knowing what Benedict knew of himself. Knowing how his body might react when that moment came.

It was too awful a conundrum.

Too terrible a possibility.

And he hadn't been able to make a choice.

And then, Benedict had heard Locky's voice. That tiny, scared little voice, asking Benedict if he was okay.

And something inside Benedict broke—shame and horror that he'd even considered the alternative. That he'd even entertained it. Because Locky was too amazing and too special. What Locky had shared with Benedict—what they'd shared with each other—was too big and too vulnerable. And whatever was coming, whichever way it went, Benedict wasn't going anywhere.

He'd told Locky it was time for someone to take care of him for a change. Benedict had meant it then. And he meant it now.

It wouldn't be easy. If that moment came, every part of his body would tell Benedict to run, to flee, to make it all just *go away*. But he wouldn't give into it. Not this time. He would fight it. *They* would fight it.

Because Benedict wouldn't abandon Locky.

Not now.

Not *ever*.

Benedict placed a gentle kiss on Locky's cheek as he reached for another stick of butter.

"What was that for?" Locky asked.

"For being so adorable," he said, low and growly, like he wanted to drag Locky to his bedroom right here and now. "And tell me, Mr. Sorenson, what's on your shortlist?"

Locky reached for a spiral-bound notepad, which had two dozen pies scribbled out in a messy script. "It's all traditional dishes. The ones people would expect. I figure that's the best bet financially?"

Benedict read over Locky's shoulder. "Apple, peach, key lime, blueberry. Sounds like the making of a great menu. Although . . . what do we have here?"

Locky tried to pull the notepad away as Benedict reached

for the next page. "Oh, those are nothing. I just thought . . . it doesn't matter."

Benedict placed a firm finger against the edge of the pad, his wingspan too wide for Locky to keep it away. As Benedict flicked the page over, he wrapped his other arm around Locky's midsection, fingertips brushing underneath Locky's shirt and over his furry belly. "Yes, I can see how unimportant they are by just how aggressively you've crossed them out. Possum Pie? Shoofly Pie? Fluternutter Pie? And on the third page we have . . . Gooseberry and banana custard? Pear, rhubarb and Earl Grey tea?"

Locky made a little grunt. "The second page are some old recipes that used to be popular. I thought they might fit the gangster-era vibe."

"And the third?" Benedict asked, kissing Locky's neck and making him shiver all over.

"Just . . . some dumb recipes I came up with myself."

Benedict tutted. The sound was more playful than disappointed. It was a sound that carried all the meaning it needed to—knowing that Locky had crossed them out because they were risky. Because they weren't proven. Because they might not sell, and people might hate them and hate him, and the store might fail and every other concern that had probably gone through Locky's head when he was making the list.

"Tell you what," said Benedict, running his hands down Locky's belly. "If you agree to make a mix of all three pages, I'll let you take me on a tour of your bedroom before we start baking?"

Locky's cock pulsed as his neck radiated warmth. "You drive a hard bargain, Mr. Owens."

"Not yet I haven't," Benedict growled, pushing his own bulge against Locky's ass.

Benedict stared at the tally in front of him. "How can we have a seven-way tie?"

"*Piccirudu*," said Evelyn, slouching over the breakfast bar, "they were all so delicious, I had to give them all full marks! It's like asking me to choose my favorite child."

"You don't have any children, you ancient hag," muttered Kai, unbuttoning his designer jeans. His belly audible plopped against the counter. "And don't blame me, I went for all the punchy ones. I'm a simple man—"

"*Very* simple," mumbled Evelyn.

"But if you're going for pies, you want them familiar and stodgy. Give me sugar and cream and flour and a massive serving spoon. Lemon meringue and sweet potato and cherry all the way. None of this experimental shit—no offense."

"Well . . ." crooned Tris, dabbing at the corner of her immaculate mauve lips, which had somehow survived the feeding frenzy. "I know I'm the new one here. But if you're going for a more memorable experience, you want differentiation. Lighter dishes. New and exciting flavors. I think pies like the strawberry and mint crème are much more likely to generate buzz."

Benedict slumped, exhausted from the hours of baking. "Well, this was pointless."

"You know," said Evelyn. "If you want a bigger sample size, you could always bring them to New Hope tomorrow night? For their Thanksgiving dinner?"

Kai groaned. "Can we *please* go ten minutes without hearing about one of your charities?"

"The shelter in the Mission District?" said Benedict, ignoring him.

He'd attended a presentation about New Hope at a charity seminar a few years back, although he'd never seen it up close. Apparently, it was a mini suburb all of its own, combining dozens of little cabins for those with nowhere else to go, alongside communal vegetable gardens and dining halls and a big centre for events. The aim was to be less an emergency bed for one night than a place to start over for a few months.

"*Precisamente!* We're catering for the community. It's a few days before the real thing, so anyone can participate and build connections. We already have a pile of pumpkin pies donated, but no one will complain about a few extra choices. Particularly when they're as delicious as this."

"That's a great idea," said Benedict, before Locky could protest. "A bigger sample size would really help."

Locky shifted nervously. "But isn't it rude to give someone day-old pie?"

Benedict waggled his finger, remembering their big lists on the apartment wall. "Oh, no you don't. That was one of the reasons pies won out, remember? Because they can last a few days between bakes. Didn't you tell me that all the pies you get in restaurants are a few days old?"

Locky's face brightened before falling suddenly. "It won't work. If Evie and I are occupied, who will lead the meeting that night?"

Kai's hand shot up. "What? Don't look so surprised. It would be rude not to step in."

Evelyn scoffed. "And the fact it would keep you from volunteering with the needy?"

Kai pinched a glistening cherry from the nearest pie dish. "Consider that an added bonus."

Locky gazed around the New Hope dining hall.

It was an hour until dinner started, but a few dozen people had already gathered among the fifty indoors picnic tables, overflowing with festive decorations. Candles flickered on gingham tablecloths, alongside full crockery place settings. Painted wooden pumpkins and plastic cranberry bunches were scattered over freshly collected oak leaves, ranging from green to gold to richest amber.

Behind one long wall—plastered with promotional signs from all the contributing businesses—was a canteen kitchen, wafting out the glorious scents of stuffing and roasted vegetables.

To Locky's surprise, there were a bunch of waiters in crisp white shirts and black bow ties, probably donated by a catering company. It wasn't something Locky had expected to see, but he thought back to what Benedict had said about his sister's business philosophy—giving people diamond service to make them feel special.

And there was no doubt that anyone attending this event would feel special as hell. Welcomed and warm and safe.

On a little stage surrounded by hay bales sat a very attractive bear in a blue flannel shirt and a bushy red beard. He was tuning an acoustic guitar between distractions from one of the waiters, an equally stocky man with honeyed skin and raven black hair. Even from this distance, the smiles they gave each other were so cheek-bitingly wicked that Locky found himself glancing over to Benedict, craving that same attention.

As if knowing the gaze was on him, Benedict looked up from where the pies had been set. Locky's stomach fluttered at the man's expression, strong and secure and so fucking happy to see him, even though they'd only been apart for a few minutes.

The music rode warm over the swell of conversation and the clinking of plates. Locky found himself listening with his eyes closed, letting the comfortable ambience wash over him.

The two of them were waiting at a little table to the side, their serving utensils at the ready. It was now the crossover point in the meal, when the last table had gotten their main course, and the first table was about to come up for dessert.

Some of the waiters were undoing their bow ties and talking with the patrons. The raven-haired bear was sat at one of the tables, surrounded by a growing group of residents as he jotted down some notes.

"What's going on there?" wondered Locky.

"Probably some interviews? Events like this love getting PR quotes."

Locky considered that. While it sounded plausible, he wouldn't have thought PR quotes would cause that many naughty laughs? Or that many blushing cheeks?

And why would a waiter be doing it anyway?

Locky glanced down at the pie dishes, marked with little name tags—Benedict's idea, to give people the confidence to try new things. "We didn't need to bring the pies I created. No one's going to want *apple, rosemary and brown sugar crumble*."

Benedict tapped Locky's arm with his spatula. "You doubt yourself, Mr. Sorenson. But I bet at least one of your creations will get demolished."

"Oh, yeah? And what's the bet?"

"The winner gets to do anything they like to the loser?"

Locky's eyes bulged—among other things. "This table isn't tall enough for you to talk like that!"

"So that's a yes?"

Locky pulled his jacket as far down as it would go. "You are so *naughty*, Mr. Owens."

Benedict winked as the first diner approached their table. "Only because you're so fun to be naughty with, Mr. Sorenson."

The stars were bright when they finally left, the evening calm broken only by the clanking pie dishes they both carried.

"*Anything I like*," gloated Benedict, juggling the ceramic into his car boot. "I can't believe you doubted the appeal of strawberry and mint."

"I didn't doubt it! I just thought people would be scared."

"And the pear and Earl Gray disappeared. I got you twice there, sucker."

Benedict wrapped his arms around Locky, one hand rubbing a shoulder blade, the other resting on the full and beautiful curve of his ass. Benedict could almost kiss the stardust from the man's eyelashes, his barely disguised glow at how the evening had gone. The way people had queued for his baking, coming back for seconds and thirds. The praise and the clean plates and the *my God, Barbara, you have to try this one*-s.

There was something incredible about the atmosphere of the night, warm and lively and brimming with good feeling. Something about contributing to that sense of community and belonging. Something in the music that felt comforting and strangely familiar—like it had always been there.

And if *Benedict* had felt that way, he could only imagine what Locky must have felt. Because, quite accidentally, Locky had just experienced the exact vibe he'd wanted for his bakery.

Comforting.

Warm.

Familiar.

Benedict's voice was sweet as honey when he next spoke. "And while *you* might have been the sucker tonight, I think *I'll* be the sucker when I cash in my winnings? If that's all right with you, Mr. Sorenson?"

He felt the welcome throb against his thigh. Confirmation that Locky was *very* much on board with that plan.

Benedict chuckled at that. Only a few days ago, that same poke of dick against his leg had sent Locky into a panic spiral. But now it only made Locky smile, no doubt thinking about Benedict's pink tongue gliding up his straining shaft.

"I . . . think he speaks for both of us," said Locky, pressing his boner even harder against Benedict. "Oh, and I had a thought."

"That we should run home immediately?"

Locky contemplated the suggestion. "That wasn't it. But I *really* like your thinking."

Benedict laughed. "What was it then?"

"I was thinking. Could you put it in the business plan that a portion of profits go to charity? And figure out a daily schedule for how I could still lead the nightly meetings and open the store? I feel bad that I've canceled on them twice in quick succession."

A remnant of Benedict's past indecision knew that he should be worried about Locky talking like that. That coming up with concrete ideas for the store meant the dream was getting even more real in Locky's mind.

But the rest of Benedict didn't feel like that anymore. He *couldn't* feel like that. Because his chest swelled at Locky's request—at his impossible generosity.

Because here was this guy, whose biggest fear was financial instability, and he wanted to put aside money for other people? To put aside time for other people? To reduce his own stability for the sake of others?

It was unbelievable.

He was unbelievable.

"You are so fucking cute," said Benedict, rubbing his nose against Locky's. "Of course we can do that. Was there anything else you picked up?"

Locky stood on his tiptoes, bringing them close to even height. "Actually, I thought the waiters' uniforms were kinda fun? Black tie and black apron?"

To Benedict's surprise, it was his turn to land a heated throb against Locky's belly.

Locky grinned. "Did you just get hard thinking about me in a waiter's uniform?"

Benedict nodded enthusiastically. "Yes. Very hard. My God, you would look so fucking cute. Is there a costume place open at this time of night?"

Locky laughed, making a big show of reaching for his

phone. "I think I have a bow tie at home. But the black apron would be—"

There was a frozen moment as Locky stared at his phone.

Suddenly, he'd dropped from his tiptoes, leaving an unwelcome distance between the two of them.

"Oh . . ." he said.

"What?" said Benedict. "Is everything okay?"

Locky looked up with eyes Benedict hadn't seen in days. Suddenly, Locky seemed so much smaller, like a balloon deflating. "One of the jobs got back to me. They want me to do an interview tomorrow."

TEN

A Sucky Plan

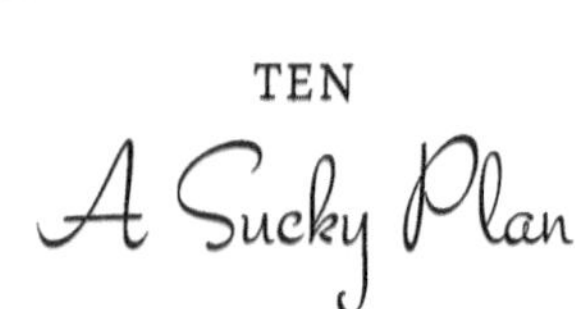

Dawn crept into Benedict's home office, the sound of birdsong mixing with the whirr of printing.

First came the media plan—websites and passwords and contact details for local journalists. Then were the sketches of potential logos and tables detailing footfall and cost projections and likely amenity prices.

Gradually, the printer tray filled with scans of permits, mostly riding on Pizza My Mind's existing accreditations. Then came the menu, only settled last night, alongside information about charitable contributions and tax status. Alongside pictures of black-tied French waiters and decor touches that could be implemented within the owners' restrictions.

Alongside . . . well, nothing.

Because there, as the background buzz of the printer faded, was the cover page.

Pie Me to the Moon.

Locky's dream bakery.

The sheets were still warm as Benedict held them—the

culmination of all their work together. A few weeks ago, Locky wouldn't have imagined this was possible. Wouldn't have let himself imagine it. But now, here it was.

The crisp orange folder waited on Benedict's desk. Ready for him to close the page. Ready for him to slide the folder into his shelf, just like all the other clients before.

But Benedict didn't reach for the folder. Instead, he stared at the paper—high quality and designed to make every detail pop. To bring the dream to life in a client's hands.

Because right now, he didn't want to shut the business plan away—all neat and tidy and ready to be forgotten. Because right now, all Benedict could think about was how devastated Locky had been about the job interview.

Yesterday morning, Benedict hadn't known where Locky stood on his bakery—whether he still thought they were just killing time, or whether Locky had started seeing it as real. Maybe Locky hadn't known either. Not until that moment last night. Not until that message inviting him to the job interview.

But now Benedict knew. They both knew.

At the Thanksgiving feast, Locky had seemed so sparkling, so hopeful. So alive with color and light.

And afterward, in the car park, he'd seemed so very empty. Gray and flat and resigned to his fate. Because Locky didn't want to go back to some soulless office. He wanted the bakery.

And he wasn't going to follow that dream.

Because Locky had said yes to the interview. Yes to the office. Yes to his old world. Yes to stability and order and a normal life—the one he'd sought all those years ago, when he'd found his peace and his sobriety.

And as Benedict had driven him home, asking Locky if he was sure about his decision, Locky had said something so bleak, so brutal, that Benedict's stomach had dropped to the tarmac below.

You know why they call them dreams, Benedict? Because eventually, you have to wake up.

Benedict's fingers tensed against the paper. A few days ago he might have been happy for Locky to take the office option. For Locky to avoid getting *complicated*.

But now . . . now Benedict was *anything* but happy.

Because Locky deserved so more than some stable, sensible life. He was extraordinary. He was creative. He was passionate and had ideas and cared for people and had endured so damn much in his life.

He deserved so much more than he thought.

He deserved this.

He deserved *the dream*.

Locky stared at his bedroom mirror. The interview wasn't until after lunch, but it wasn't like he'd slept. He'd tossed and turned and glared at the ceiling until the breaking dawn had forced him out of bed.

And this was his reward—a stranger staring back at him.

It was weird. He'd worn this same corporate uniform for years. Business shirt and inoffensive tie. For years, he'd trudged to the office and sat down at his desk, lights so bright he could almost hear the hiss of the fluorescence, and he'd lived in his spreadsheets. Numbers he didn't care about. Projects that didn't matter. A career he didn't like.

All so he could take home a reliable income. All so he

wouldn't have to worry about making it through to another day.

And now, in just a few short weeks, he barely recognized the man in front of him.

His hair felt strange, being forcibly brushed into something halfway neat. The shoes crushed his toes into an unnatural point. And the tie. How had he tolerated this awful choke for so long?

Locky breathed as deeply as he could with a polyester noose around his neck—trying to banish those negative thoughts. Because there was no point thinking like that. Because *this* was where he needed to be.

These last few weeks had been . . . well, they'd been a lot of things. At first awful, but finishing so much better, with last night being so perfect it was almost magic.

Which, unfortunately, was a fitting word. Because that's what it had been. Magic. A *fantasy*. Something that had no place in the real world.

Had it been amazing? Yes, of course it had. Had it been scary and strange and incredible to explore all those things? Yes, of course it was.

But it wasn't *real*. And nothing he'd done could change the fact that *this man*—the one staring back at him—was the man who paid his bills and had a roof over his head and didn't have to worry about where his next meal would come from. The one who turned up on time and who people could rely on and who didn't get involved with reckless behavior.

All the other stuff? The bakery? The dream? That was just a trip to another world. A trip to another Locky.

And besides, it wasn't all bad.

This way he might keep seeing Benedict.

Not that they'd . . . God, they'd only slept together a few

times. And it was just kissing and jerking off. But no one had ever made him feel so safe before. No one had known when to push him and when to hold him close. No one had given him the space to express and to explore.

And Locky didn't know if he and Benedict were going anywhere. Whether Benedict even wanted it to go somewhere. But it sure wouldn't happen if he opened the bakery, as much as Benedict had hinted otherwise. Because that would tear Benedict apart—making Locky just another one of the clients he'd left behind.

After a long stare, Locky decided the tie wasn't right. Even if it had only been fifty cents, khaki stripes were a terrible idea.

He flicked through his hanger of thrift shop staples. Muted reds and dark greens and—

His fingers brushed against black satin as he pulled out the long bow tie. The fabric sparkled—stars against sunlight.

Locky cradled it for long, silent seconds.

Maybe . . . it would help to say goodbye?

With hasty hands, Locky swapped the khaki tie for a badly tied bow. The button around his throat was no less choking, but the discomfort faded when he caught sight of himself.

He laughed low as he turned on the spot. "Benedict was right. I do look fucking cute." Locky let the seconds tick by, allowing himself this brief moment of magic—this brief moment of possibility—before finally whispering, "See you, Mr. Sorenson. You would have been a lot of fun."

And just as he was reaching to untie the bow, there came a knock at the apartment door.

It was Benedict.

"Please don't take that job," he panted, gathering himself against the door frame. "Sorry. I planned . . . to do that more professionally. But too many words. Not enough breath."

Locky didn't bother to ask stupid questions like *what are you doing here*. Not when he'd just been interrupted giving a farewell speech to an alternate image of himself.

Just like he didn't stop Benedict from monologuing about how happy Locky had looked last night. How he'd come so far and changed so much. How he was brave and brilliant and better than some awful desk job.

Just like he didn't argue as Benedict stepped him through the finished plan, bright and professional and somehow *his*. All those little moments and little ideas, brought together into something that looked almost possible.

Just like he listened when Benedict ran through the financials one last time. The lack of contracts. The temporary setup. How everything—every single thing—would let him try this idea without risk. To dream briefly. To let the real world rest for another few months, not gone but *sleeping*, ready to wake if needed.

Just like he let Benedict pitch him the big opening event: A New Year's Eve party without alcohol, and how the local media would jump all over that as a novelty, scoring tons of free publicity and a packed house that guaranteed success.

Just like he let Benedict take his hand, fingers interlocked against the shakes, and say the words that finally settled Locky's resolve.

"I think . . . I think a decade is long enough," whispered Benedict, on the verge of tears. "For both of us."

"You can't mean—" Locky started, before Benedict kissed him deeply, seemingly knowing what Locky was about to say and silencing those doubts before they could be spoken.

"I *do* mean for both of us, Locky. I don't want you to have to choose." Benedict's lip quivered, his face flooded with shame. "You've been so brave. You've faced all these things that scare the hell out of you. And I want to do that as well. I *need* to do that as well. I'm not saying it will be easy—I'm not saying *I'll* be easy. All of this is still so fucking new to me."

Locky raised Benedict's hand to his lips, kissing his skin, slow and soft. "Not new. Just forgotten."

"Yes," laughed Benedict through the tears. "And I want to remember. I want to remember what it was like to make connections with my clients. To let myself care about my clients. And . . . I don't know how it will affect me. I might freak out. I might panic. I might melt into a fucking puddle. But I want to try. And I want to try all of that with you. If . . . if you'll have me?"

If you'll have me?

Locky kissed Benedict on instinct, passionate and warm. Because he couldn't let those words hang unanswered—not for a single breath. Not for a single second. Because this incredible, supportive, beautiful man, actually thought that *he* might not be worthy of Locky?

"If *I'll* have you? It's the other way around, Benedict," said Locky between kisses. "If I open this store, I'll probably be just as bad! I'll get freaked out about every expense and I'll be difficult and just . . . messed up."

Benedict ran his fingers through Locky's hair, drawing him close. "How many times do I have to tell you, Mr. Sorenson? Things are better if they're a little messed up."

"Even as your *boyfriend*?" Locky said, daring to breathe the word out loud.

The grip in his hair firmed, holding him tighter. "*Especially* as my boyfriend."

Locky exhaled, barely believing this moment could be real. Because how could it be. This man? This dream?

A month ago, he'd had neither.

And now, he could have both?

It didn't seem possible.

And yet, right now, possible seemed like a promise.

A promise that he wanted to accept.

"Yes," said Locky. "To everything."

Benedict laughed, freeing an arm long enough to wipe the tears from his own cheeks. "Can I please drag you to your bedroom?" he said. "I tried not to notice your bow tie, but if I don't suck the cum out of you right now, I think I might *literally* die."

"Green, Mr. Owens," growled Locky. "So fucking green!"

Locky groaned as Benedict kissed him hard against the bedroom door, lips and earlobes and softly across his neck. His mouth was hasty and demanding, barely giving Locky time to imagine this beautiful, impossible man on his knees worshiping him.

That thought made Locky's cock so hard he felt like the fabric of his business pants might tear in two.

Benedict's mind was clearly in the same place, giving a low growl as he slipped fingers into the black satin bow, letting the fabric fall loosely across Locky's chest.

Locky undid his top two buttons quickly, grateful for the release against his throat. But before he could undo the rest, Benedict slowed him, looking him up and down, like the whole world should be lucky enough to see him right now.

"Like that," said Benedict, running a knuckle over his collar. "That's how you should wear it in your bakery. Like you've finished for the night. Like everyone can just relax."

"You don't think it's too messy?"

Benedict kissed across Locky's Adam's apple. "You know my opinion on that, Mr. Sorenson."

His lips traced slowly down Locky's chest, undoing each button as he passed, revealing staw-colored fur and delicate white skin, until Locky's shirt hung open and Benedict was on his knees.

On reaching the swollen shaft in Locky's pants, Benedict extended his tongue, running it up Locky's full, caged length.

Locky melted into the sensation as the heat traveled up him, longer and longer, until it finally reached his head—straining hard against the fabric and leaving a nickel-sized patch of precum, dark and wet.

An old instinct told him to wipe that sticky patch away, so Benedict didn't have to deal with it, but he knew better than that now—by the way Benedict licked his fingers clean each time he'd jerked Locky off.

The growl only got deeper as Benedict realized how wet Locky was, swirling his tongue across the sticky patch, letting the precum coat his lips. Benedict moaned approvingly as he tasted it, his face going soft and happy, like he'd just swallowed a mouthful of the sweetest candy imaginable. "I love how much you drip, Mr. Sorenson."

Those words, dirty and delightful, caused a fresh drop to form. Benedict lapped it up eagerly as he reached for Locky's belt, sliding a finger between leather and buckle, getting enough leverage to pop the belt open with just one hand.

"How did you do that?" asked Locky, impressed.

Benedict repeated the trick with the top button of Locky's pants, the pressure making the straining wool snap open. "Your boyfriend is *very* good at what he does."

Locky shuddered again at that exclamation—that

promise. At how Benedict had made sure to use the word. *Boyfriend*. Making sure that Locky knew that it wasn't some mistake or moment of madness.

After ten years of avoiding this—all of this—Locky had a fucking *boyfriend*. One that was about to willingly suck the cum from his balls.

Warm fingers gripped either side of Locky's hips, grabbing business pants and white briefs, slipping all the way against his skin, taking full hands of both waistbands and pulling them down.

Locky's cock sprang out with a big bounce and an even bigger throb. Curving up all the way to the ceiling, the head thick and parallel with his belly button.

Locky experienced a brief moment of conflict at that sight, the shadow cast by a decade of shame.

Because on the one hand, his cock looked so *wrong* next to Benedict's face. It was so big and so thick—with veins full and snaking, like a bodybuilder's biceps. His foreskin had already rolled back from the throbbing, revealing glans of pastel pink. A long strand of precum arched from where his cock had been resting against his hip, forming a clear and crescent moon.

The image was filthy, but it also made Locky feel *powerful* —dominant and free and deserving of all this attention.

A big part of that feeling was how Benedict was staring at his cock, awed and so fucking happy. Like he'd finally discovered the divine—already on his knees and ready to worship.

Which Benedict soon did, running the flat of his tongue across Locky's furry balls, so big that Benedict's free hand could barely hold them. Benedict maintained eye contact as he traced along the underside of Locky's shaft, the warm sensation making Locky's cock throb away from the contact, only to slap back down against Benedict's tongue, wet and engulfing.

The heat of Benedict's breath wrapped around the sensitive skin, close but not yet swallowing. The teasing against his frenulum made the urgency in Locky's balls grow, throbbing so hard that Benedict had to wrap a finger around Locky's shaft, holding his cock in place as it tried to escape. The sensation was so intimate and so intense that it made Locky feel like his knees could buckle at any moment.

His viewing angle was perfect to see the copious precum drool from his slit and onto Benedict's lips. "Fuck you taste good," whispered Benedict, his voice so happy that Locky's thighs shook.

More precum spat unexpectedly across the man's nose and forehead. Benedict looked shocked in the best possible way at the sign of unrestrained pleasure. It seemed to spark something extra in him, some loss of patience.

And in one shocking movement, Benedict swallowed Locky's cock.

Locky's legs actually did buckle this time, the sensation so unexpected and so overwhelming that he couldn't stand upright. But Benedict seemed to expect this, pinning Locky back against the door, making the hinges squeak and the wood groan.

"Fuck!" Locky barked, unable to control his volume, unable to control his *anything*. Benedict slid his mouth up and down over his long shaft—suddenly fast, suddenly ravenous. Locky's eyes were clenched shut, too overwhelmed to handle it all.

The sensation was like nothing he'd experienced. His entire body felt like it was being sucked into a vortex—like every part of him was being pulled into Benedict's expert mouth. Even back in his partying days, he couldn't remember anyone deep throating him properly, taking him all the way down until they were slobbering over his nuts.

It was all combined with the most visceral sounds that Locky had ever heard. Unable to open his eyes, all Locky could hear was slurping and throat noises and bubbles of spit bursting. It was so loud and so graphic that he felt like he should intervene, wrenching Benedict's head away.

But Locky's hips had other ideas, bucking deeper into the sensation. Locky's back and shoulders curled down toward his cock. His feet involuntarily strained on tiptoes, pushing his knees toward the man's fast-moving jaw.

The gurgles became even more intense as the pleasure grew bigger and hotter in his balls. Unexpectedly, those big, slippery noises were replaced with guttural gags.

Locky opened his eyes at that.

And if he hadn't been pressed hard against the door, he might have taken a shocked step backward. Because the scene that greeted him was like nothing he ever thought he'd see.

Benedict's nose was pressed flat against his pubes. Tears of effort were streaming down his cheeks. And threaded through Benedict's thick hair were both of Locky's hands. Grabbing him. Forcing him deeper onto his cock.

Locky felt like he was floating above his own body. Like he was watching a scene from a horror movie.

"Oh, God!" he said, yanking his hands away and releasing the man's head. "I'm so fucking sorry, I didn't mean to—"

Benedict snatched Locky's retreating wrists as he pulled his mouth off the aching cock, great strands of slime and drool arching between shaft and chin and balls.

Benedict made gagging noises as he cleared his throat.

"Sorry," he spluttered, voice deeper and more lubricated. "I didn't mean for you to stop!"

Locky's eyes bulged as his dick made another leap into the air, almost spearing his belly. "Wait . . . what?"

Benedict gently brought Locky's hands back down against his head, still looking up at him lovingly, eyes wet with effort. With his hands now free Benedict gave a little rap against the bedroom wall. "One knock for yellow, and two for red? Sorry, I should have done that earlier."

"You *want me* to fuck your throat like that?"

"You have no fucking idea, Mr. Sorenson," said Benedict, between little licks against his swollen pink head. "If you're okay with that?"

The throb that followed was so hard that Locky felt like his cock was straining against shackles, yearning to break free of its restraints. And yet, as much as his body was saying yes, Locky was struggling to form complete sentence. He hadn't had his cock sucked in almost a decade, and this beautiful man wanted him to go as deep as possible, as hard as possible? To brutalize him and take control and force him down hard?

He . . . he couldn't be serious?

And yet, there was no lie in Benedict's expression, no pity or obligation. He looked up at Locky like a man starving. And further down, past thick shoulders and between splayed knees, Benedict had taken his own cock out. It was rock-hard and dripping heavily in his grip, streams of precum running down his piercing, mixing with the long stands of drool that poured down Benedict's chin and across his chest.

He really does want this.

Locky thought back to what Benedict had told him at the Pizza My Mind kitchen. How he'd said he was into various kinks. And how he hadn't second guessed Locky's decision when he'd said green. How he'd respected his choices.

Locky's cock throbbed hard again as the realization took hold. What he was about to do. What he was about to experience! Because if Benedict—this amazing, supportive, beautiful man—wanted him to be rough . . . well, wasn't it the least Locky could do? Particularly when his own body was urging him forward.

Tentatively, Locky gripped harder in Benedict's hair, pulling the kneeling man's tongue halfway up his spit-slicked shaft, teasing him, testing him, before finally shoving Benedict's mouth back down over his cock.

Locky winced as the hot grip returned with furious pace, clamping and grinding and making him shudder. Locky could feel a jet of precum pulsing out of him, confirmed when Benedict gave an eager swallow, his voice box sliding slickly across the sensitive underside of Locky's cock.

Inch by inch he forced himself down Benedict's throat, stopping only when he felt the tightness and resistance get too strong, afraid he might break something. But Benedict did the job for him, struggling through those last few inches.

Locky groaned, deep and animal. The tightness and heat felt like a gateway to a whole different world, making Locky's balls pull up against his body, boiling and building their load.

Benedict was stroking himself faster now as Locky repeated that slow throat-fucking motion—back and forth along the full length of his shaft. This time, when he came to the final inch he didn't stop, forcing Benedict all the way down until his lips were smeared against Locky's nuts.

It felt . . . God, it felt incredible. Not just the sensation, but the sheer power of it all. The feeling of hair through his fingers. The realization that he could do whatever felt best for him. That he could fuck this throat how he wanted, when he wanted, and Benedict would only thank him for it.

It was so fucking *wrong*. Locky knew that deep in his guts. It was the opposite of everything he usually believed. He *cared* for people. He didn't take advantage of them.

But in this moment, he couldn't deny the angry growl of his own desire. "You . . . you like it when I do this?" he said, under his breath. He wasn't used to being verbal, wasn't used to any of this, but the words came out like a demon muttering through him.

Whether it was the questions or his tone of voice, Benedict's cock gave its answer, spraying a clear jet of precum between Locky's legs.

Oh . . . fuck, thought Locky. *I'll take that as a yes.*

Locky moved one of his hands from Benedict's hair around to his jaw, holding his mouth open with firm pressure.

He fucked hard against the man's already stuffed throat, finding an extra half inch by twisting Benedict's head on the diagonal, giving Locky an unblocked view of the sick scene.

He'd never seen himself so hard before.

Locky shoved Benedict's head roughly against his pubic hair, as deep as it was possible to go. He waited for the inevitable knock against the wall, the message to stop. But Benedict made no such movement. One of his hands was rubbing lovingly up Locky's thigh, the other was gripping hard around his own cock.

When the man finally gagged, Locky let Benedict's mouth rise to halfway along his shaft. Desperate breaths whistled through Benedict's nose. The tears down his cheek were pouring now.

Benedict stopped jerking himself off suddenly. But it wasn't because he was turned off and wanted to reach for the wall. Locky could see that Benedict was having the opposite problem. His cock was so hard, so urgent, it looked like he could spray his load at any second.

And a nasty little thought overcame Locky.

I wonder if I can make that happen?

Gripping his fingers tighter, hair and jaw alike, Locky gave Benedict the full length of his cock again. But this time, he didn't move the man's head. Instead, he held it in place, letting his hips do the work.

Every thrust made Benedict's throat grip him hard, squeezing the blood from his cock head until there was nothing but an electric vice of pleasure. Each pull out was slick and slippery, disgusting and drippy.

"You like having my huge cock down your throat?" he said, louder this time, feeling things he'd never felt, saying things he'd never say. "You like having your throat fucked like this?"

Benedict gagged approvingly as Locky's pace quickened, spending longer on the depth and shorter on the withdraw, the feeling too good to slow down. He controlled the pace with loving brutality, giving Benedict just long enough to catch his breath before jamming his cock into his spit-soaked face once more.

Benedict's gags grew heavier as Locky bashed his dick into his esophagus. Suddenly, those gags were joined by a *growl*. The sound was muted but the cause was clear.

Benedict was *moaning*. Loving every second of his throat being destroyed.

Locky looked down through the carnage of slobber. Benedict's cock was straining against his belly now, hard as granite and veins snaking angrily.

"Oh, fuck," said Locky, without slowing. The vibrations

of Benedict's growls intensified, humming inside his cock, down his shaft and deep into his overfull balls. It was like his cock was being massaged from all sides. Like Benedict was summoning the cum from his aching nuts.

The growls and the gags merged as he fucked even faster, feeling the pressure gathering. Feeling the cracks of lightning before the roar of thunder.

Benedict reached down for his own cock, desperate to finish himself off, but Locky stopped him, grabbing Benedict's hands and shoving them behind. "Hands against the wall! If you want to cum, you'll cum like this!"

Benedict's cock pulsed in surprise, like it was screaming for the attention it wasn't going to get.

But he obeyed immediately, hands pressed flat against the wall.

The realization that he wasn't in charge of his own orgasm seemed to make Benedict's eyelids flutter, ecstatic and overwhelmed and so fucking grateful.

The rumble through Locky's own dick became urgent as he fucked Benedict's throat in long, angry strokes. Pounding him. Slamming him. Taking him!

The fire built to a fury as he watched Benedict struggle not to pull his hands back and grab his cock, so desperate to jerk his dick to completion.

Benedict's cock looked so hard it might shatter now. The precum stream was torrential, collecting in sick drips and sticky pools all over his thighs and balls and floor. Every now and then it twitched, screaming for attention, screaming for someone to finish it off.

But Locky didn't stop.

Because he was too busy using Benedict's throat.

And soon, Benedict wasn't trying to get his hands back.

Now Benedict's eyes were fluttering constantly.

Now Benedict's whole body was shaking.

"That's it," Locky growled, low and commanding. "You want to cum just from my cock in your throat? Is that what turns you on, you sick fuck? The thought of this big cock breeding your mouth?"

Benedict nodded furiously as the shaft slammed past his lips.

"Then say it!" Locky barked. "Tell me what a naughty little slut you are for my cock!"

Benedict tried to speak with a mouthful of cock, the muffled buzz fizzing up though Locky's shaft.

That obedience, that domination, made something inside Locky swell. The sense of control. The sense of power.

"Louder!" Locky roared, gripping Benedict's hands harder against the door, making both of their cocks bounce. "If you want my cum, I want to hear you beg for it!"

Benedict's guttural growls were deep and strangled, trying to comply but overwhelmed by just how brutally his throat was being used.

And then, suddenly, that growl of throat-fucked compliance built into something louder, something more desperate and disbelieving. First it was a roar, panicked and piercing. Then it was a bellow, like an animal roaring into the wounded night. Soon it was like the man was screaming into the depths of Locky's soul through a mouthful of dick.

Benedict's expression grew shocked, eyes looking up at Locky, overwhelmed and unable to comprehend what he was feeling.

"Yeah, that's it," snarled Locky, slapping his face hard. "You're feeling it now, aren't you? I want to see you to cum for me! I *order* you to cum for me! Cum for me now! Blow your load, you little bitch!"

And those filthy words were too much for Benedict, shaking and screaming and sobbing through a full throat of cock.

The kneeling man jolted hard as he shot his cum hands-free, huge jets blasting up through the space between them, coating his own chest and chin in a monstrous spray of white. One rope found the gap between the furious fucking and slapped Locky across the lips and beard. He opened his mouth and caught another fat splat on the underside of his tongue.

The taste of sweet salt made his own thighs shake, barely able to keep his brutal thrusts going. Because his brutality was making Benedict cum like a maniac. Was making him feel this amazing and this incredible and this much better than anyone had ever . . . had ever . . .

Suddenly his own balls were boiling.

Suddenly the pressure was rising inside Locky like a torrent, unable to be stopped.

Suddenly Locky was screaming too.

The first shot of cum exploded down Benedict's throat. The sensation shook Locky to the core, racking him with a full body pulse. The next jet was even bigger, even more intense.

Locky's limbs shook independent of each other, spasming out of his control. Benedict choked and breathed and spat all at once, splattering streams of cum across Lock's wet pubes and balls. Each time Benedict gagged it was joined by a wet eruption of cum down his lips and chin as the overflow cascaded onto his chest.

Benedict pulled his hands from the wall and grabbed his own cock, still hard and straining. His eyes rolled back as Locky's cum poured from his mouth. Within seconds,

Benedict was shaking once more as he shot his second load, his high-pitched whimpers hissing hard through Locky's cock head.

Benedict swallowed heavily for a full ten seconds after Locky's cock finally stopped pulsing, bubbles of spit and cum popping on the space between lips and shaft.

Sweat streamed down both of their faces. They were wet and humid and sticky as hell.

"Benedict . . . Jesus . . ." Locky started, trying to breathe through his own gasps. He was holding himself against the jambs of the door, afraid he might collapse.

Suddenly the heat which had spurred him to those brutal places vanished, leaving a cold hollow in its place—regret and guilt and shock at his own brutality. At the things he'd just done. At the things he'd just *said*.

But before those feelings could intensify, Benedict rose on shaking legs and planted the wettest, most cum-soaked kiss of Locky's life. He kissed like a long-forgotten lover. Like he'd lost the ability of speech and had to communicate all his appreciation with his tongue alone.

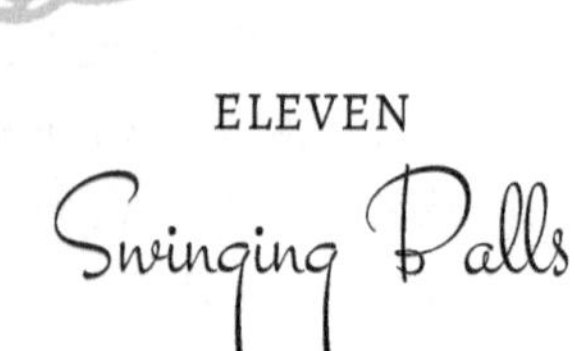

While stuck in the bank line, Locky reflected on the weirdness of the human brain.

Because, on the one hand, everything in his life was perfect. He was about to pursue his dream, creating a magical, unique experience in a low-risk way. He was lining up to withdraw his own money—money he could spare, rather than taking on debt or trading equity. And yesterday, he'd had the soul sucked out of him by his *boyfriend*, a man so handsome and so supportive and so adorable and just—*gah, everything!*

It was more than Locky could have hoped for. More than he deserved. And it should have left him skipping through the streets.

Instead, he found himself with a lead weight in his stomach, and a nagging sense that he was making the biggest mistake of his life.

Not about Benedict—*God no!*—that part was still gooey warmth and goofy smiles whenever he thought back to what they'd done. To what they now were.

Boyfriends.

Boyfriends.

Locky knew it was stupid to feel this way, like some middle-school kid scoring their first kiss. But he couldn't deny that he felt alive and giddy and *happy*. Knowing that he had a man who cared about him and found him sexy and supported his ambitions and was kind and patient and affectionate and all the other Benedict-scented words that Locky could have guzzled right now.

But the *money* situation? That was another matter. Deep down, he knew he was making the right call. And that he'd regret it every day if he didn't. But that didn't make this moment any less terrifying. Because he was about to withdraw an insane check. One with five figures on it. Seven if you counted the decimals.

And that would be the biggest payment Locky had made in his entire life. After all, Kai had never demanded an upfront payment when he'd first moved in. And he didn't own a car, so he'd never dealt with one of those scary loans.

This, right now, was the big test.

Then, Pizza My Mind would vanish for the winter.

And Pie Me to the Moon would be born.

But that would just be the start of the spending. Yes, Benedict had been amazing to keep the costs down, but soon there'd be food suppliers and utilities and a million things that would cost money, money, *more money*.

The heavy feeling wasn't helped by the setting. The Bay Bank was strangely eerie in a way that Locky had never noticed before—a long line of people in almost funeral silence.

Evelyn squeezed his hand, bringing Locky back from a blank stare at the well-dressed teller, helping a customer three ahead of him. "You're making the right call, *Picciriddu*. You know that, yes?"

He looked at her for a moment before returning the squeeze. "I know," he said, not very convincingly.

"You'll see, I promise everything will work out. Although, I do wonder why your man isn't here to support you?"

The truth was that Benedict had offered to come—leapt at the chance—but Locky had turned him down. "He's got his own stuff. He . . . doesn't like seeing his clients struggle. He's really supportive, I swear! And he's going to work through that stuff over the next few months. But . . . I didn't want to scare him off by seeing me like *this*. Not yet, anyway."

Locky reflected on that—about how freaking out in front of Benedict would be the worst thing he could do right now. Yes, Benedict had seen him at all kinds of lows. But that had been when he was just exploring his options for the store. When things had been easy and low risk.

Not when he'd decided to actually open it.

Now Benedict would look at him differently, even if he didn't want to. Because every freakout by Locky would light the spark of panic in Benedict too. Wondering if he'd made a mistake. Wondering if there was something he'd missed. Wondering if he was forcing Locky into taking risks he couldn't afford and making choices he didn't want. Which would, in turn, only freak Locky out more, like they were trapped in some endless echo.

Evelyn chuckled. "I still can't believe my little *Picciriddu* has a *boyfriend*."

Locky's spirits lifted at that. Sure, he'd been the one to tell her about Benedict. But hearing her say it out loud still made those giddy feelings kick back into high gear. "He's pretty great," said Locky. "There's no way I'd be doing this without him."

"Speaking of, how can I help with the big opening? No,

don't fuss. Let me gather support across the meeting network. They'll be so excited! And I'm sure many people from SunSpark would love to help with—"

"No!" said Locky, much sharper than he'd intended, causing several people to turn. "Sorry! I just mean . . . I haven't told anyone else from the meeting yet. Or anyone from work."

"*Picciriddu . . .*"

"I know! It's stupid. And there'll be lots of media going around before the party. So if they hear about it naturally, that's fine. But I just . . . I don't want anyone to feel obligated to help. Everyone has their own issues at the moment—they don't need to waste their time on me."

What Locky left out was how much needless pressure it would add if all his close connections started focusing on a launch party that might flop.

Eventually, Locky shuffled to the head of the line. For all his mixed feelings, the issuing of the check was clinical. Not that he should have been surprised. It wasn't like *Hello, my name is Jasmine* was going to ask follow-up questions like *Are you sure this is a wise investment?* or *Is accounting really that bad a job?*

The details and signatures came and went until the paper slid across the stainless-steel dip.

Locky picked it up gingerly, looking down at the figure—an amount he wouldn't have considered a few months ago.

And rather than sobbing, his chest swelled as he thought of the man who'd made all of this possible. Who'd given him the courage to choose the scary path.

Who'd made him the luckiest man on the planet.

His distraction was broken when Evelyn didn't step away with him, instead being served at the window herself.

When she returned, she had her own check in hand,

tucked quickly into an unknown crevice around her bra. "What? You aren't the only one who had their stock bought out."

"Your tithe, madam," said Benedict, sliding Locky's check across the polished walnut.

Tris glanced over her Yves Saint Laurent tortoiseshell glasses—absent of lenses and unapologetically there just for the fashion statement. She was sitting in a high-backed leather chair at an intimidating desk, too large even for her oversized office. Chatter and ringing phones filtered in from the work floor. Tris's eyebrows shot up whenever there was a dip in activity from her fifteen staff. "What the hell is a tithe?"

"I don't know. I saw it on some Tumblr meme."

"You and I occupy very different parts of the internet," she said, spearing the corner of the paper with a sharp nail and dragging it toward herself. "And about time you got him over the line. How will you handle the opening? Christmas Eve?"

"New Year's. More likely to get novelty headlines and the uniqueness buzz. *A New Year's Eve party without booze?* The press will eat it up."

"Clever," she said, before returning to her keyboard with a *clickity-clack*.

Benedict laughed under his breath. It always amazed him how different Tris was in the office. The second she put on the power suit and the stilettos, all her sass and playfulness was replaced with a sharp-edge that screamed, *don't fuck with me, fellas!*

Not that Benedict could judge her for that. Not when

she'd taken her business from a ramshackle operation run out of their parents' basement to one of the biggest estate agents in the city, specializing in innovative leasing arrangements for those overlooked by traditional providers.

"See you at home, Ms. Executive Realness," he said, making to leave.

"Benedict," she said, when he reached the door. "You did good with this one. You know that, right?"

Benedict's cheeks warmed as he looked away, uncharacteristically shy. "Yeah, I really did."

"Okay, what's with that smile?"

"Locky and I . . . well, we're kinda boyfriends now."

Tris's mouth dropped open for a long moment before she shot up, grabbing Benedict by the arm and dragging him through the office.

"Gah! Where are you taking me," he said as the startled faces rushed past, clearly not used to seeing their boss skip between desks.

"Shopping," she said. "The shoes are on me!"

It was a week later when Benedict found himself following Locky through an overstuffed dollar store, fighting through the cascading racks of streamers and foam signs and tacky decorative stars, the glitter so cheap that it smeared across Benedict's vintage sheepskin jacket at the lightest touch.

The party planning was going . . . well, it was certainly *going*.

In so many ways, Benedict was incredibly proud of how grounded Locky had been in his first few days of having his own store. With barely an eye twitch, Locky had accepted Benedict's advice to get some expensive-but-excellent electricians in to check the heating system and ovens and coffee machine, leaving time for spare parts to be ordered if needed. Locky had let his social media accounts go live with only minimal griping. And he'd even agreed, after the smallest amount of bargaining, to order a few thousand napkins with the store's logo printed on them—an easy way to get branding onto every plate, without the cost of monogramming the crockery.

But for whatever reason, the decorations for the big party were a sticking point. Because Locky seemed convinced that it should be done as cheaply as possible.

"Ohhh," said Locky, as he snatched a bag of balloons in lifeless gold. "Fifty for five dollars! What a bargain!"

Benedict opened his mouth to protest but shut it again quickly. It was something he'd found himself doing a lot these last few days. Just like he'd done when Locky turned down the idea of hiring a swing band for the big night, opting to play records through the speakers instead. Just like Locky had turned down the suggestion of hiring additional waitstaff to deal with the bigger crowds.

Benedict felt stuck between two worlds—the business adviser who knew that a dozen really good balloons would look better than fifty crap ones, even if they were twice as much for half as many, and the boyfriend who understood Locky's issues with money and didn't want him to spend more that he felt comfortable with.

It was just like he'd noticed Locky being more controlled with his own nervous energy, letting it escape briefly before appearing to trap it away again. Nodding a little too enthusiastically and constantly saying that he was fine in a voice from a hostage tape.

Benedict couldn't even get mad about that—because it made perfect sense. If Locky started freaking out too much, then he'd start freaking out as well, which would only freak Locky out more, which would freak *him* out more, and then they'd both end up as great big panic puddles on the ground.

Benedict sighed internally. They should have had the conversation earlier about how to not spiral off each other, particularly as the costs mounted and the opening day drew closer. Unfortunately, they'd both defaulted to the more familiar and more comfortable groove of *not talking about it*.

That was, until Benedict finally snapped.

"What do you think?" said Locky, holding up the cheapest New Year's banner Benedict had ever seen, eight feet of generic party colors against a nasty silver material that was even thinner than the bag it came in.

"Oh God, burn it!" said Benedict, flinging it back onto the messy shelf. The two of them stared wide-eyed at each other for a second, before Benedict relented. "Sorry! Really sorry. But . . . can we just sit and talk about this for a second?"

"Or, counteroffer, we could just keep pretending everything's fine?"

Benedict nodded. "Yup, I hear what you're saying. Great offer. Excellent instincts. And if we were just doing the whole client-adviser thing, I'd totally buy it. But as your *boyfriend* . . . we should probably figure out a way to talk about our mutual fears without melting down."

"You had to play the boyfriend card, huh?"

Benedict ran fingers through Locky's hair, delighting as the man's eyes softened and he leaned into the touch. "What can I say?" said Benedict, more gently. "It's a really nice card to have."

Locky sighed through the beginnings of his familiar blush, his voice more warm than worried. "Yeah. It is."

They found a couple of camping chairs at the back of the store, the cheap metal groaning under their weight. And it groaned even more as Benedict, still sitting, shunted his chair beside Locky's in distressingly loud thumps against the old carpet. He stopped when they were close enough to hold hands across the armrests, like they were at the movies watching a mushy rom-com.

Benedict ran his thumb across Locky's palm. "Now, call me crazy—"

"Pretty sure we both are. Sorry. You may continue, Mr. Owens."

"Thank you, Mr. Sorenson. It seems . . . Look, it seems like the party is giving you even more nerves than usual? I'm not trying to make you feel pressured, but I'd usually recommend making big a splash for your launch. Spend a bit extra to get the attention and the buzz and leave a powerful first impression. But I feel like that idea isn't connecting for you?"

Locky tapped his foot against the floor. "It's just . . . I can understand the electricians and the napkins and all that stuff. They'll pay for themselves over the full three months. But spending thousands of dollars on one night? One party? A band and expensive decorations and extra staff? It's just . . ."

Benedict ran his fingernails up Locky's forearms. "It would all be wasted money if no one came?"

Locky half-exhaled, half-laughed. "I know it's stupid. I know we've got novelty on our side. A sober New Year's party? I can see people talking about that. But that whole *spend money to make money* thing is really scary for me. Because what if it doesn't work?"

Benedict nodded. He'd found himself in this position so many times before. When no amount of logic could shift the nervous instincts. When no amount of talking could calm the crazy.

Benedict looked around the store, not sure what he could say in this moment to make it better. His gaze fell on rack of costume jewelry, including a pair of pearl earrings. They were far cheaper than the real thing, of course, but their shape was very similar to the pair Tris had picked out in Prada—the ones she'd be wearing to their parent's winter gala in under a week.

And Benedict had an idea.

Because maybe Locky didn't need to hear about a successful event.

Maybe he needed to *see* it.

"Would it help," said Benedict with a playful shove against Locky's shoulder, "to see the principle in practice?"

"I can't believe it!" said Kai as he worked the unknotted bow tie around Locky's collar. "My baby boy's going to his first gala!"

"I will stab you so fucking hard," muttered Locky.

"Ohhh, *stabbing*? So now you've broken the curse, I can finally get a taste of that big swinging D?"

"Eww! Gross! No!"

Kai twisted the black silk in precise motions, a finesse that stood in contrast to his own outfit of hoody and gray sweats.

"Wow, so unappreciative. And after I made you who you are today."

"How did you *make me*, exactly?"

"Face it—you wouldn't be starting the bakery if I didn't push you into it. And you wouldn't have met your little smoochy snuggle bunny without me introducing you. I'm basically your fairy God-Daddy at this point."

Locky rolled his eyes affectionately. It all seemed a lifetime ago. Before he'd met Benedict. Before he'd even allowed himself to start thinking about the store. But Kai was right. If not for him, this whole journey would never have started. "Thank you, Kai. Genuinely."

"What? No. Stop it!" he said, pulling the last of the knot through. "But I do expect to be your best man when the wedding comes around. And I want my pick of the groomsmen."

Locky almost choked on his tongue. "What! We only started dating a few weeks ago. No one is talking about marriage!"

"Of course. What was I thinking?"

The doorbell rang as Locky was admiring the perfectly symmetrical knot—far better than he could have tied himself.

He was about to rush for the door, but Kai took him unexpectedly by the shoulders, looking him over with a rare, brotherly affection. "Genuinely, Locky, I'm so fucking proud of everything you've done these last few months."

Locky gave him a sincere smile in return. As playfully combative as their relationship was, Locky had always known that Kai cared deeply about him. That he'd look out for him and protect him and push him to succeed as much as he could. But it still made Locky melt at hearing the words out loud.

With anyone else, this might have been a moment for hugs

and affirmations and grand reflections on their years of friendship.

But Kai was never going to let that happen.

Instead, he slapped Locky hard on the ass. "Hello! Didn't you hear the doorbell?"

Locky snorted as he adjusted his lapels, making sure his belt was properly aligned before swinging the door open.

It wasn't Benedict.

There were two unfamiliar men on the doorstep. One was a mountainous muscle daddy with silver hair poking out of his floral button-up. Beside him was an early twenties otter with tattoos that stretched from his wrists to his neck, fully visible through his pink mesh shirt.

Only when Locky looked past the shorter one did he see Benedict standing awkwardly behind them, dressed immaculately in his own bow tie and suit, giving Locky a cute little wave.

And Locky completely forgot about the two strangers.

Because he'd ever seen anyone look quite so beautiful.

"Oh, those are mine," said Kai, reaching past Locky and dragging the two men inside. "What? I prefer my balls a little less fancy and a little more furry."

Locky spun on the spot, unable to process the scene. Even in his full black tie he felt criminally underdressed, like he needed a top hat and a silver-tipped cane.

The rotunda was three stories of white marble, getting progressively more decorated on each level. It shifted from ornate iron railings to grand Greek columns to an arched, bone-white ceiling carved with dazzling figures that probably belonged in some European palace.

The grand staircase swept down from the first floor, spilling into a circular base for the last third, like the gathering of a bride's dress. Combined with the dozens of flower-covered tables and ornate, golden-lit lamps, it felt like a duke might wander into view at any moment, sword on his hip and a lovely daughter on his arm.

Locky gave Benedict a disbelieving look. "When you said money wasn't a problem in your family, I didn't think you meant *this*."

"In our defense, we don't *own* City Hall. The mayor just lends it for the night."

"If you're on *can I borrow your building* terms with a mayor, you've reached a certain level of wealth."

"Indeed," said Benedict, holding out his arm with a glowing smile and a terrible attempt at a British accent. "Then look lively, Mr. Sorenson, for tonight you'll be dining with *royalty*."

Locky played along, taking the arm and allowing Benedict to lead him around the grand space. In one corner, a string quartet bowed classical music, lively and warm. Women in crips jackets weaved effortlessly through the chattering crowds, carrying silver trays with morsels so tiny that Locky thought he might crush them accidentally.

Every now and then Locky had the surreal experience of seeing an in-person face he'd only previously seen through television glass. Famous football players and highly-strung newsreaders and one of the two federal senators for California.

In the distance, standing proud among the most elite of the guests, they spotted a tall black man with silver dusted hair standing alongside a curvy woman with box braids and a bright fuchsia dress. The resemblance was immediate, and aided by the fact that both were currently talking to Tris, who was wearing a blue-and-red-striped pencil dress, worn off the shoulder and etched with black hatching, accessorized by a matte silver belt in the bow of her hourglass figure.

They were Benedict's parents. They had to be.

Before Locky's heart could leap into his throat, Benedict stopped them, still about thirty feet away, and gave a low chuckle—a sound which only intensified as his mother eyed Tris's ensemble. "Look all you want, Judith," he muttered. "But that dress has only been on the rack for a month. Even you can't find fault with it."

After a long inspection, Benedict's mother give Tris a reluctant smile. Benedict's chuckle turned wicked as he led Locky in the opposite direction. "We'll grab them later, when they've done the other introductions."

"You don't have to introduce me, you know? I mean, I'd like to! But don't feel obligated. If you don't want to. If it's . . ."

Locky let the words fade—born from the fear of knowing his life had become too good, too suddenly.

Because how had he intended to finish that sentence?

If it's too soon?

If you aren't sure?

If you don't want to commit?

But before any of those fears could take proper hold, Benedict banished them with an easy warmth. "Of course I want them to meet you. You're amazing, Locky."

And that was that. No more words were said. And it was clear to Benedict that no more were needed.

Because Benedict was certain.

And so, with a flush of red and a silent prayer to anyone who might be listening, Locky let himself to be certain too.

As they moved through the dignified hustle of the gala, they eventually found themselves at a silent auction table covered in clipboards, alongside a handsome young man tending a velvet sack that guests were tossing little envelopes into, no doubt filled with checks for God knew how many thousands of dollars.

And standing here, Locky had to admit that Benedict had been right. There was something about this space, about the ornate expensiveness of it all, that made the charitable aspects feel *fitting*. Like they belonged. And like it would be the height of rudeness not to contribute a little extra money to a good cause.

"Funny how we accidentally ended up at the *open your pockets* part of the ball, huh?" said Locky.

Benedict grabbed two glasses of a non-alcoholic punch from a passing waitress. "I'm sure I don't know what you mean. But was I right, or was I right?"

"Yes, yes, Mr. Business Adviser," said Locky, feigning annoyance. "Very clever. Now do your victory lap. Tell me how you'd set up the New Year's party to capture all of this."

"God you're sexy when you pout," said Benedict, before glancing downward. "Please Mr. Sorenson, not here! An erection? Control yourself!"

Locky's mortifying boner problem had mostly resolved itself over the last few weeks, now that Benedict was sucking the frustration out of him at every available opportunity. But comments like that could still set Locky on the pathway to public humiliation. And cause the flush of red that Benedict relished.

But rather than panic, Locky waited until Benedict was

taking a sip of his drink. "How about I control your throat instead?"

Benedict spluttered. "*Stop it!* That's so naughty!"

"You're the one who started the battle, Mr. Owens. I just wanted to know about party planning."

"Fine, truce!" said Benedict, waiting until he could stand normally again. "Well, for starters, I'd ticket the event. Yes, I know, you're worried that people won't even come to a free event, so how can you charge for entry? But it creates exclusivity and a sense of time pressure. Plus, charge enough and you can make it 'all you can eat and drink.' That way you don't have to deal with money on the night, freeing up a ton of serving time."

Locky pondered that suggestion. "Could we give some of the ticket proceeds to charity?"

"Yes, that's perfect. It actually helps with marketing. And we can do a velvet bag as well, if you like. Grab a few extra contributions."

"And . . . the decorations?"

"Oh, that's easy. I know a guy who can set it all up. Decorations, band, an extra waiter. Do the whole thing as a package. He'll even provide ropes for the VIP area."

"We're going to have VIPs?"

"Of course! There are plenty of celebrities around town who've spoken about their sobriety journeys. Send out gold ticket invitations to a dozen or so and have a few tables behind ropes. Trust me, if the influencers start talking about their invites, everyone else will too. And speaking of which . . ."

Locky followed Benedict's gaze to the unexpected figure of Grace Liu, leading anchor on the Channel 7 news. Usually, she was a sharp-eyed figure of authority, all silver bob and rimless glasses. But in the flesh, she was barely tall enough to reach the clipboard for the silent auction.

To Locky's horror, Benedict guided them both toward her. "Let's go say hi."

"What!?" hissed Locky, trying to press his heels down, but finding no grip against the polished marble. "You can't be serious!"

"You've got journalists from television and radio and newspaper here tonight. I've worked with them all—they love a good *in lighter news* story."

Locky could feel the sweat beading on his forehead. It had been bad enough knowing that he had social media and a website, without being interviewed on the biggest nightly news broadcast! "But that doesn't mean we can just go up and talk to them!"

"Why not? Schmoozing is half the point of these events."

"Yes, but . . . but . . ."

"Locky," said Benedict, gently running his hands up each of Locky's biceps, just like he had on their first meeting. "You want people to know this event is happening, right?"

Locky relaxed at the steadiness of Benedict's touch. "Yes, of course."

"Well, we can either talk to the powerful people who could give us thousands of dollars of free publicity. Or we could wait until tomorrow and call whatever oblivious intern they've got working the hotline?"

"Okay, *fine*," he breathed. "But do we have to talk to the most famous journalist in the city first?"

"She's actually the perfect person to talk to first."

"Why?"

Benedict leaned in and placed a kiss on Locky's forehead.

"Because the tall blond woman beside Grace is her wife. And I happen to know that she's been sober for the last thirty years."

Tomorrow's the big day, thought Locky, steadying himself on the ladder.

It had been a crazy few weeks since the winter gala, and even with Benedict's help, the work had seemed never ending, a million snowflakes bunching into a blizzard. What had originally seemed like a perfectly clean store turned out to be anything but, once you really got close and saw the gathered grime from months without regular scrubbing.

Seriously, how did it get that way? The store had been shut tight the whole time, so it should have been pristine. But the marble tables had needed a damn good polishing, and the various bits of chrome buffed to sparkling, and the lighting rig on the stage serviced and a few bulbs replaced, and the ovens given a good scrub, and everywhere there'd been dusting, dusting, so much *dusting*!

Not that Locky was complaining, it had been a good distraction as the big day creeped closer.

And now, this was finally it, the last touch, replacing the

old green glass lampshades with big paper moons—swapping the speakeasy aesthetic for a little jazz-era twinkle.

The full decorations for the New Year's party would come later today, but these moons would be here for the next few months, a reminder that this was his store now.

His business.

His dream.

Locky grunted as he tried to force the final shade over a misshaped ring. "Oh, come on, you bitch. Just . . . get . . . in . . . there!"

"So many things I could say to that," sniggered Benedict from the other side of the ladder, using his weight to counterbalance the sway of Locky's jamming. Before Locky could break the light in two, Benedict joined him on the middle rung, swiveling the shade in small, precise movements until it clicked into place. "Patience isn't your strong suit, is it?"

Locky leaned over the apex for a kiss. "No. That's what I have you for."

The old radio from the kitchen crackled as they got down from the ladder. It was some top-thirty rubbish that Benedict had put on, more as background music than anything else.

It wasn't that Locky hated modern music, he'd just always gravitated toward songs with mood and melody—that could fill a room and bring life to a lonely space.

However, no sooner had he packed the ladder aside, than a familiar voice wafted through the room, interrupting the songs.

It was himself—higher and reedier, like nails on a chalkboard. *"Well, Janice,"* said radio Locky, sounding so smug it made real Locky want to hide under one of the freshly polished tables, *"for a lot of people, the only option on New*

Year's is a bar or a nightclub. Which is great for some. But not everyone wants that kind of atmosphere, you know? That was the inspiration for creating Pie Me to the Moon, a late-night bakery with a jazz lounge vibe, to give people who want a different—"

Benedict caught Locky as he tried to sprint for the kitchen, pulling him into a forced hug. "What's the matter, honey bun? It sounds like a fascinating news report, *you know?"*

"Benedict!" sobbed Locky, his arms thrashing about at a full zombie stretch. "I sound like a fucking dork!"

"No, you sound sexy and smoochable," said Benedict, giving machine-gun kisses against his cheek. "And am I a good interview coach, or what?"

Locky slapped his hands over his ears. "How did you know it would be on now?"

"If I can get you an interview on the city's top-rated morning show, I can find out when they're planning on airing it."

Locky huffed, still blocking the worst of the noise. He knew he should be grateful—and he was, really. He never thought he'd have a store at all, let alone having an almost sold-out opening night. And despite there only being a few dozen tickets left, Benedict had convinced Locky to keep doing media. That way, they might get a crowd gathered outside, even if they couldn't get in—generating enough buzz to tide them over until the end of the lease.

Muffled breath brushed across Locky's fingers. "It's over, Mr. Sorenson."

Locky lowered his hands and was blessedly met with a song he'd never heard.

Rather than release his bear hug, Benedict shuffled them

both toward the wall, like they were trapped in an indecisive wrestling hold.

"What are you doing?" said Locky, confused but still stepping in time.

"Just being cute."

"Well, you're succeeding."

When they finally arrived at the wall, the two of them reached over and clicked the light switch on.

Locky exhaled as the room glowed to life. The new lights had lifted the space in the most beautiful way, adding a dreamy softness and a touch of the night sky. Now, every surface glinted like a moonlight sonata. Like he could almost hear the music and the conversations and the dancing.

Locky could have stared across the dining floor for hours —had his attention not been caught by an unexpected glow over the counter. Because, in place of the old neon sign was a brand new one, all soft amber swirls and familiar words.

Pie Me to the Moon.

Locky slapped Benedict's chest. "What! How did you do that? How didn't I notice!?"

"Trade Secrets, Mr Sorenson. Trade Secrets."

"Benedict!"

"What? I'm sneaky! As soon as you picked the logo for the napkins, I rang a friend. And don't worry," he said, before Locky could protest, "it won't cost you anything. Think of it as my store-warming present."

Locky gave Benedict a loving kiss. "Thank you for that. For everything. I couldn't have done this without you, Benedict."

"Just glad to be of service," said Benedict, with a waggle of eyebrows and a slight swivel of bulge against bulge. "Speaking of . . ." At that moment, Benedict's phone buzzed. "Can you hear something?" he said, placing hot kisses along Locky's neck. "Because I sure can't."

Locky groaned as Benedict's rapidly hardening cock started sliding against his own. "Okay, I *really* love where this is going, but that's probably your party planner."

"*Fine!*" said Benedict, half releasing his embrace. "Doug, how are things? Ready to start setting up?"

Benedict's other arm fell away from Locky's shoulders. It was so sudden, and the absence so sharp, that Locky felt like he'd been thrown in cold water. It was a feeling amplified by the way Benedict's expression fell, and how he shuffled into the corner, giving increasingly sharp hisses into his hand.

"What is it?" asked Locky, heart pounding, once Benedict hung up.

When Benedict finally turned around—slowly, like he was standing on roller skates—he looked small and sweaty, like he didn't know where he was.

Like he was about to faint.

Locky rushed to his side, bringing him safely to a seat. Benedict's movements were stiff, his eyes vacant. "Everything's fine. I'm here," said Locky, feeling the pulse pound through his boyfriend's clammy wrists.

Benedict looked up to him—looked *through* him. "I'm sorry. I'm sorry. I'm—"

"It's okay, just breathe," said Locky, doing his best to grasp the fraying shreds of his own calm. He remembered what they'd talked about, what they'd promised each other over these last few weeks—that they'd try and avoid panic spiraling off each other if things went wrong. "Tell me what happened."

"Some . . . some big corporate New Year's gig. Band and barista. Last minute. Getting paid triple. *Can't say no . . .*"

Locky's eye twitched.

Oh shit.

They had no band.

No barista.

And it was one day until opening.

It was the worst news they could get right now, but Locky tried to keep a lid on his own panic. Because, yes, this was bad for him. Apocalyptically bad. But it would be even worse for Benedict. Because this was his biggest fear—that he might give bad advice and ruin Locky's big night, starting a cascade toward total failure.

And just like Benedict had been there for him so many times, now Locky needed to be there for Benedict.

"Have you used these people before?" Locky asked, slow as he could manage.

Benedict looked up from the middle distance, taking a few moments to find Locky's face. "I . . . recommended them. I told you they were reliable . . ."

Locky took Benedict's cheeks in both hands, his own touch hot against Benedict's frosty skin. "I know. And I can't imagine how much that's hurting you right now. But have they ever done something like this before?"

"No, they've . . . they've always been good. But that doesn't—"

Locky leaned in, laying a warm kiss against Benedict's freezing forehead. "Then it's not your fault, Benedict. You recommended someone you trusted. You couldn't have known this would happen."

"But—"

"Benedict," Locky insisted, using his thumb tips to gently brush away the tears running down Benedict's cheeks. "Things happen. I don't blame you. And you shouldn't blame yourself. Okay?"

Benedict searched his face, as if willing Locky to scold him. Clearly wanting the confirmation that he was wrong. That he'd failed. That he was a fuck-up. Because that would confirm every dark and terrible thing that Benedict believed about himself. Because Locky knew better than anyone, sometimes it felt better to confirm your failures than accept forgiveness.

But Locky wasn't going to do that. He wouldn't let Benedict believe that about himself.

Not now.

Not *ever*.

Eventually, weakly, Benedict nodded.

"Okay," said Locky breathing out the top layer of his own terror. "What the hell do we do now?"

Benedict rubbed his temples, feeling better—though far from perfect—after a brisk walk through Union Square. "How is *every* band in the city booked?"

"I can't imagine," said Locky, kicking a rock down the footpath, almost skipping over a railing and bouncing into the nearby ice rink, full of carefree sounds.

The three-story Christmas tree hadn't been taken down yet, showering festive warmth over a scene of holiday revelry. A warmth that Benedict really wasn't feeling.

Their situation was hopeless. Absolutely hopeless. He'd rung all his usual contacts who'd, of course, been booked up months ago. They'd gone top to bottom through the local directories with similar results. Even when they'd dropped their expectations from a jazz band to any band, to any breathing person who could halfway carry a tune, they'd still had zero luck. Even begging bands playing in public places had got them nowhere.

Usually, he'd have told Locky to just play CDs in the background and make the best of it, but they'd made such a big deal about the live music during their promotions—hammering home that the only thing missing from this party was the alcohol.

Which was another fuck-up on his part.

Overpromising and underdelivering.

Just like he always did.

Benedict tried to push that frustration away, even if he was about ten minutes from asking someone's Aunt Lola to bust out a few verses of "Do the Funky Chicken."

"What about a fancy hotel lobby?" said Locky, after they'd wandered around aimlessly for another half hour. "They sometimes have bands or string quartets playing around the holidays?"

Benedict sighed—it was better than any other option they had right now. "Might be worth a shot? I think there's a Hilton around here somewhere? If we cut through this street, we should—"

Benedict froze at the entrance to a narrower lane, lined with shops.

Lined . . . with *familiar* shops.

Locky walked ahead a few paces before turning back, giving him a look of concern.

But Benedict didn't hear his questions. Because the street ahead was fading into a singular tunnel, like a whirlpool sucking everything into its vortex. And all Benedict could see was the entrance to a distant bar, tucked into the slope of the street.

Over the doorway was an illuminated sign reading *Hops and Honey.*

It was the brewery and bar he'd helped Dan the football coach create. A store he hadn't seen in six years.

Frost stabbed into every part of him, distant and sudden and close and slow, everywhere and nowhere all at once. The feeling of pressure, of icy water crashing over him, flooded his eyes and nose and mouth, wrapping tight around his chest. Unable to breathe. Unable to speak.

He felt like he was withdrawing from his body, from this moment. The world whistled in the distance as he floated back, *wrenched* back.

Because it couldn't be real. It couldn't be *now*. He couldn't be face to face with a client's store after so long, after being so careful.

It just . . . it just couldn't be happening . . .

A million questions hooked in Benedict's throat, threatening to drag him deeper into the swirling water. Was the bar doing okay? Did Dan achieve everything he wanted? Had he made those three different beers for his three little girls?

Did I give good advice?

Did I do a good job?

Was I worthy of your trust?

Are you mad that I disappeared without warning?

Do you blame me?

The surrounding howl told Benedict that he didn't want the answer to those questions—that he couldn't *handle* the answers to those questions. Because of course things had gone wrong! Of course he'd fucked up. That the only reason the bar was still standing was because Dan had probably remortgaged his house. Or spent his daughters' college funds. Or sold the bar to someone else, just to try and pay of all the debt that he'd—

Breath, sudden and sharp, returned to his lungs. A guiding light against the cold. A beacon against the bitter dark.

Locky had taken his hand. His grip was strong enough to drag him from the vortex. Warm enough to vaporize the freezing swell.

Locky looked up at him with a certainty that Benedict knew he didn't deserve. An expression that said more than words ever could.

Because Locky knew. Benedict had never told him about this place. About Dan or this bar or any of it. But somehow, Locky just knew.

"I'm not going to make you go into a bar, Locky," said Benedict, each syllable feeling like a speech.

The squeeze Locky gave him brought a tear down Benedict's cheeks. A wordless promise burned into his flesh.

You aren't alone, Benedict.

You're never alone when you're with me.

"We don't have to go inside," said Locky, bringing Benedict's hand to his lips and laying a kiss so soft it might have been from an angel. "But we can still walk by? If you want?"

Time seemed to stand deathly still, cold as the winter breeze. There was no one else on this street, in this entire city.

Only them and this moment.

Only them and this decision.

Benedict knew that he could turn around. Forget this ever happened. Go another way and feel this terrible pressure unravel, just like he had so many times before.

He felt the familiar twitch in his feet, like pins and needles.

The well-known swivel of heel. The moment of flight. The relief of running away from all of *this*.

It was inviting him. It was calling him.

And it would be so fucking easy.

Locky's hand felt so heavy in his, undeserved. Because Locky was brave—so much braver than Benedict. Because he hadn't cowered in his moment, had he? When the decision between the familiar and the terrifying had finally caught up with Locky, he'd taken the brave path. He'd been through so much more than Benedict, so much worse and so much more brutal. But he'd still found a way to fight through it. Because he was better! Because he was stronger! Because he was—

It came like a ringing bell, a single, clear strike, echoing sweet and bright through the still street.

The chains around Benedict's chest unraveled.

The flood through his throat subsided.

And the words, sweet words, glowed through him.

I couldn't have done any of this without you, Benedict . . .

Because it was true that Locky was brave and strong and amazing. That would always be true. But Locky hadn't managed to overcome his fears alone—he'd told Benedict as much. He'd needed someone to help pull him through. To give him the strength and the confidence to take that final, terrifying step.

He'd needed Benedict.

And maybe, just maybe, it wasn't so bad if Benedict needed Locky as well?

Every fiber of Benedict's being begged for him to turn around, but Locky stood firm beside him.

His anchor.

His light.

His warmth.

There for him. No matter how this went.

And in this beautiful, terrible moment, that was enough.

Benedict stepped forward.

It wasn't a good step—no confident bound into the unknown. It was hesitant and strange, like his body didn't understand what it was doing. Why it was walking toward the danger, not away from it.

Locky kept his pace, neither dragging Benedict forward nor leaving him to walk on alone. He stayed steadfast beside him. Fixed. Two ships against the storm. Two lights among the raging dark.

As the store grew closer, his soul screamed for him not to do this. To stay safe. To get out while he still could.

Quickly.

Now!

And if it hadn't been for Locky, Benedict was sure he would have turned back.

But he didn't.

Because Locky was with him.

As they drew parallel with the storefront, Benedict didn't have the heart to stare directly through the window, to see how busy it was or catch a glimpse of the owner—the man he'd abandoned.

But he still walked by.

And like the rain passing into sun, the store was soon behind him.

And he'd survived.

He'd *survived*.

He just he'd gone past a client's store for the first time in almost a decade. Something so many people would think of as tiny, but something he hadn't dared to do, hadn't imagined himself doing.

And he'd just done it. *He'd done it!* Something huge and important and impossible.

Benedict sped up, not in his eagerness to get away, but because there was suddenly too much inside him to walk slowly. Too much excitement. Too much relief. Too much . . . *everything*!

By the time Benedict got to the end of the lane he was floating through starlight, skipping like a little kid and pulling Locky into passionate kisses and dancing them both in wild circles like they'd just won the lottery.

In fact, Benedict was so swept up in the hugs and the kisses and the words of congratulations, he almost tripped into someone on the corner of the street.

He was a stocky man, his camping chair taking up most of the sidewalk. His beard was copper and streaked with a few flecks of silver, a little darker than the curls that poked from his beanie. He was wearing a blue flannel jacket, teamed with well-scuffed jeans and a pair of Timberland boots that looked like they'd climbed through every mountain in the country.

Benedict immediately recognized him, even though they hadn't had a chance to talk.

It was the musician from the Thanksgiving dinner.

But that wasn't what had caused Benedict to stop, as unexpected as this encounter was.

What made Benedict stop was the song. It was soft and light and surprisingly gentle against the sounds of the street. It was pretty, yes, but more than that, it was *fitting*. The notes that shimmered through the air felt like they belonged to this place, to this season. Like they were being pulled from the air and woven into song.

The stardust over Benedict was still sparkling so bright that he found himself blurting out. "How are you with jazz?!"

The notes drifted to a stop as the man looked up, taking Benedict in with more curiosity than annoyance. "Yeah, I'm a fan," he said, in a voice of honey and campfire smoke. "Although I usually like to know the guy first." To Benedict's furrow-browed he added, "Oh, *jazz*. Sorry. I thought you said something else."

Locky cleared his throat and introduced the two of them —and their Thanksgiving connection—not attempting to hide the desperation of their situation.

The man—Artair was his name—scratched his chin. "Innnteresting. I'll be honest, I've never tried a jazzy, big band vibe. But I've got some synth equipment in storage. I could swing by later and test it out?" He chuckled to himself at that. "Get it. Swing by? *Swing* by? 'Cause swing music? No, nothing?"

Benedict exhaled hugely, the biggest part of their hunt now over. "Thank fucking God. Musician down. Now we just need to find a barista."

To his surprise, Artair chimed in. "I don't want to be all forward and stuff, but this might be your lucky day?"

"Okay, now slide the steam wand into the jug at a thirty-degree angle. Then you ease the pressure up until it's rolling around and you can hear a rumble."

Locky blinked at the instructions from Artair's husband, Luca, the raven-haired waiter-slash-journalist they'd also seen at the Thanksgiving dinner. The one who'd been making— now understandable—goo-goo eyes at Artair all evening long.

He had piercing brown eyes, inquisitive and ever so

slightly judgmental, staring out at Locky from messy waves. And Locky had the strangest feeling that he'd seen this man before—not just at the Thanksgiving dinner, but somewhere long before that.

Artair sniggered as he shuffled by, lugging some kind of speaker. "Lol, *slide in the wand.*"

"Maybe later, babe," said Luca, voice softening as he leaned over the counter. "If you're lucky."

Artair made a deviation on his journey and stole a passing kiss. "I'm always lucky with you," he said, as the snigger grew louder. "Lucky? Locky? Luca? There's a song in there somewhere."

Locky didn't have time to absorb their cuteness, because he was too busy staring at the intimidating machine. He liked his coffee as much as the next person, but he'd always been happy with a communal pot of drip. He'd never got into *espresso*, and didn't have the first clue how the levers and dials worked.

They were interrupted by a teeth-chattering roar of electronica from the back corner. The sound was long and high and slightly distressing, like someone jumping on a lamb with a pogo stick. "Sorry! That's *definitely* not the vibe," yelled Artair, as the noise morphed into something even more unpleasant. "Can you turn the amp down, Benny Boy? I still have it set from the last concert I did, but I don't think they need to hear us from across the Bay."

"How do I do that?" roared Benedict, over the din.

"That little twizzly knob thing. No, the other one. Third from the left. *My* left."

Locky's eye twitched as the sound jagged even louder, before finally settling to a more reasonable level.

"You're doing great, babe!" said Luca, halfway between

exasperation and adoration. "Sorry, about that. The steam wand?"

Luca moved Locky's wrist under a long metal straw. With an effortless *click-whack-swoosh* of levers, the cold milk started to swirl in the jug. Still gripping tight, Luca yanked Locky's hand up and down in slight motions, letting small hisses of steam break the milk's surface. "Okay, now on your own."

Locky panicked as Luca removed his grip, accidentally dropping the jug a full two inches. A great jet of steam hissed across the milk's surface. Locky desperately reached for the lever, only to flick it in the wrong direction, making the geyser grow bigger, spitting lukewarm milk all over the place, like a bubbling white volcano.

Without any great haste, Luca reached up and clicked the lever off, bringing the steam to a halt. "Well, that went badly," he said, wiping some stray milk splats from his beard. "And the screaming isn't *strictly* necessary to make a good latte."

Locky put the jug down on the bench like it was a grenade with the pin pulled. "If I pay you, can you make sure I never have to touch this thing again?"

"*Never?* Probably not. But I can keep it away from you for the winter. After that we're heading up north to rebuild a cabin in the mountains."

"I . . . have way too many questions," said Locky, overwhelmed by this manic day and struggling to process new pieces of information—like how someone could be a waiter, and a journalist, and a wilderness carpenter?

"That's the usual response, yes," said Luca, before glancing down at the empty cocktail bar by his knees. "Are you planning on using those?"

Locky raised an eyebrow. "This is an alcohol-free place. Sort of a big part of the identity."

"Yes, sweetie, I gathered. But mocktails also exist."

Locky considered that. *Pie Me to the Moon* was already a huge departure from what most people would think a "bakery" was. Adding mocktails would only make the store stranger and harder to describe. "Do you think we need them?"

"Need? No. But they could help people stay longer. There's only so much coffee you can drink. Particularly at one in the morning. And I can take care of setting it up. It's just a few juices and garnishes, given you already have the equipment and the ice machine. It's literally a hundred bucks and a trip to the grocery store."

There was another wall of sound from the back corner, but this time the electronic harshness had softened to something strangely fitting. It wasn't jazz—lacking the big band sound you only got from brass instruments—but it still somehow carried the warmth of the place, the moonlight sparkle and the fireplace crackle.

Benedict was dancing a little jig to the music with no idea —*no care*—that he was being watched. He'd been like that ever since they'd walked by Hops and Honey. Like he was drifting on a cloud.

Locky turned back to Luca, who was eyeing him, keen and inquisitive and clearly waiting for a decision.

Mocktails weren't something Locky had considered, and they definitely weren't something he'd planned for.

But then again, had *any* of this been?

He was standing in a store he never would have created, with a boyfriend he never would have met, if not for scary and unfamiliar suggestions.

Suggestions that had turned out pretty damn okay.

"Sure," said Locky. "Let's give it a go."

No sooner had he said it than Benedict was unexpectedly at the counter, his phone in hand. "Doug messaged!" he said, panting. "He says we can have the decorations. He can't help us set up, but he'll give us the materials at no charge."

"Oh, shit. I completely forgot about the decorations."

"Yeah, and I know you still haven't told everyone in your life about the big opening. But I think this might be an all-hands-on-deck situation?"

Locky sighed. "Yeah, you're probably right. Let's gather the troops."

Pie Me to the Moon was a hive of activity.

Kai and Evelyn were standing ten feet apart, on ladders of very different heights, bickering about where to hang these complex brown paper banners with intricate cutouts and built in orange lights, which gave an effect like firelight dancing though the window of a log cabin.

Tris and Benedict were assembling upside-down fishbowl things for each table, with twinkly golden lights on fishing line, giving the effect, when dark, of fireflies moving under glass. The two of them were laughing together, relaxed and comfortable, with Tris clearly delighted and so damn proud after Benedict told her of his success today—finally breaking the curse that had plagued him for so long.

Artair and Luca, who'd graciously offered to help, had taken on the daunting task of constructing a big, crescent moon seat, which could be used by guests to get memorable photos, hopefully posted to social media to keep the buzz train going.

And Locky was being yelled at.

"How could you not tell us you were opening a store, Boss Man!?" said Adriana, her anger somewhat softened by her need to take deep breaths between blowing up balloons. "This whole time I thought you were applying for accounting jobs!"

"Yeah," said Jared, from one of the booths, weaving fairy lights into a wire template for the moon seat, which would—eventually—say the name of the store. "We could have helped out with this months ago."

"I know, and I'm really sorry about that," said Locky, trying to figure out the best position for a guest book—another thing that Benedict had recommended, making each visit feel extra special, and giving an opportunity for any VIPs to leave a lasting mark. "But I didn't want anyone to feel obligated."

"*Obligated?*" Adriana groaned. "Seriously, you've done so much for so many people. This isn't obligation. We care about you. We want you to succeed. And you've earned everyone's support."

Locky waved a dismissive hand, the praise making him feel embarrassed. "Well, it doesn't matter anyway. We're almost sold out."

"Yeah, and everyone from work will have their own parties to go to. But they'll still want to be here when you open. Even if just for a few minutes."

"I don't want people to stand out in the cold when they can't even come in!"

Adriana bounced the balloon off his head. "Just let me ask them!"

Locky looked around the room, at all the people helping out on his store, his project. Every instinct told him to feel guilty about that. And yet, among the laughs and good nature, no one seemed like they were being forced. No one seemed like they were feeling *obligated*.

"Okay, fine," he said, rubbing the back of his neck. "You can ask. But I'm not expecting anyone to say yes."

Locky collapsed on one side of a booth, lying flat on the length of leather. Benedict followed on the other side, landing with a loud *floomph*.

This day—draining and dramatic—was finally over. Artair and Luca would be coming in tomorrow for opening night, and the decorations were all sorted, meaning the disasters had been averted as quickly as they'd come.

"Please tell me that's the last thing that can go wrong," said Benedict, flopping an arm under the table. From down here, it looked like the two of them were in some kind of secret table cave, away from the rest of the world.

"Not sure I can make that promise," said Locky swinging his hand between marble and tile. "And you did really well today. Facing your fears like that."

Benedict smiled back, soft and tired. "Only because of you. I couldn't have done any of this without you."

"Hey, that's my line," said Locky, flicking Benedict's fingertips with his own.

"I'm pretty sure it's both of our line," said Benedict, returning the gesture.

With an exaggerated groan, Locky forced himself back to standing. Benedict followed, collapsing onto Locky's shoulder dramatically. Both of them were clearly ready for food and snuggles.

Unexpectedly, Benedict turned around so his thick ass was rubbing against Locky's lap. The bigger man let out a soft groan. "You know, in all this commotion I didn't tell you that my regular tests came back clean."

Locky perked up in more ways than one. Despite how badly they both wanted it, Locky hadn't got around to sliding his cock into Benedict's willing ass yet, with both of them collapsing into an exhausted puddle these last few weeks.

But now, everything was ready with the store.

And there was nothing holding them back.

This might not have been how Locky thought this night would end. But he certainly wasn't complaining.

"Oh *really*?" said Locky, rubbing his bulge against Benedict's cheeks, up and down over the big bubble curves. That feeling made him shudder, reminding him of how long it had been since he'd last done this.

"Maybe it's my reward for breaking the curse?" said Benedict. "You taking me home and fucking a load into me?"

Locky's cock throbbed hard at that. Suddenly, all thoughts of sleep were gone. All he could think about was doing that— sliding his bare cock into his boyfriend's beautiful ass. Making him moan and shudder as he emptied his full, neglected balls into his tight hole.

A sly grin brought dimples to Locky's cheeks. "You know . . . this might be the last time the store is empty for a while?"

Benedict looked over his shoulder, grinning wickedly. "You really are full of surprises, Mr. Sorenson."

Sparks crackled across Benedict's skin, urging haste. Urging *immediacy*. Those sparks told him to tear his boyfriend's clothes from his body and lick all the way up his furry chest, stopping at the hard peaks of his pink nipples, making Locky shake under his attention. They told Benedict to lay Locky down and take what he needed, what he'd desired since the first moment he saw this incredible man, all those weeks ago, awkward and nervous and so horny he'd gotten rock-hard from just a hug.

But he didn't rush the moment. Because Benedict wanted to savor this man. To bring life to all the emotions running through Locky's face—excitement and nerves and anticipation.

Because Locky couldn't remember most of the sex he'd had. That meant he probably didn't remember what it felt like to top—the pleasure and power and the incredible passion of it all.

And if this was the first time Locky remembered fucking someone, Benedict wanted him to remember it *right*.

Locky gave him the cutest smile as Benedict brought their lips together, blond eyelashes closing softly as their tongues met, stoking Benedict's fire. And they were stoked even further by the soft moans that left Locky's mouth, vibrating through their connection, tongue tip to tongue tip.

They'd been far too busy these last few weeks. Neglecting each other. Neglecting their needs. And now, all that pent-up desire was boiling inside them both.

Locky grabbed at Benedict's belt, fingers fast and clumsy. Benedict laughed against Locky's teeth. Clearly, he wasn't the only one who'd been looking forward to this.

"Sorry," said Locky, moving the leather more slowly through the belt loops.

"You've been thinking about this ass a lot, huh?"

Locky grabbed hold of Benedict's butt, rough and hungry. Each hand covered barely a quarter of a cheek. "You have no fucking idea," he growled.

"And what do you want to do to it?" said Benedict, swiveling against Locky's fingertips and making the nails dig deeper. It was a sharp bite through fabric, making Benedict shudder.

Locky's cock throbbed hard against Benedict's thigh. "I want to taste you."

"*Fuck yeah*," said Benedict, bringing their lips together again, relishing the haste of Locky's tongue and thinking about him sliding it deep into his tight ass.

Suddenly, *incredibly*, one of Locky's hands shot up and grabbed the back of Benedict's collar, yanking their mouths apart.

It was a forceful act. A *welcome* act.

Locky's eyes were hungry now. No, not hungry. *Starving.*

All of Locky's shyness was replaced by something more primal. More yearning.

Now it was Benedict's turn to groan. At Locky's force. At his command. At the steel that now filled those sky-blue eyes.

His own cock pulsed hard in its cage, wanting more of *this* Locky. Wanting all of *this* Locky.

Because, suddenly, Locky was staring at him like a carnivore eyeing his prey. Like he hadn't fed in many, *many* moons.

And never in his whole life had Benedict felt more desired.

As if overcome with an unholy heat, Locky licked up Benedict's neck, fast and rough. Tasting his scent and his sweat. When he came to Benedict's mouth, he kissed hard, ravenous for every inch of him. "You know what I want?" Locky said, steel and fire in his voice.

"Tell me," whispered Benedict.

"I want to fuck the cum out of you," he growled, grabbing either side of Benedict's business shirt and tearing it open, buttons clattering to the floor around them. "I want to hear you scream as I fill you with my fucking load."

Benedict's whole body shook at the power in Locky's voice. "Green, Mr. Sorenson. *So fucking green!*"

Before he could even catch his breath, Locky pushed Benedict onto the booth table, back flat against the marble.

The stone was cold against Benedict's hot skin, visceral and delicious in its contrast. Another hand pulled hard on the hem of Benedict's pants, not even bothering to undo them— the hunger too great, the desire too demanding. There was an animal scrape of stitching as the suit pants tore over Benedict's ass, the sensation of ripped fabric sharp and sensual.

Because Locky needed him.

And he didn't have time for niceties.

A big wave of cold hit Benedict's bare ass as what was left of his pants and briefs were tugged down to his ankles. His cock sprung out, wet and harder than he'd ever seen it before, the silver piercing glinting clear and pornographic in the warmth of the moonlight shades, a corona dazzling on his slick precum.

Locky pulled his own jeans down with equal haste, his godly dick pouncing out, hard and hairy and pointing to the ceiling with its intimidating curve.

Before Benedict could praise him, Locky had hoisted himself fully onto the table. It creaked under their shared weight as Locky prowled toward Benedict like a tiger through tall grass—the metal buttons of his ankle-bunched jeans clanking on the marble like a summoning bell.

"Open your fucking mouth," Locky growled, grabbing Benedict by the shoulders and spinning him 180 degrees on the smooth surface, until Benedict's head was by the edge of the table. Locky climbed over the top of Benedict, into a 69 position. "Stick your fucking tongue out!"

Benedict obliged, spreading his lips wide and extending his tongue tip. As Locky's beefy, blond-thatched thighs spread over his face, Benedict wasn't sure he'd ever seen anything as beautiful. Locky's big balls were hanging just inches from Benedict's nose and smelling of their busy, sweaty day. Over the top of his obediently open mouth was the most incredible cock he'd ever played with, so long that both of his hands wouldn't be enough to hold it all.

Locky's cock was twitching in anticipation, a clear drip of precum bobbing from his foreskin, growing longer with each throb.

Slowly, Locky lowered his hips until those big balls were dipped against Benedict's waiting tongue. A low growl came from overhead as Locky moved his hips back and forth, allowing Benedict's tongue to trace the full weight of his nuts.

He tasted of salt.

He tasted of *beast*.

As the heat of the Locky's cock radiated against Benedict's chin, close but not yet touching, it was like Locky was measuring Benedict's throat for length. Benedict couldn't see it from this angle, but he knew the pink and white shaft measured down past his neck, reaching all the way down to the notch between his collarbones.

Suddenly, Locky shuffled the slack of his bunched jeans under Benedict's head, cradling him between Locky's ankles in a makeshift hammock of denim and cotton. The leverage was such that Benedict's head was held firm, trapped and unable to escape. If Locky moved his ankles up or down, Benedict had no choice but to follow.

Locky lowered his hips further, sliding his hard cock across Benedict's face. The warm wetness of Locky's swollen glans left a trail of excitement dripping onto Benedict's chin. The veins of his shaft ground against Benedict's lips and tongue as Locky drew his hips back, making as much room as he could. Trying to slide his cock down Benedict's throat.

The heft of the dick strained hard against Benedict's cheek, with Locky being so hung that he could barely make room to reposition himself. It was a realization that made Benedict's own cock jump, stickiness gathering all across his lower belly.

Because the pressure against his cheek, the strain of the effort, was a visceral reminder of just how big the man really was. Just like it made clear the promise of the position, with Locky's hips locked over him, and with Benedict's helpless head stuck between Locky's shoes, moving up and down whenever Locky shifted his ankles.

Benedict savored that incredible view for one last moment: cock and balls and furry pink asshole.

And just when he couldn't handle the anticipation any longer, two things happened that overwhelmed Benedict with heady perfection.

The first was an upward shift in Locky's hips as he leaned his body forward, allowing his big, slippery cock head to pop into Benedict's grateful mouth, filling it quickly and forcing his jaw to stretch in accommodation.

The second was a warm sensation around his own cock, as Locky eagerly returned the favor.

Benedict groaned at the welcome relief, a salve to a burn, as Locky's tongue glided over Benedict's piercing in slow, deliberate circles, making Benedict twitch involuntarily.

That incredibly, squishy warmth was accompanied by the slow thrust of Locky's own cock across Benedict's tongue, rolling back his foreskin as it crept, inch-by-patient-inch, down his throat.

Benedict's cock pulsed as Locky slid deeper into his throat, the thickness of the shaft filling him. Benedict used his experience to control his breath as the cock reached the choke point, where breathing was no longer possible. Benedict felt a jet of precum spurt from his own cock, a full shot rather than a drip, which was confirmed by the unexpected throaty noise that Locky made, swallowing that salty gift.

All the sounds Locky made were driving Benedict wild—growls of animal joy at everything he was experiencing. And that sound only intensified when Locky decided to join in with the deep throating, struggled his way about halfway down Benedict's girthy cock, forcing through the gags of his own inexperience.

Not that Locky seemed to mind that effort. Instead, Locky's full balls were already gathering closer to his body in anticipation of the massive load he would soon shoot.

Benedict ran worshiping hands across the godly heft above him, down the broad back and big, blond-furred ass. There was so much there to feel—so much power and weight that Benedict felt small underneath it all.

Small and dominated and *wanted*.

The fullness in Benedict's throat grew as Locky filled him further, and even Benedict had to fight against the gag. It was a sensation that always made his skin prickle. Scary and hot at the same time. That feeling of your lungs being cut off. Of wanting to breathe, needing to breathe, but having so much cock in your mouth that you couldn't.

Benedict's voice box quivered as he tried to hold the cough, before finally gagging hard on the slab of cock.

Locky pulled his cock back fast, and Benedict was worried he might withdraw it completely. But Locky had learned from their recent experiences, pulling his cock out just far enough to free Benedict's windpipe, making Benedict gasp wet breaths through a full mouth of slippery skin.

He'd barely got his breath back before Locky was forcing his dick deeper. His thrusts were faster this time—the sensation of dominance making Benedict's eyes roll back into his head.

He knew that he could knock against the table at any time —making Beng Locky stop. But no part of Benedict wanted Locky to do that.

He wanted this.

All of this.

The warm slipperiness around Benedict's own cock shifted, no longer swallowing him but running a heavy tongue down his shaft and across his balls.

Locky's tongue didn't stay on Benedict's balls long, because no sooner had Locky reached the full depth of Benedict's throat, than he grabbed the back of Benedict's knees and forced them against Benedict's belly, turning him into a bearish pretzel.

Locky spread Benedict's ass even wider until Benedict could feel Locky's hungry breath brushing against his tight ring.

Benedict gasped through his full mouth of cock as Locky's tongue came hot and hasty onto his hole. The hungry tongue was joined by an even deeper thrust down Benedict's throat, pushing for depth where none remained. Locky tongued him deep and hard, mimicking what he was doing to Benedict's mouth. Mimicking what he so clearly wanted to do to Benedict's ass.

Benedict's gag was met with another withdrawal, the movement coming from Locky's hips alone. But the rimming didn't stop, deep and probing. There was just enough time for Benedict to rasp a single hot breath before the next thrust came, finding the full depth even faster than before, taking advantage of his vulnerable position and his well-lubed throat.

Benedict gave a muffled groan as Locky forced his elbows into the back of Benedict's knees, opening him up even wider, trapping him even more, making him feel even smaller and more commanded.

Locky's tongue was like fire against his ass, and Benedict wanted all of it. Wanted Locky's tongue to loosen him. To make a contract with his ring, promising just how hard he'd soon be fucked.

That feeling of being commanded only increased when Locky brought his own ankles up, all the way to the back of his knees, with Benedict's head still trapped by the denim sling. Benedict gagged hard as he was forced up into a crunch, unable to escape the quickening thrusts down his throat. The straining fabric against the back of his head was like a firm hand shoving him onto the cock, letting Locky throat fuck him in long, powerful strokes.

Benedict gagged and breathed whenever he could, but no sooner was his throat empty than the next thrust came—a thump of weight against his chin and nose. Locky was so hard now that Benedict could feel the cock pulsing against his esophagus.

Locky's own hunger was proved by just how deep his tongue was jamming into Benedict's ass, his lips pressed flat against the full stretch of the hole.

As Locky moved into a rhythm, Benedict's mind started to converge on the two points of pleasure. Taken from both ends. Dominated from both ends. The urge grew like a fire in his belly, magma in his balls. The urge to have this man unrestrained inside him. To be pinned down and fucked deeper than he could take, more overwhelming than anything he'd previously experienced. To have his limits pushed, pain and pleasure and discomfort and the urge to be fucked harder, harder, *harder*!

He wanted it.

He needed it.

And he needed it now!

"Fuck me!" Benedict spluttered when his mouth was next free. Spit dripped down his chin and pooled over the marble. "I need you to fuck me, Locky!"

Locky leaped down from the bench, the creak of table

mixed with the wet slap of curved cock against his ample belly. Benedict barely had time to get his bearings before Locky spun him around again and yanked him ass-first toward the edge of the table. Through the whole motion, Locky kept Benedict's knees pinned to his chest, hole up in the air.

It was the perfect position for Locky to rub his throat-slicked cock head against Benedict's tongue-fucked hole.

Benedict groaned at the initial sensation of pressure, teasing his tightness and making his belly ache in anticipation. He looked up dreamily to Locky, who'd lost none of his dominance. But now, that dominance was joined by a look of contentment, warm and glowing. A complete confidence in what he was doing.

Locky's strong, bread-maker's hands rocked Benedict's whole body back and forth, letting Benedict's tight hole bob up and down on Locky's swollen glans. At first it was just a wet kiss against his ring, delicate and velvety, a promise given and taken away. Then, that rocking was followed by the slightest spark of depth, no more than a half inch down Locky's slippery head, but enough to make Benedict gasp.

Locky did that far longer than Benedict expected, keeping him at his mercy, entering him shallow, in a torturous tease. Each grip around Locky's dick made Benedict's ass scream for more. For every long inch of this big, beautiful man. To have him slip fully past his first ring, stretching him wider than he'd ever been taken.

It was a desire that was only increased by the way Locky's cock bounced up at each withdrawal, half from the momentum, half from the vein-bulging throb of sensation as Benedict's hole gripped him tight, not wanting to let him go.

They both grunted in unexpected unison when Locky got

a little deeper than he'd anticipated on one thrust, slipping almost all his bulging head inside.

But Locky didn't take it away. He let it stay there, thick and hard and stretching Benedict wide.

Benedict panted at the incredible sensation, feeling his ass gripping hard against it, too rigid to yield against his strangle.

He didn't know what Locky would do next—pull out or push deeper. But after all the taunting of his hole, first tongue and now cock, Benedict was in no mood for teasing.

Locky's arms shuddered as Benedict pressed his hips down, stealing the depth he craved. It was like his ass was starving, like it was wolfing down a slab of juicy steak.

"Fuck!" Locky barked in surprise as Benedict got his ring past the full cock head.

Benedict whimpered at the unbelievable fullness in his guts. And now, it was his turn to tease Locky, gripping his ass as hard as he could, making the man jolt at the tight, warm throttle.

As if trying to regain the upper hand, Locky dug his fingers harder into Benedict's thighs, holding him in place as he finally slid his shaft into Benedict's ass, having to angle his hips to push his upward-curved cock in, inch by slow inch.

Benedict's eyes almost bulged out of his head as the huge glans slid past his prostate—the sensation so intense, so sudden that it made his whole belly burn. His own cock, which had been lying rock-hard in a pool of precum on his belly, bounced up to full attention, like it couldn't believe the sensation either. It wasn't just Locky's girth that was making his own face twist in joy. It was the curve of his length, pressing forcefully against his G-spot. It filled him so hard, and with such an overwhelming pressure that Benedict's cock felt like it might burst in two.

Benedict couldn't believe the intoxicating, immediate effect that Locky's cock was having on him. He'd been fucked plenty, and enjoyed it too, but never like *this*. Like he might piss himself or cum and didn't know which was more likely.

Locky paused at just the right spot that Benedict could feel Locky's heartbeat through his cock head. "Is that what you want?" he snarled. "You want me to slam this cock into you?"

Benedict moaned incoherently. The heat and the hardness made his body melt into the marble. His mouth wasn't working. His hands weren't working. If he'd been holding something it would have clattered to the floor. Because all he could feel was the thickness and the pressure against his prostate, the heat and hunger in his ass.

"Fuck . . . me," he moaned, from somewhere distant and hazy, where the world was nothing but a sweet and sticky sensation.

Benedict found himself gripping his ass hard, as if coaxing Locky deeper, as if begging him to give over all he was holding back.

Through the haze, he saw Locky's eyes fill with a momentary panic. "I don't—*fuck, Benedict*—I don't know how long I'll last if you keep gripping me like that."

The words warmed Benedict even further—that even in this moment Locky was looking to be selfless. Wanting to last as long as possible. Wanting Benedict to feel this forever.

And yet, in this moment, no part of Benedict cared how long Locky lasted. Because he felt like he could cum at any second.

Locky's hands were still pressed against the back of Benedict's knees. Into one hand, Benedict threaded his own fingers. He drew Locky's other hand into the slick of precum at his belly, viscous and clear, before wrapping Locky's grip around his own thick shaft, drawing Locky's thumb against his piercing.

And in that moment, full and overwhelmed and like every inch of his skin was crackling, Benedict wanted to say *It's okay if you cum, baby*. He wanted to say *Be with me in this moment*. He wanted to say *Feel what I'm feeling, Locky*.

Instead, Locky's cock head throbbed hard and angled against Benedict's swollen prostate. And the only thing he could manage was a whimpering, sobbing, "Fuck the cum out of me!"

And Locky obeyed.

Benedict's back arched as the remaining inches were driven into him hard. His mouth was locked in a voiceless scream as Locky squeezed Benedict's cock, rubbing it slippery from thick base to electric tip, sending ripples of pleasure all through Benedict's body. By the time Locky's full length was buried to his balls, Benedict was gripping so hard against Locky's other hand that he feared he might break both of their fingers. It wasn't in pain, but in a pleasure so indescribable that his consciousness blurred into heat.

"Oh, fuck," came Locky's voice, warm and wavering. "You want it?"

Benedict nodded furiously, unable to speak.

"You want this cock?" said Locky, suddenly fast. Thrusting from still to slamming in a matter of seconds. He pulled his whole cock out with a pop, only to jam it back in with a slam—the sheer length and the unbelievable hardness causing Benedict to convulse.

It was beyond.

It was transcendent.

It was. Oh, God, it just *was*.

Benedict grunted at the brute force behind each thrust—

the kind of slam you only got when being fucked by a big boy. One who had the heft in his belly and ass and thighs to really lay the dick in *hard*. Who had some weight behind their slams.

Benedict's whole body screamed as Locky picked up his pace—his depth. Benedict's core was on fire, stoked bright by the coordinated timing of Locky's deep thrusts and the slick jerks of his dick. It was like his prostate was being massaged on both sides. Like his granite-hard cock was being used to build the brutality of the pleasure.

"Harder!" Benedict screamed, staring down at his straining cock, slippery and solid in Locky's furious grip. The view was mesmerizing—the slam of Locky's furry belly moving back and forth, driving his cock deeper than anything Benedict had ever felt.

Locky met the pace that Benedict demanded. Brutalizing his ass. Stretching it wide and deep like Locky was rearranging his insides, hitting squirmy spots with his massive horse cock that Benedict didn't even know he had.

Locky was grunting just as much as him now, desperate and fevered. That thought burned in Benedict, just like the fire that flickered up in his well-stroked cock. That this beautiful man was about to flood his guts with his huge load.

Somehow, Locky found even more pace, hitting so deep that Benedict flinched. It was too deep, too hard, leaving him overwhelmed and overheated, like the cum was being drilled out of him with heavy machinery. The slamming pressure made Benedict go cross-eyed, until all he felt was the rumble in his bowels. It grew and grew as Locky fucked the hell out of him.

Harder.

Harder!

Harder!

The feeling was suddenly so urgent that Benedict couldn't even draw breath. It was a fire in his balls. It was a heat in his heart.

"Oh, fuck, Benedict," panted Locky. "You want me to breed you? You want me to fuck this load into your ass?"

"Give me your cum!" screamed Benedict, tears streaming down his cheeks. "I want all of you!"

"Oh, fuck, Benedict. Fuck, fuck, *fuck*!"

Locky pounded him harder and harder, stroking Benedict's cock so fast that he couldn't see properly anymore. The monstrous pleasure was eating his body from the inside. He felt like a can of soda shaken up, straining at the sides, about to burst.

And his boyfriend was right there with him.

Locky roared as his first jet of cum exploded into Benedict's ass, the hot flood sliding slick across Benedict's prostate, bashing it with such ferocity that Benedict lost control of all his remaining senses.

It was too much.

It was too good.

It was . . . it was . . . oh, *fuck*!

Locky!

Benedict's load was so strong that it almost broke him in two, the convulsions making him seize up against the steel bar in his ass, strangling Locky's cock with each convulsion, as wet warmth splattered hard against his belly and chest. It slapped across his face, so hard it felt like he was getting punched.

But Locky didn't stop, slamming his cum-slick cock deep into Benedict's guts, punching his insides out and making another involuntary jet explode over Benedict's shoulder.

Benedict sobbed as the pleasure overtook him, the orgasm that wouldn't end. That he didn't want to end. It was like he was burning from the inside. Only getting more explosive as Locky stroked his cock faster, sliding his piercing through the molten jets of white, making his whole body shake as a sprinkler of cum splattered all over the booth.

Until, finally, sticky and sweaty and overwhelmed with pleasure, they both collapsed onto the table.

Locky exhaled as Benedict's hands came soft against his sweaty back—drawing him in, small and safe.

The fury of moments earlier was still hot against his skin, joined by the radiating warmth of the panting man beneath him. The man that, in this moment, couldn't have looked happier.

"And you . . . said you wouldn't be any good the first time," breathed Benedict, kissing Locky's damp forehead and giving a vague gesture toward the flood of cum across the table.

Locky laughed into Benedict's armpit. "I can't believe I lasted as long as I did."

"Me either. I could've cum the second you slid in."

Locky grinned. It was a strange feeling—success, victory, relief. A sense of pride that he'd been up to the task. That he'd made Benedict feel like *that*—cum like *that*.

As a warm silence pooled in the room, Locky waited for the turn in his core, the long-grooved instinct of the past decade. The one that would prey on just how brutal he'd gotten. How animal they'd both been.

And those voices did come, the tiniest whispers. Familiar and furious.

But they didn't last. They *couldn't* last. Not against the overwhelming glow of his satisfaction. Not against the look on Benedict's face—the one that said he never wanted this moment to end.

Locky could feel the drum of Benedict's heart against his cheek, the rise and fall of his breath—the lifeblood coursing through him. It was the beating drum of the man who had made all this possible. Who could have run away on that first meeting, when Locky had embarrassed himself. Who could have let Locky flee when he'd tried to give up, not chasing him down or convincing him to follow through with his dream. Who could have let him return to an office job, rather than taking this terrifying, wonderful leap of faith.

Instead, Benedict had given Locky so much more.

Instead, Benedict had given Locky *everything*.

A feeling came hot by Locky's ribs—too sudden and too shocking. The glow of Benedict's sun, the warmth of his embrace, and the comfort, *Good Lord, the comfort*, of just being here with him.

Words were forming against his lips, confused in his throat.

I love him . . .

His breathing stopped as his heart quickened. Because it was too much. Too dangerous. What if saying the words would make Benedict withdraw. What if saying the words would break this spell and make Benedict realize what a terrible mistake he'd made. What if—

Locky caught himself spiraling on the thought. But this time, he fought back. Because these words weren't meaningless. And he felt them—with all his heart and all his soul, he fucking felt them. Even if they were big and scary and new.

Because that was why they needed to be acknowledged.

That was why they needed to be said.

But . . . that didn't mean they need to be said *now*. That wasn't how it worked in the movies. The lovers didn't blurt the words out the second they realized them. They agonized over them. They took long walks through winter streets. They made sure the feelings were real. They tortured themselves with doubt—because that meant those feelings had been tested. That meant they'd been validated.

And yet . . . Locky didn't want to *test* these feelings. He didn't want to wait weeks just to string the moment out.

Because that was who he'd been his whole life—indecisive and uncertain.

And he wasn't uncertain about this.

Because how could it not be true?

How could Benedict *not* deserve these feelings?

Locky glanced up at his boyfriend, who was still in the soft light of his afterglow. Benedict didn't seem to notice Locky's dilemma. That meant Locky could stay quiet. He could shake these thoughts off and move on without Benedict ever knowing.

But if he did that, what would it make him? If he couldn't say words like this, then what had he really accomplished? He would be no better than the man from months ago. The man who'd been too scared to do anything, risk anything, be *anyone*.

And that wasn't who he was anymore.

He was brave. He'd done brave things.

And he could be brave again.

He *needed* to be brave again.

"I love you, Benedict," Locky whispered.

It couldn't have been more than a few seconds before

Benedict responded, but those moments felt like millennia. His chest pounded even harder, wondering if he'd made a terrible mistake.

And then Benedict laughed—warm as a summer breeze. "Awww, I love you too, Mr. Sorenson," he said, giving kisses all over Locky's face.

The scattered smooches settled on one long, hot one—at first giggly, and then, as it lingered, more fiery. Locky's dick sprung back to life, sliding against Benedict's cum-slick belly.

Benedict separated from the kiss just long enough to say, "Round two?"

All the ingredients were laid out before Locky, ready for opening night.

He'd love to say that the bench looked cozy, but it didn't. There was simply too much stuff, industrial quantities stacked high.

On the steel bench was a whole sack of baker's flour, so heavy he could barely lift it. Alongside that was huge white tub of superfine sugar and a teetering tower of butter sticks, alongside container after container of carefully labeled white powders, all to ensure he didn't confuse his cream of tartar with his baking soda.

And yet, clinical as it was, the sight still made Locky stand a little straighter. A little prouder.

Because this wasn't meant to look *cozy*. Cozy was an aesthetic for an amateur baker. And, quite by accident, that wasn't who Locky was anymore.

He'd become a professional.

Strictly speaking, he didn't need to start baking this early —just after eight in the morning, and especially not when he'd be staying up until God knew what hour in the evening. For the next few months, his normal days would start around midday, baking and cleaning and doing the books and getting everything ready until 7 at night, when he would ride the eight blocks to his nightly meeting, back in time for an 8:30 opening.

Still, despite not needing to be here this early, he definitely preferred it. He had thirty pies to make today, with enough time for everything to set and cool and be ready to slice. And the last thing he wanted was to be running late on his very first night.

An unfamiliar feeling spread through Locky—nerves, yes, but also a sense of excitement. Because that urge to be here early, that urge to prepare, wasn't out of fear. Shockingly, there was no panic to the process. Only power. Familiarity. The knowledge—strange and new—that he *could* do this. That whatever might come on this night, these months, he would find a way to push through.

Because he'd proved that.

Benedict kissed the back of his neck, wearing a plain white t-shirt beneath his own apron, looking relaxed and weekend perfect. "A few more ingredients than your old Sunday bakes, huh?"

Locky clicked his tongue. His old Sunday bakes? It was hard to believe it had only been a few months—working at SunSpark for long weeks. Stealing a few moments on the weekends to find some peace. Being single and chaste and trapped in his little world of shame.

"You know you don't have to help out?" said Locky leaning back into the Benedict's warmth. "If you've got other things you need to do?"

Benedict slid his hands under Locky's apron, making a

contented little noise as he held him close. "But then I'd miss out on all the fun. Besides, I have to support my client on his big night."

Locky placed his own arms over Benedict's, skin and fabric melding together. He didn't want to ruin the mood, but he knew how big a test the opening would be for Benedict. "How are you feeling?"

Benedict rested his head on Locky's shoulder. "It's weird. Part of me is scared. But I feel like a bigger part of me is excited? Because tomorrow is literally a new year. I can take on new clients and start doing things properly again. No more rejections. No more distance. I know I've got a long way to go —there are so many people I need to make things right with— but tomorrow is a new start. And that feels kinda nice, you know?"

Locky rubbed the back of his head against Benedict's chin. Because he did know. With every fiber of his being, he knew.

"And I was thinking," said Benedict. "Maybe I could host a get-together here down the line? Create a regular networking event with my former clients? That way they could help each other out—share all the expertise they've acquired from their own businesses—rather than me thinking I have to do it all for them?"

Locky turned his head and kissed Benedict softly, proud as hell that he was still pushing himself into uncomfortable spaces. "I think they'd really appreciate that, Benedict."

As the morning drifted on, the two of them moved around the kitchen in a slow dance, side by welcome side. They kneaded and mixed and rubbed in unhurried sways. Flour into butter. Cinnamon into sugar. Spice into cream.

There was no rush to their routine. After all, there was enough time to take the necessary care. To put love and attention into each and every dessert.

Eventually, Locky shuffled the final pie dish to the countertop, the lattice crisp and golden and stained a beautiful indigo from the still-bubbling juices.

Benedict mopped his brow with the skirt of his apron. "That's the last of them, right? For the love of God, tell me that's the last of them?"

Thirty pies were laid across the counter. Red glistening cherry and toffee-rich pecan, meringue-topped lemon and deeply spiced pumpkin. They'd made them in record time, doubling up on the flavors most likely to go first. Admittedly it had still taken close to *six hours*, but the time had flown in the pleasant warmth of each other's company.

"I hope so," said Locky. Even with his love for baking, the effort had been quite a haul. He'd never done so much in one stretch before.

"Thank God. I'm steaming."

"And so are they!" said Locky, checking his watch. It was just after two, giving them five hours until he would head over to the nightly meeting. "But they should have plenty of time to cool."

"And when are Artair and Luca coming in?"

"Four?"

"So . . . we have a few hours alone?"

Locky chuckled. He definitely liked where this was going. "I suppose so? What were you thinking?"

Benedict waggled his eyebrows. "That we should add some cream to these pies?"

"We probably shouldn't cum on the desserts."

"What? No! I just meant . . . oh, shut up and fuck me."

Locky ran a finger down Benedict's chest. "I was thinking, Mr. Owens, that we could maybe go the other way round this time?"

Benedict was honored to see Locky lead a meeting. Yes, it was Tuesday night, open night, and he could have just wandered in anyway, but it was still sweet of Locky to invite him—wanting Benedict to see this side of him for the first time.

The room was packed, so full that they'd run out of chairs. It was a crowd that seemed to shock even Locky, although Benedict figured that New Year's Eve was probably a complex night for this community, and there were lots of people looking for support.

And he had no doubt that Locky would provide it. He had a unique ability to make people feel welcome. To make them feel wanted.

Benedict wasn't disappointed in Locky's performance, although he was a little surprised. Because here, in this place, Locky spoke just like he did in the kitchen, clear and comfortable with his topic, authoritative and warm and with a surprising amount of humor, drawing great laughs from the group in well-punctuated beats.

It was the same after the sharing was over, when the group broke into coffees and conversation—things Locky could have excused himself from, given the rest of his night. Instead, there was no apprehension, no checking the time. The people came to Locky in singles or groups, seeking out his guidance and his advice. And even though Benedict couldn't hear what they said, Locky radiated strength. The handshakes and hugs seemed to come effortlessly. Strangers greeted like old friends.

And in that moment, Benedict realized that Locky hadn't really changed over these last few months. He'd just become the person that was always there, waiting for him.

It was only when Locky looked over to Benedict, stealing a little glance, that the shy smile emerged. Benedict returned it, his chest swelling at the slight blush that kissed Locky's cheeks.

And Benedict's breath caught at a strange realization—at the way Locky was looking at him, so different to everyone else in the room. Benedict wasn't sure why he'd never made the connection earlier, given he knew there were two different versions of Locky, the confident one who baked and the turbulent one who hadn't let himself explore his dreams. But Benedict hadn't realized how deep that duality ran.

Because this, right here, was the version of Locky that most people saw. They didn't think of him as quiet or nervous or scared. To his group members, his employees, Locky *was* the confident teacher. The powerful guardian. The pillar of strength to all those around him. The one who soldiered on when others fell. The one who would carry the fallen, even if it broke him down.

Because Locky didn't show most people that other side of himself. He wouldn't allow them the burden of worrying about him.

But he had shown Benedict.

If only through unexpected circumstance, Locky had revealed a side of himself—a deep and honest aspect of his soul—that perhaps no other person on the planet had ever seen.

Benedict's heart pounded as the implications overtook him. Because Locky wasn't the sort of man to explain the significance of what he'd given Benedict, the insight and the vulnerability that he'd entrusted him with. Because Locky was too selfless to acknowledge how precious and how fragile a piece of himself Benedict now held. It was delicate crystal in a world full of smashing strikes.

A shiver went up Benedict's spine. And right now, with Benedict cradling that delicate crystal close to his chest, he knew that he would guard it with his life. Because he would never, *ever*, let anything hurt Locky again.

The voice came low beside him—in height at least, if not volume. "He's quite something, isn't he?" said Evelyn. "He is lucky to have found you."

Benedict shook his head. "Not as lucky as me."

Evelyn patted his forearm, bony fingers against broad muscles. "On that matter, I understand you take new clients from tomorrow?"

"I will indeed," chuckled Benedict. "And let me guess, you've spent long enough volunteering for other people's causes, and you've received a stock payout even bigger than Locky's? So now you're thinking about starting your own charitable organization?"

Evelyn led him through the throng. "You're even better than my little goat said, Mr. Benedict."

They ran into a familiar figure among the crowd. Kai greeted Benedict with a slap on the back and gave a surprisingly restrained eye roll toward Evelyn. "Well, I've done my bit. Packed to the rafters, and with more on the way."

Benedict took a second to realize that Kai wasn't talking to him. He was talking to Evelyn.

She turned up her nose, although Benedict could have sworn that her heart wasn't completely in it. "*Congratulazioni*. But I think *my* efforts will yield more fruit."

Kai plucked a stray piece of lint from his suit. "We'll see, old woman."

Benedict swiveled a finger between the two of them. "What's going on here."

Kai and Evelyn looked briefly toward each other, before snapping their heads away in a mutual huff. "Consider it a temporary truce," they said, in unison.

"Kai! I told you not to make the meeting come!" said Locky, loud enough that his best friend could hear him, but hopefully quiet enough that the horde of people behind them wouldn't. Almost every single person from the meeting had joined the procession, with a good number of them apparently hoovering up tickets to the event long before they'd sold out. "I didn't want anyone to feel obligated!"

"Who's obligated?" scoffed Kai, jamming his hands under his armpits against the cold. "This isn't communism, buddy. You're offering a service that people *want* to experience. And you've been all over the news? Most of them already knew this was happening."

"Yes, but—"

Benedict gave him a playful shoulder shove from the other side. "I think this is where you say thank you, dear."

"Yes, sorry, thank you, Kai."

Kai gave a self-satisfied snort. "Oh, don't thank me until you've seen the rest of it."

"The rest of it? What's the rest of—"

As they rounded the last corner, they were met by a wall of a cheer.

Locky gasped, his mouth hanging open.

There were hundreds of people. Maybe a thousand.

First were faces he recognized from the nightly meetings. Those who didn't attend all the time, and others who usually went to different locations around the city.

Beside them was group who were even more familiar. Half the employees from SunSpark had to be there, with Adriana and Jared waving through the crowd.

And then, somehow even larger, were people he'd never met before. Crowding around the entrance and thronging the street—packed so tightly they were flowing between two different news crews that were setting up out front, turning on big camera lights and conducting interviews with excited patrons.

Locky gaped at the impossible scene. His first feeling was guilt, that so many of his old coworkers, so many people from the meetings, had been forced into supporting him. "You didn't . . . you didn't need to . . ."

Evelyn rubbed his back. "*Piccirudu*, for seven years you were there for them, celebrating every birthday and every anniversary and every single promotion. Remembering when others didn't. Asking nothing in return. Believe me when I tell you, I didn't have to twist any arms."

A tear rolled down Locky's cheek. "I . . . I don't know what to say."

Benedict squeezed his hand. "I think, Mr. Sorenson, you should declare the city's first nighttime bakery officially open."

Locky rested his head against Benedict's chest, turning slowly alongside the music—soft as the night, warm as their embrace.

It might have been one or two or three in the morning. Locky didn't know for certain, but it was late enough that they'd sold out of practically everything. Late enough that Luca had insisted Locky get out on the floor and enjoy his opening night.

Around him, the room glowed with the sound of laughter and music and happy memories being spun into stories— stories that they'd created together.

Benedict pulled him close as they swayed to the song.

Their dance wasn't perfect, with fumbled feet and tiny trips. But that didn't matter. Because, in so many ways, things where better when they were a little messed up.

"I love you, Mr. Owens," whispered Locky, rubbing his forehead into the space between Benedict's neck and shoulder. The safest place in the entire world. The safest man who'd ever lived.

Benedict placed a long kiss into his golden hair. "Not as much as I love you, Mr. Sorenson."

And then, hand in hand, they danced through moonlight.

Epilogue

TURNING THE PAGE

February 2014

Locky's eyes bulged at the magazine. "Oh, my . . ."

"Yeah, I don't hold back in my articles," said Luca from the other side of the counter. His face was lit by the dappled light of mid-morning. The store wasn't technically open yet. In fact, none of them would usually be here at this hour. But there was something special about today. And nobody wanted to miss it.

"Did you read page three?" hissed Tris, dropping her ruby glasses to the end of her nose and sipping on a double espresso. "These three screwed on the observation deck of Coit Tower! How? They lock that place up at night!"

A grunt came hidden from a far booth. The only sign of life was a pair of Armani loafers propped on the edge of the table. "Yeah, but the padlock is set to 000. Everyone knows that," said Kai, popping his head over the seat in the silence that followed. "What? Sometimes I like to treat a date to a scenic view!"

Locky rolled his eyes. "You can't call what you do *dating*, Kai."

"It is *very* pretty up there at night," agreed Artair, sitting on the visible side of Kai's booth and slowly strumming his guitar. He glanced to his husband with a grin that was somehow all sweetness and all filth at the same time. "I wrote a song about it a few years back. *Climbing the Tower*. You remember, babe?"

Luca's voice suddenly went all growly. "How could I forget? An amazing build and a really deep beat. Like it could last all night."

"And that climax!" sniggered Artair. "Gosh, I wish I was playing it right now."

Locky blushed at the thought, arousing and scary and exciting—resolving to ask Benedict if he wanted to take a trip out there one night and see it for themselves. "Okay, but why did they tell you all of this? Aren't they embarrassed about it?"

"Why would they be embarrassed?" said Luca, a wicked glint in his eyes. "Are people without houses not allowed to feel horny? To feel desired? To want to experience pleasure? Should they deny themselves affection, and be ashamed of sharing their stories, just because people like *you* find it uncomfortable? I never took you for a sexual elitist, Locky. For shame."

Locky's mouth gaped. "I'm . . . not going to win this conversation, am I?"

"No. But it's always cute watching you try."

Locky flicked back and forth through the story. "I still can't believe I hired an award-winning sex columnist as a barista . . ."

"*And* a number one artist as your house musician."

"Whoa," said Artair, a shy look on his bearded face. "It was just the Independent Artist charts. It wasn't one of the big ones, with like, Lady Gaga."

"Babe, you've sold three million records and headlined festivals on four continents. I'm not sure you can pretend to be some unknown artist anymore."

"I mean, I *am* still technically unknown! Given I wear a mask on stage."

The banter was interrupted by the tinkle of the bell above the main door. Evelyn, the CEO of the Abruzzo Charitable Trust, walked in wearing a bright blue cloak with a half dozen buttons for various causes pinned on the chest. "There's quite the crowd out there. Lovely people. All very excited to see him again." She looked around the room. "Where is he hiding?"

Kai grabbed his knees theatrically. "Close the door, you old hag! You're letting the cold in!"

"He's out back," said Locky. "I'll go grab him. Evie, if you can bring everyone in. Artair, upbeat classy, please. Luca, whatever they want is on the house."

Benedict stared at his warped reflection in the oven door, adjusting his crisp navy tie. He knew the speech on his palm cards, he'd practiced it enough times after all, most recently a dozen times into this solitary steel audience. But somehow it just didn't feel . . . *enough*. Somehow if felt like he was going backward.

In many ways he'd had the perfect start to the year. He'd taken on two clients so far, Evelyn first, and now a young gaming nerd with dreams of creating a mobile van for board games, coming around to parties and hosting table-top games for people who didn't know the rules. And in both cases, the darkest parts of his panic had stayed away. For the first time in forever, Benedict felt like the worst of it might finally be behind him.

That had definitely been helped by the roaring success of the bakery over these last two months, not just getting a good and loyal customer base during the evenings but also having plenty of lucrative business bookings for companies wanting to host fun and inclusive events that wouldn't rack up a bar bill. It had been especially inspiring how Locky had signed the long-term lease just last week, extending the lifespan of *Pie Me to the Moon* for the next three years.

Benedict had expected sleepless nights and tortured talks over that. And Locky had experienced a little of that—passing and brief—before finally putting ink to paper.

Because in so many ways, Locky had reckoned with his fears. With his past. Those worries might still be there—they might *always* be there—but he'd found ways of dealing with them. Of proving that he was stronger than them.

And now, it was Benedict's turn.

His home office still contained his shelf of folders, all his former clients, closed off and complete, exactly as they were on the day they'd opened their stores. Each one was a little tombstone to his past, never allowed to change.

But things *had* changed. Over these last ten years, some of those stores would have thrived. Others would have limped by in mediocre success. And some . . . well, some wouldn't have made it.

As much as that thought made Benedict's pulse pound, it was reality—the world moving and choices mattering. And he'd never be able to move forward properly until he accepted that reality. Until he made things right with his past clients. Until he owned the past that had plagued him for so long.

And that's what this event was—the first meeting of a monthly get-together with his past clients. The meeting that had seemed like such a good idea a few months back. And now, in just a few minutes, he'd be face to face with all those people he'd abandoned. All the people he'd disappointed. All the people he'd—

The cold through his veins warmed as Locky joined him in the kitchen, wrapping strong arms around him, holding him close. "Ready, Mr. Owens?"

Some part of Benedict wanted to say no. To cancel the whole thing. To put it off for another month or another year or another decade.

But a bigger part of him, newer and stronger than he gave it credit for, managed to nod.

"This is a good idea, Benedict," said Locky, kissing his shoulder blades. "I'm sure they'll learn so much from each other. This is a great thing you're doing. A *brave* thing you're doing."

In his heart, Benedict knew that was true. He'd walked through fire already on this journey, and he'd survived. He'd fought through terror, and he'd survived. And on the other side of both, he'd found this man, this place, this *life*.

And he liked this life.

He *loved* this life.

Benedict turned around in Locky's embrace, kissing him close, holding him like he never wanted to let go.

Somewhere between those kisses, Locky reached up, at first holding Benedict's face, then running fingers against his tie, undoing the knot and allowing the silk to fall from his collar. "That's how you should wear it with your clients,"

Locky whispered. "Like you've finished for the night. Like everyone can just relax."

In the distance came the chime of the doorbell. Then the rise in noise and voices beyond the threshold.

His former clients were here.

The meeting was now.

"Will you be there with me?" Benedict asked, knowing the answer but needing to hear it. Because he needed a little of his boyfriend's strength right now.

Locky took his hand, fingers safe and strong. His harbor in the storm. His anchor against the crashing waves. "Always, Mr. Owens."

THE FINAL SWEET & STOCKY BOOK

Kai Kimura always gets his way. As a high-powered executive, he's used to fucking his rivals (in the boardroom and the bedroom).

But all that changes when he inherits a half stake in his family's failing dive shop in Hawaii. His co-owner? A handsome but scatterbrained surfer daddy, more used to bonfires than business ventures.

Kai wants to sell up to a property developer. But Surfer Stud has other ideas. Neither can act without the other's agreement, so they'll have to wrestle for control. In the boardroom. And the bedroom.

Daddies & Dive Boats is a sweet and spicy enemies-to-lovers romance about beefy boys getting deep, wet, and salty.

ABOUT THE AUTHOR

Dylan Drakes is an Australian writer of beefy boy romances whose books usually end up twice as long as planned. Let's blame the ADHD for that.

When not waking up at three in the morning to write about thick thighs and furry bellies, Dylan can be found with a controller in hand, cursing the existence of the Soulslike genre.

He also enjoys eating any and all carbohydrates, drinking far too much tea, acting a fool on his socials, and snuggling up to his cavoodle, Sven.

To sign up to my newsletter (and receive a free ebook) visit
www.dylandrakes.com

facebook.com/thedylandrakes

instagram.com/thedylandrakes

tiktok.com/@thedylandrakes

youtube.com/@thedylandrakes

Thank you, Pixies!

Thank you so much for reading my sweet and spicy story about big boys frosting each other's cakes. This book was a blast to write. And if I did my job right, it should have been a blast to read as well! (Get it? Blast? BLAST?)

If you enjoyed the story, why not leave a review on Goodreads, your socials, and/or the place of purchase. Your reviews play a massive role in other people finding my stories and spreading the beefy boy love.